The Possessor Wars

Book 1

I0520165

The Boy
Who Fell
into
the Sky

Chad Spencer

This book is a work of fiction. Names, characters, places, and incidents used or described herein are either the product of the author's imagination or are used fictitiously. Any resemblance to actual events, locales, or persons, living or dead, is entirely coincidental.

No part of this book may be reproduced in any form without the permission of the publisher.

Editor: Keilani Conger
Illustrator: David Conger

Official Web Site: http://possessorwars.com/
Facebook: https://www.facebook.com/chad.spencer.165
Twitter: https://twitter.com/PossessorWars
To be notified of new releases, please sign up for the author's newsletter at:
http://possessorwars.com/subscribe.html

The Boy
Who Fell
into
the Sky

Part 1

IN A SMALL WORLD

"All moments in time are not created equal. Large events often begin in small, very personal ways. The monumental forces of history often hinge on the individual choices of the people involved. There's a proverb about the flapping of a butterfly's wings that sets off a chain of events that causes a hurricane on the other side of the world. So it was with the events that preceded First Contact. The choices made by one, seemingly unimportant boy in the lower reaches of one, seemingly unimportant arcology completely changed our view of both the universe and human race itself." *First Contact, an Eyewitness Account,* Hugh Benson, p. 14. © 2776 Megalon Interstellar Media, All rights reserved in this and all other universes, parallel or unparallel realities, unrealities, and planes of existence.

1

A small robot, which was shaped very much like a dog, scanned its surroundings keenly. Hiding under a thick clump of bushes, it was unnoticed by the people strolling along the nearby path. They were too busy enjoying the afternoon sun, which shone brightly through the clear dome hundreds of feet above the park.

The robot, the park, and the dome were on the top of a building that was on the plains of the American Midwest. It was a tall building, standing 3,000 stories high. This building, called an arcology, was cylindrical and a mile wide. It towered above a vast grumbling city that stretched across most of the state.

The building itself was not unusual. Neither was the city around it. For the last 120 years, most states in the U.S. were nearly covered by cities. And most cities had many arcologies just like this one. Each arcology housed millions of people. Every arcology was like a city unto itself, with apartments, schools, stores, recreation centers, and more. This arcology, like all the others, had a huge, clear dome on top. Inside the dome was a park filled with trees, bushes, ponds, streams, and paths. And in this park stood the secretive, dog-like robot.

The dogbot swiveled its ears, which had built-in microphones, in every direction. It peeked out through the bushes, examining its surroundings with its camera eyes. It did not, however, look up. If it had, it would have seen a robot shaped very much like a small monkey lowering itself stealthily from a tree by its tail. Hanging upside down, the monkeybot paused and gazed intently at the dogbot.

Slowly, quietly, the monkeybot moved closer to the dogbot. It was not in a hurry. In its hand-like paws, the monkeybot clutched a Swiss ultra knife, which was a modern version of the Swiss army knives people had used for centuries. When it was close enough to touch the dogbot's back, it opened the knife and took out a power decoupler, the modern equivalent of a screwdriver. Quickly, and very gently, it removed a panel on the dogbot's back. Next, the monkeybot passed the Swiss ultra knife up and gripped it with its left foot, leaving its hands free. With both hands, it lifted the panel and transferred it to its right foot.

Two thousand, one hundred and eighty-three stories below the monkeybot, Jeff Bowman smiled. He peered attentively at the 3D video feed that he was getting on his datapad from the monkeybot's camera eyes. He peeked warily up at his teacher, Sirsen Bering, sitting in the front of the room.

Although Sirsen Bering was looking around at the students in the room, Jeff was pretty sure his teacher didn't notice what he was doing. With 300 students in the class, Sirsen Bering didn't usually focus on an individual student unless that student made either noise or trouble. Jeff made neither.

Looking back at the datapad, Jeff rapidly sent commands to the monkeybot. The datapad, which was a powerful computer that every student carried, was about the size of a large clipboard and just less than an inch thick. It transmitted Jeff's commands through the building's network, called the grid, to the monkeybot up in the park. Following Jeff's directives, the monkeybot reached into the opening in the dogbot's back. It pulled loose a thin cable.

Jeff glanced quickly over at Dirk Highborne, who sat eighteen rows to his left. Highborne was clearly stunned. After a moment's hesitation, he furiously typed commands into his datapad to try to reconnect to the dogbot. Jeff smiled, knowing it wouldn't do any good now that the dogbot's wireless network antenna was disconnected.

'He'll never control the dogbot again.' Jeff congratulated himself.

Jeff sent a text message to his friend, Hugh. "Got your robot disconnected from the grid. Stand by."

Jeff commanded his monkeybot to pull itself back up and retrieve a cable it had left dangling in the tree. The monkeybot opened a panel in its own chest. It then connected one end of the cable to itself, and the other to the dogbot's innards.

Working steadily, Jeff reprogrammed the dogbot. When he was satisfied, he had his monkeybot reconnect the dogbot's wireless network antenna. It then disconnected the cable and replaced the panels on both itself and the dogbot.

"Hugh," Jeff texted, "You can get control of your robot again. Log on with the user name of MyDog and a password of DirkIsALoser. When you're done, send your dog to the farm. I'm sending my monkey there now."

Hugh sent back a smiley face and a thumbs-up icon with the text, "Thanks!"

Glancing back at Highborne, Jeff saw him turning a furious shade of purple. Smiling, he started the Science lesson he was supposed to be working on already. For about the hundredth time that day, Jeff pushed his wavy brown hair out of his eyes and mentally reminded himself that he needed a haircut.

Just then, Jeff received an ominous message from his teacher. "Jefferson Bowman: Come to my office after class," it said.

'Uh-oh,' thought Jeff. Being called into Sirsen Bering's office was usually not good news. And he hated it when his teacher called him Jefferson instead of just Jeff.

At the end of the school day, Jeff presented himself at Sirsen Bering's desk at the front of the room. "Let's go in my office," Sirsen Bering said. They stepped through a door behind Sirsen Bering's desk and sat down in his small office.

Sirsen Bering looked at Jeff gravely. "Jeff, did you know that there's a program on the school's network that notifies the teacher if any of the students are sending messages when they shouldn't?"

Jeff shook his head, but didn't say anything. 'I'm toast,' he thought.

Sirsen Bering continued, "I know you were getting a robot back for Hubert Benson that Dirk Highborne had stolen."

Feeling that he was in serious trouble, Jeff tried to explain. "I … well, you see … I …" Jeff looked down at his feet and stammered. "Uh … he likes to be called Hugh instead of Hubert," he finally said.

'Idiot,' he thought, 'what a stupid thing to say.'

Sirsen Bering smiled gently and waved him silent. "I know. I also know that Dirk Highborne is a bully and a thief. But, as I'm sure you know, his mother's a vice principal at this school. Every time he gets into trouble, she gets him off. She's also on the Sector Council, so if he gets into trouble with the police on any floor within this sector, she protects him from them as well. As a result, there's nothing that I or the other teachers can do to help you kids deal with Dirk. We'll lose our jobs if we try, and jobs are too hard to come by these days. I appreciate you stepping in and helping Hubert, uh, Hugh. But please don't do it again during school hours. School is neither the time nor the place for the kind of 'adventures' that you had today. Do I make myself clear?"

"Yes, Sirsen Bering."

"Good. You can go now. Goodbye Jefferson. I'll see you tomorrow."

Out in the corridor, Hugh immediately scurried up to Jeff. "Did you get your Science assignment done?" he asked.

Even though Jeff was slightly tall for his age, he towered over Hugh, who was much shorter. "Almost," Jeff lied. He didn't want

Hugh to feel bad because he spent so much time getting his robot back.

"I can help you with it," Hugh offered eagerly.

"Thanks, but it would help me more if you would do my weeding on the farm tonight."

"Sure," Hugh smiled. He hesitated. "Jeff, thanks for getting my robot back."

Before Jeff could answer, his friends Akio and Harriet walked up. Harriet, who everyone called Harry, asked, "Did you get it?"

Triumphantly, Jeff flashed a smile and answered, "Yup. Highborne is *so* predictable. He heard you two talking just like we planned and had the dog up in the park looking for the farm. He probably still doesn't know why he was disconnected. He just kept pounding on his datapad." Jeff imitated Highborne's furious pounding. The others laughed.

Together, the four of them walked home. As they rode an elevator down twenty-five floors, Hugh made jokes about Highborne. They dropped Hugh off at his apartment first. Although no one said so, everyone knew why. Hugh was a year younger and a full head smaller than all the other guys in their grade. His slight build made him an easy target for bullies like Highborne.

Dirk Highborne was a coward. He never went after anyone in groups. Instead, he targeted kids he knew he could beat up. So they all moved together when not with an adult.

After going up to their floor, Jeff and Akio dropped Harry off next. Highborne was not above bullying girls. The two boys lived next door to each other so neither of them had to be alone when going home.

Arriving at their flats, Akio waved as he passed through his front door. Jeff paused. All around him, kids were just getting home. Younger children, whose school days ended earlier, were already playing along the sides of the pale corridor. As always, the 10-year-old Telford twins were bouncing a ball off of every passing hovertram that floated by. The drivers routinely shouted at them, but that didn't seem to deter them any.

Jeff went inside the small flat. It had only one bedroom, which was Jeff's. When he was little, the bedroom had been his parents' and Jeff slept on a bed that pulled out from the couch. After Jeff's mother died, his father traded with him. "I really don't need a room of my own," he told Jeff. "But now that you're getting to be a teenager, you need some space for yourself."

Because of his homework, he wouldn't be able to do anything besides water his parts of their hidden farm. Hugh would have to use his dogbot to pull Jeff's share of the weeds tonight. Weeding was a daily chore. The air currents inside the dome brought up the seeds of many types of plants from the park below.

Half an hour later, Jeff was well into his Science lesson. He read about primitive methods of space propulsion. The examples showed video of the early rockets to Jupiter. "Until gravity mirrors were invented," a voice from the video said, "deep space missions used fission-powered rockets that superheated water until it turned into highly pressured hot gasses. The gasses were then allowed to escape through the nozzle at the back of the rocket. This method of propulsion enabled pioneering ships to travel without carrying so much fuel. When they reached Jupiter, the ancient astronauts of the 21st century refueled their ships by digging up the water ice that covers Europa, one of the giant planet's moons."

Abruptly, an evil-looking dragon popped its head into the upper corner of his datapad and blew fire. The fire turned into a text message that read, "Are you busy?"

Jeff smiled, paused the video, picked up his datapad, and slid open a little compartment on the back. He removed a small earpiece with a microphone attached to it. Placing the earpiece in his ear and adjusting the microphone, he tapped the Talk icon on his pad. "What's up?"

Akio told him, "Harry and I were talking." Jeff looked down at his datapad. Sure enough, Harry's red-haired fairy appeared in the message section of Jeff's datapad.

She broke in. "The three of us can't keep watch over Hugh forever," she said. "Dirk's going to find him alone sometime— probably sometime soon. Jeff, I think it's time we started asking some of the others to help out with him."

"I suppose you're right," Jeff sighed. "I just haven't done it because the others don't seem to like him much."

The fairy on Jeff's datapad made a stern face. "You've got to give them a chance. I know Hugh's really ... awkward around people. But he's got to start to make friends with everyone so he can help out too."

"She's right," Akio agreed.

"Yup, I know. Look, I've got to finish my Science lesson. Let's have an eChat with everyone together the day after tomorrow. We can get together after dinner. What chatworld shall we meet in?"

Akio shouted at once, "Dragon's Crag! Dragon's Crag!" His dragon excitedly shot a pillar of fire upward.

Harry's fairy stuck out her tongue. "We always go there. I want something different."

Knowing which virtual world she wanted them to meet in, Jeff suggested, "We haven't been to Merfolk's Keep for awhile."

The dragon stomped off the screen while the fairy did a dance. "I'll send the invitations," Harry told him, and she signed off.

Returning to his Science lesson, Jeff continued working on the assignment. The datapad was another advantage of living in an arcology. Everyone got one for free. They contained hundreds of thousands of books, school lessons, games, songs, and entertainment programs when the residents received them. For a fee, you could get regular updates broadcast directly to your datapad over the network. The updates had newer and better content. However, most people Jeff knew just got by with the free stuff.

At 5:30, Jeff put his homework aside and began cooking dinner in the small kitchen section of the flat. He took out blocks of synthpaste and cut them into bite-sized chunks. Jeff chopped up vegetables from his portion of the clandestine farm and mixed them into the bland stew he was cooking.

Because of the vegetables and fruit he grew, he was able to use only half of their monthly ration of synthpaste. His father didn't know because he left all of the shopping and cooking to Jeff. Jeff didn't like keeping secrets from his dad any more than the others in the group liked keeping secrets from their families, but the farm was too important to their futures. He and his friends did the same for their school lunches. Their parents just thought they didn't eat much at lunch. It left more synthpaste for their families. They sold the rest of the food they grew to a store on level 2811. The store's owner was glad to get their fresh fruits and vegetables—and he didn't ask many questions.

As always, Jeff's dad, whose name was Kent, walked in at exactly 6 p.m. "Hey kid," he said as a greeting.

"Hi, Dad. How was work?"

Kent scratched his thick, slightly graying hair, scrunched his face and replied, "Ok. Same old thing. Dinner smells good. Whatcha makin'?"

"Nothin' special. Just beef-flavored stew," Jeff replied.

"Kid, your cooking is *always* something special," Kent told him as he sniffed the bubbling mixture. "I swear you can do more with a chunk of synthpaste than anyone I know."

"Thanks, Dad. Dinner's almost ready. Can you set the table while I finish it?"

Kent stretched his muscular frame, stood, and folded down the table from the kitchen wall. Then he grabbed two chairs, unfolded them, and put them up to the table. He went to the cupboard and pulled out some bowls and large plastic cups.

"Hey Dad," Jeff commented.

"What?"

"A really good space combat simulator just got released as public domain. Wanna play it with me tonight?" Jeff invited. Like all his friends, Jeff anxiously kept track of games, movies, music, and computer programs that passed into the public domain because anything in the public domain was free.

"No thanks," Kent replied, "I'm going out for a while tonight. I have some things to do." Jeff knew what his dad was really saying. About four years after Jeff's mother died, Kent had started dating. In the beginning, it was only once a week. But things changed shortly after Jeff turned 14; his dad seemed to want to get out of the flat almost every night.

'We played games together lots until he started dating,' Jeff recalled, withering a little inside. He told Kent, "Ok. I guess I can work on my assignment until bedtime anyway."

Although his dad seemed to be dating regularly now, he didn't talk with Jeff much about the women he was seeing. Jeff recalled that when Kent started dating, he told Jeff that he wouldn't bring any women home until he was serious about one. Because his dad seemed to be going out so much, Jeff figured Kent was dating one woman in particular lately.

It seemed strange to Jeff that his father was dating. But Harry assured Jeff, "Your dad is a handsome man, even though he's 40. He's not fat and bald or anything. I'm sure a lot of women his age think he's good looking."

Jeff thought that was weird. But when he said that to Akio and Harry, Harry replied, "Even old people get lonely, Jeff. I'm sure your father would rather be married." Harry seemed to know about those kinds of things.

While Jeff finished setting the table, Kent got out his datapad and typed a short message. He seemed happy with the reply.

During dinner, Jeff asked Kent to tell him some of his stories from when he was a Senior Engineer on a starship. Kent was always pleased to repeat his tales, which seemed to get taller with each retelling. Jeff enjoyed hearing them, but he sometimes wished they could find more to talk about.

As Jeff listened again to his father's adventures, he dreamed of the day when he could enter the Academy and have a career in the

Space Corps. 'Thanks to my farm,' he thought, 'I might just be able to make that dream come true.'

When they finished their meal, Kent did the dishes while Jeff returned to his datapad to complete his schoolwork. Before Kent left, he went in the bathroom to shave. He waved cheerfully to Jeff as he went out for the evening.

2

"Jeff, your angle of descent is too steep. You're going to ..."

An alarm blared and the panel in front of Jeff turned into a blaze of red lights. His shuttle pod lurched to the side. Jeff was saved from being tossed against the wall by the straps that held him to his seat. Frantically, Jeff's hands flew over the controls as he tried to slow the careening pod's descent. It didn't work; the pod lurched again and flipped upside down.

"Jeff, this is Control. You're going to have to abort."

"No! No!" Jeff shouted back. "I can handle it!" He was sure he could complete the landing.

Working the shuttle pod's controls like a maniac, Jeff managed to get its nose pointed straight down. Its speed was increasing dangerously. The hull shuddered sickeningly as the control panel flashed insane patterns of red lights at him. Jeff hastily wiped the sweat from his brow and continued his efforts.

"Hull temperature increasing," said the pod's computer in a calm, monotone female voice.

Slowly, Jeff managed to pull the pod into the correct flight position and got control of it.

"Hull temperature at maximum," the computer told him blandly. "Warning," it continued, "hull breach is imminent."

The air outside the pod's front window glowed a bright orange. Jeff was worried. If he didn't get the pod slowed down, it would burn up in the atmosphere.

Drenched in sweat, he applied a strong reverse thrust. The window went blank. The computer said, "Thrust too strong. The hull has breached and the pod has exploded."

The program ended. Jeff opened his eyes and the simulated spacecraft was gone. The door to the artificial reality pod was open, so he sat up. Jeff's instructor for his Young Pilot's Association class stood next to a screen near the pod.

"That started out as a good reentry," he told Jeff. "But your angle of descent got to be too steep. You can't come in that fast and stay alive. You'll burn up every time. I was impressed how you handled things when it flipped over though. Not many of my students could have got their pods right side up like you did. If you had applied a smaller reverse thrust, you would have been ok."

Still shaken, Jeff climbed out of the AR pod.

"Don't worry about it Jeff," his instructor consoled cheerily. "Almost everyone fails their first reentry in these little pods. They're not like the freighters you're used to. They're much lighter and more maneuverable. That's why so many pilots like them. But they're also much harder to handle during reentry. You can try again next week."

Sadly, Jeff left the AR suite. He was surprised to find Akio waiting for him. "You're done already?" he asked.

"Yup," Akio told him. "I crashed my shuttle pod five minutes ago. My trajectory was off and I hit a passenger liner. Killed nearly 300. It was so sad." Akio sighed melodramatically.

Leaving the AR suite together, Akio commented, "I wish we could get some extra money together."

"Why?" Jeff asked.

"I want to go to the AR suite. There's a new game out called 'Brice Yee: Frenzied Feet of Flaming Fury' and I want to give it a try."

Jeff commented doubtfully, "They charge more for playing in new programs."

"Tell me about it," snorted Akio. "It costs an arm and a leg to play."

As they walked, they met Harry, who was returning from playing powertennis with her sister, Ruth Ann. The two girls were nearly mirror images of each other, except that Ruth Ann was taller, a couple of years older, and Ruth Ann's hair was a deep auburn rather than dazzling red like Harry's.

Together, they took an elevator to their floor. The elevator, which ran along the outside of the arcology, was made of a clear, super-strong plastic. It enabled them to see the vast city Outside as they descended. The May sky was clear and the setting sun turned it a deep orange-red color.

"I always like riding an outside elevator," Harry sighed.

"You say that every time we ride these," Akio shot back.

Harry stuck out her tongue. "I do not."

Before Akio could answer, Jeff broke in, "What do you want to do tomorrow before the study session?"

"Surf-ing! Surf-ing!" Akio shouted immediately. An older couple on the other side of the huge elevator scowled at him severely. Ruth Ann giggled.

"Shhh!" Harry hissed, turning an embarrassed pink. "You always want to go surfing. Let's do something else. How about hovercarts?"

"Surf-ing! Surf-ing!"

"I want to do something else!"

"Surf-ing! Surf-ing!"

Jeff looked at Harry. She was right, they did surf a lot. But the water park was free and riding the hovercarts cost money. "You chose the eChat world. Why not let him choose this one?" Harry scowled. "Besides," he continued, "I'd kind of like to surf too."

"But my bathing suit is so old," Harry objected. "And I haven't saved enough money for a new one yet."

"What's wrong with your bathing suit?" Jeff asked. "You look good in it." Ruth Ann smiled at him approvingly.

"Oh, alright," Harry yielded, but she looked happier.

Jeff and Akio dropped Harry and Ruth Ann off at their flat. As they arrived outside their own flats, Akio said to Jeff, "You sure know how to talk to girls."

Jeff shrugged. "I don't know. I just say what I think. Harry seems to like that."

"I say what I think too," Akio observed, "but she doesn't seem to like it *near* as much." He had a sly look on his face.

Jeff shrugged again. He didn't know what Akio was getting at, but he didn't think he wanted to talk about it. He said goodbye and went in.

Kent was sitting on the sofa watching a show on his datapad. "Hey kid," he greeted Jeff and paused his show.

"Hi, Dad."

"I was thinking," Kent began, "since Friday is the start of a three-day weekend, why not go do some camping?"

Jeff was surprised. "Really?"

"Yup, we haven't been in a couple of years. I booked some artificial reality pods for us. We'll get to hunt buffalo with an Indian tribe in the ancient West."

Jeff thought silently, 'We haven't been camping since just after Mom died.' Out loud he said, "Thanks, Dad."

Kent smiled and returned to his program—at least until he got a message on his datapad. Then he said, "I think I'm going to duck out for a while. Are you ok on your own again tonight?"

Woodenly, Jeff replied, "Sure, Dad. I'll be fine."

Jeff turned away and went dejectedly into his room. Out of the blue, he remembered how happy he had been each time his father came back from space. 'He always did a lot of things with me back then,' Jeff thought sadly. 'It made up for all the time he was gone.'

Settling onto his bed, Jeff played a game for about half an hour. Suddenly, his bedroom door burst open. Jeff nearly jumped out of his skin when two men with white-blond hair stormed in. One of the men pulled a handheld scanner from his pocket and scanned Jeff.

"This is the one," the man said to his companion.

"Wh ... what are you doing here?" Jeff demanded in alarm. "How did you get into our flat? The door isn't supposed to let people in unless we say so."

The pair didn't react. The man with the scanner ordered, "Take him." The other man pulled a stunner from his pocket.

Leaping to his feet in near panic, Jeff screamed, "Take me? Take me where? Who are you? Why are you in our flat?"

Abruptly, two towering figures appeared in the room. They were humanoid but clearly not human. The upper portions of their bodies resembled humans, but they each had four crablike legs.

Both Jeff and the intruders were frozen at the sight of the aliens. This was clearly not what the intruders had expected.

One of the aliens reached out its strange-looking hand. There was a gold band around its wrist. Surprisingly, a gold ball appeared and floated above its cupped palm. Weird symbols crawled in moving bands over the surface of the ball. The alien twitched its fingers and the symbols changed in response.

The two human intruders immediately went stiff. It was as if they had turned into living statues. Then the aliens turned toward Jeff.

Too panicked to even scream, Jeff stumbled backwards until he bumped against the wall. One of the aliens waved his hand and Jeff collapsed unconscious and face down onto the bed.

Gliding to Jeff's side, the alien gently laid him on his back. Checking to ensure that Jeff would be comfortable until he awoke, the alien then touched Jeff's forehead for a moment. It turned to its companion.

If Jeff had been conscious, he would have heard the alien click, clack, and hiss to its companion. If, somehow, he could have understood the alien's speech, he would have heard it say, "The boy is safe. All things will proceed as they should. Causality is preserved."

The alien's companion hissed his approval. Then he asked, "Will he remember the encounter?"

Clacking its negative response, the alien replied, "No. I have removed the memories. If any are left, he will think he fell asleep and had a bad dream. Now we must take these intruders and depart."

Clicking agreement, the alien's companion grabbed the two white-blond humans around the waist and hefted them easily. All four disappeared.

The next day was very ordinary, at least until lunch. As usual, Jeff, Akio, and Harry ate together. Jeff wolfed down his lunch while Harry nibbled hers. Between gulps, Jeff asked, "Harry, could you cut my hair? It's *really* getting long."

Harry's green eyes sparkled, "Sure, Jeff. Come on over right after school and I'll cut it then." She flounced her long, red curls.

Akio poked at his food silently. After a minute or two, Harry noticed and asked, "What's the matter with you?"

Startled, Akio ran his fingers though his short, thick, spiky black hair. "What makes you think something's wrong?" he asked warily.

"Duh," Harry shot back. "You're not eating *or* talking. Normally you do both *all* the time."

Akio's eyes drooped down to his food. After a moment he said, "My family's colonizing."

Both Jeff and Harry were stunned. Jeff stammered, "Wh-what? You're what? Where? When?"

Heaving a slow sigh, Akio answered, "My parents told me last night. We're going to the New Tokyo system. A planet called Yokohama. Most of my relatives from Japan and Hawaii are already there."

Jeff was speechless. Harry asked, "Will you ever come back? Will we ever see you again?"

"No," Akio replied. "At least not until we're grown up. The New Tokyo system is 259 light years from Earth. You don't just drop by for a visit. It's way too much money."

Jeff questioned, "Why is your family colonizing now?"

"Dad's probably going to be laid off. He's one of the newest ones there and they always lay off the newest ones first. We leave in a month, right after school's out."

"Wow," was all Jeff could say. He had known Akio as long as he could remember. Not having him around was something he couldn't imagine.

Harry, as she always did, tried to make the best of things. "Maybe it'll be nice there," she offered.

Akio shrugged noncommittally. "That's what my mom says. The whole planet's an ocean. No land at all. People live in floating arcologies. There's lots of jobs and most people do well there. They raise fish in big floating pens—fish farms. They make big money selling fish."

Gloomily, Jeff moaned, "Who's got money for real fish?"

"People all over the colonies are making good money. They buy fish," Akio replied. "There's even people on Earth who have enough money for fish, but it costs a lot."

With a pained expression, Akio continued, "My relatives bought us tickets and all the synthpaste we need for the trip. They've even bought a flat for us. We have to pay them back, but Dad thinks we can do that in six years."

Jeff was surprised. "You have to take your own food with you?"

"Yup," Akio nodded. "When you go steerage class you do. Those are the cheapest tickets. They give you water on the ship, but you have to take your own food."

Harry broke in, "And you leave in a month?"

Even more dejectedly, Akio nodded again. "Yup. Dad put our flat up for sale this morning. My mom just emailed me and said they sold it already to a family from Outside the arcology. So we're all set to go. We just have to pack up our stuff."

Jeff, Akio, and Harry didn't have much to say to each other throughout the rest of the day. The trio had been inseparable for years. Now Akio was leaving, probably forever. They spent a very glum day.

After school, Jeff dug into his homework. As soon as he sat down to his lesson, the doorbell rang. When Jeff answered it, he found Kevin Gibson and his ten-year-old brother Logan. "Hi guys," he greeted. "Come on in." The Gibson brothers entered and plopped onto the couch. Jeff pulled out a folding chair and used that.

"So here's the thing," Kevin began immediately. "You know my dad left Earth to find work right?"

Surprised at his abruptness, Jeff nodded and asked, "Did he find anything?"

"Yes," Kevin answered, "but he's still traveling. He'll be on a ship for another three months. That's the problem. My dad took a job with a mining company, but they don't pay him until he gets there and starts working. But now my mother is sick and can't work. We can't afford to take her to the doctor."

"Wow Kevin, I wish there was something I could do to help."

"Well actually Jeff, there is. My mother and my brother are both living on less synthpaste than one person normally eats. I've been spending all of my 'robot club' money on food for them. If things keep going the way they are, I won't be able to pay my share for lessons unless you let Logan into the group."

Hesitantly, Jeff asked, "You mean into the robot club, don't you?"

"No. I mean into the *real* group. We need the food and the money or both Mom and Logan will starve. I've been trying to mix in some of my food from the you-know-what. But if I do too much of that, my mom will find out the secret."

Jeff looked at Logan thoughtfully. Logan seemed puzzled by the conversation. Standing, Jeff retrieved his datapad and turned it on. He sat back down, faced Kevin and queried, "Can he keep the secret?"

"Absolutely. Right Logan?"

Logan asked, "What secret?"

"Logan," Jeff explained, "you have to absolutely promise that you won't tell anyone our secret. Everyone's future depends on this."

"Everyone?"

"Everyone in our group. If you blab, we're all going to be poor the rest of our lives. This is the most important secret you'll ever keep. If you can't keep it, say so now."

"I ... I can keep the secret," Logan gulped, wide-eyed.

Jeff used his datapad to log onto his monkeybot. He held it on his lap so Logan could see. "We tell everyone our group is a robot club and that we fix up and sell robots to make money for lessons and books that will help us get into better high schools. If we go to a better high school, we can get into a better college. That means better jobs. Understand?"

Logan nodded.

Jeff continued, "Now here's the secret part. Fixing and selling robots is not how we make our money—at least not most of it. We really keep most of the robots. We all have one. Our bots don't really have much brains. I put wireless network adapters in all of our bots so we can control them from our datapads. But we use our datapads as the brains and the datapads send commands to our bots across the grid."

In awe, Logan questioned, "How did you learn to do that?"

"My dad taught me the basics. I taught myself the rest. Now look here. You see that door my monkeybot is going into?"

"Yeah."

"I wrote a program to make my bot go there when I was 12. The program guides the bot to that door. And that door is an entrance for maintenance robots. It leads to a series of ramps. The ramps go up among the big support beams that hold up the dome on top of the arcology, the one that covers the park."

"You mean your bot is all the way on top of the arcology?"

Jeff nodded. "Yup."

"Isn't that against the rules?"

"That's why we have to keep it secret."

"Oh."

Jeff continued, "When I was 11, I was in the park and playing with my monkeybot. I looked up and noticed the ramps. I got curious and did some research on the grid. The ramps used to be used by maintenance robots that rolled around on wheels. These days, they have gravity mirrors. You know what those are?"

Logan nodded and replied, "They make things float in the air?"

"Right. So the maintenance robots don't need the ramps anymore. But no one took the ramps down. The maintenance robots never look at the ramps when they float by. They're programmed to repair the beams that hold up the dome, but they ignore everything else. I searched for weeks to find the door you just saw. But once I did, my robot was able to follow the ramps way up near the top of the dome. The ramps are in the sunlight every day so they're the perfect spot to grow food."

"*Grow food*?" Logan gasped. "You know how to grow food?"

"Sure," Jeff answered, "we learned about it in school. You put seeds in dirt and add sunlight and water."

"Dirt? You grow food in *dirt*?"

"Yup. And that's the secret. We're growing food up there on the ramps to eat and to sell. We use the money to buy lessons. And you can never, *never* tell anyone or our farm will be closed down. None of us will have the food *or* the lessons. Our entire futures are riding on this, Logan. You can't tell no matter what."

Nodding, Logan swore, "I'll never tell. No matter what. I promise. But ..."

"But what?"

"Where did you get the dirt?"

"Well, there's no dirt in the arcology, except for in the park on top. But taking dirt from up there can get your whole family kicked out. So my friends Akio, Harriet and I pooled our money to buy a small bag of potting soil and a bag of compost starter mix at an expensive store on level 2831. That was the only place we could find it. People near the top of the arcology have money for things like dirt. They have flats big enough for potted plants and even gardens."

"What's compost?" Logan interrupted. "What does that mean?"

"It's a way of making dirt from organic garbage like food scraps."

Logan scratched his head and cast a confused look at his brother. Kevin assured Jeff, "I'll explain it all to him later." Logan shrugged and then nodded.

Jeff continued, "We started with that one bag of dirt and composted our kitchen scraps to make more. It took us months of working at it, but we finally got enough to plant a couple of short rows of vegetables. We've kept going and now our farm stretches over lots of ramps. It's hundreds of feet long."

"Whoa! For real?"

"Yup. And every day we have to do chores on our farm if we want to get food. Watch." Jeff tapped commands into his datapad to run a program that made his monkeybot fetch a container of water and carry it up the ramps. The water came from a faucet not far inside the robot maintenance door.

"See that faucet? It used to be used for cleaning the dome. These days, it's ignored so we use it to water our crops. We use our bots to plant crops, carry water, do the weeding, and harvest."

Kevin interjected, "Logan and I can share my bot. I'll get up early and do my chores in the morning, and Logan can do his after school."

Jeff nodded. "That works," he said. "At least until you can buy Logan a bot of his own. I'll get some money from the seed fund to buy you starter seeds. After that, everything depends on you, Logan."

"Me?"

"Yeah. Whether your farm works or not depends on how hard you work. Some of us make pretty good money. Others just barely get by. It all depends on you."

"I'll work *really* hard," Logan promised.

Jeff smiled and told him, "I bet you will."

Jeff stood. Kevin and Logan copied him. "Ok Logan," Jeff told them as he showed them toward the door, "you're in the group. But remember, if you tell the secret, you'll starve. And everyone else's future is gone. Never, never tell the secret."

"I won't. I swear."

Kevin and Logan thanked Jeff, said their goodbyes, and left. Jeff returned to his homework. By evening, Jeff was ready for the group meeting. It would take his mind off of Akio's departure.

After dinner, Kent did the dishes and then went out again for the evening.

Going into his room, Jeff folded up his desk and chair, inflated his bed, and plopped himself down on it. Pulling out his datapad, he put in his earpiece, adjusted the microphone, and called Akio.

"Ready to go?" Akio's dragon asked as soon as he answered Jeff's call.

"Sure," Jeff replied. Jeff's avatar was a wizard dressed in leather and shaggy furs, and carrying a magic staff. Jeff made it climb onto the back of Akio's dragon. "Let's go."

With a jet of flame and a roar, Akio's dragon ponderously flapped its wings. It rose into a clear blue sky.

Harry was hosting the eChat on her datapad. Jeff used a link in the invitation to connect. When he and Akio were accepted, a shimmering circle of light appeared in the air in front of their avatars. The dragon flew into the circle, and instantly their avatars were transported to Merfolk's Keep.

Akio's dragon circled above the lush, green island a couple of times. Looking down, Jeff could see Harry's fairy sitting on a rock in the lagoon. They were too high up to tell, but she was probably playing her flute while the mermaids sang. Jeff and Akio descended and landed on the white-sand beach. Jeff made his wizard avatar climb down from Akio's dragon.

Everyone in the group had their own avatar. As Jeff looked around, he could see that most of the group was already there. Some of them were on the balcony of the ornate golden castle above the beach, but most were on the beach itself.

As usual, Ally Wilson, whose avatar was a warrior princess, was having kickboxing matches with several of the guys. And as usual, she was winning. Further down the beach, Kevin Gibson was trying to get into the volleyball game. The other players didn't want to let him in because his avatar was a 24 foot tall giant. It gave him an unfair advantage. Eventually, he wandered off and went to wrestle the sea monster in the lagoon.

Harry's fairy flew to them, her pale blue wings shimmering. Her fairy's knee-length red hair flowed gently behind her. "You're late," she scolded.

"Nice to see you too," Akio said sarcastically. The fairy stuck out her tongue in reply.

"Everyone's here but Hugh," Harry told them. "I tried calling him, but he doesn't answer. His datapad says he's busy."

Jeff said simply, "Then we wait."

Akio heaved a sigh and said, "Whatever." He wandered over to Kevin Gibson's avatar, shot a jet of flame at the giant's rear end, and challenged him to a fight. Within moments, they were happily knocking the stuffing out of each other.

As they watched Akio and Kevin duke it out, Jeff asked, "Were you playing your flute with the mermaids?"

Harry's voice brightened, "Yeah. You wanna hear the song?"

"Sure."

At that moment, an icon flashed on Jeff's datapad. "Wait," he said to Harry. "I'm getting a call from Hugh."

Jeff tapped the icon and said, "Hugh, where are you?"

"Jeff," Hugh answered excitedly, "I struck gold!"

"What?" Jeff asked, puzzled.

"Yesterday I was exploring with my dogbot after I did your farm chores. I transformed it into humanoid mode so it could climb. I found an access shaft that runs up the building next to the main garbage chute. There's a side shaft that runs right to a restaurant on level 2998. They serve *real food* there, and you wouldn't believe what they're throwing away."

Hugh's dogbot, like most toy robots, could transform into a human-like figure with hands and feet. In humanoid mode, the robot could climb and walk like a small person.

"Wait, Hugh. How do you know they serve real food?"

"The side shaft runs along the outside of the chute. I pulled off a panel like we did in the school cafeteria. I'm using my net to catch garbage. I just got an *entire* head of lettuce that they threw away because part of it was a little brown."

Shortly after starting their farm, Jeff, Akio, and Harry realized that the little blobs of leftover synthpaste they scraped off of their family's plates when they cleaned the dishes would never provide enough compost. With their robots, they found an access shaft that ran just outside the garbage chute of their school's cafeteria. When they wanted to collect food scraps for compost, they had their robots remove a panel on the garbage shoot and use a homemade net to catch blobs of synthpaste going by. The entire group took turns collecting garbage from the cafeteria for their compost piles.

"You're kidding," Jeff said.

"Nope. I got a whole big bag of real food. All my bot can carry. This is more than I get in a week from the cafeteria."

"Man," Jeff breathed, "you *did* strike gold."

"Everyone else should get their bots up here too. I'm sending a map. Seriously, Jeff, we can double the size of the farm in a few months."

Hugh hung up while Jeff sent a broadcast message to everyone in the group explaining what Hugh found.

Harry was pleased. "Hugh will be a hero," she said. "It won't be hard to get the others to watch out for him now."

Like the other members of the group, Jeff immediately disconnected from the eChat and activated his monkeybot. Far above him in the ramps on top of the arcology, the monkeybot made its way toward the maintenance shaft on Hugh's map. As it began its downward climb through the arcology's service tunnels, Jeff plotted a course for it that would take it to the restaurant's garbage chute. When it arrived, it would automatically begin collecting compostable garbage.

Happy with how the evening turned out, Jeff spent a couple hours playing the battered old guitar his uncle gave him for his fourteenth birthday.

4

The public water park wasn't crowded as Jeff, Harry, and Akio made their way to the surfboard booth on Saturday morning. They each checked out a battered surfboard from an automated service stand and then headed toward the wave pools.

Akio, of course, went straight for the Heavy Surf Pool. Able to out-surf most people twice his age, Akio was always a wild man on a surfboard. It was an image he liked. In fact, whenever he went surfing, he always wore a shirt that said "Surf Maniac" on it.

All three of them had their bathing suits on under their clothes, so they took off their clothes and put them into a locker. They also stuffed the locker with their lunches and towels, deposited a coin, closed it, and removed the bright orange key. Harry fussed a bit more about how old her bathing suit was. Jeff and Akio both reassured her again that she looked good in it, which seemed to satisfy her.

At the wave pool, they stopped to watch the few other surfers that were in the water. Akio ran his fingers through his jet-black hair, which stuck up in every direction as usual. His piercing eyes were such a dark brown that they were almost black. "Mmm," he observed with an almost professional air. "I think most are under seven feet. Stinks. I was hoping for 12 to 14."

Although Akio was slightly shorter than a lot of other guys his age, including Jeff, most of the guys at school were too smart to pick on him. Strong and lean, Akio was known for being a swift and agile fighter. He was deeply tanned from the many hours he spent under the water park's sun lamps.

Jeff, who was a bit tall for fourteen, towered over Akio. He had always been bigger, and people sometimes commented humorously about it. But neither of them paid attention. They had been lifelong friends from the moment they met.

Without a word, Harry jumped into the long pool with her surfboard and paddled toward the end where the waves were created. Akio quickly followed with Jeff close behind. By the time they got to the other end, Harry was already catching her first wave. Perched on her board, she rode toward the shallow end of the pool.

Jeff admired Harry's light agility on the surfboard. She wasn't as good as Akio, but she was a lot better than Jeff, and he knew it. Jeff was never bothered by the fact that the other two were better surfers. 'I'm better with robots,' he told himself.

When the next wave came, Akio hung back to wait for something bigger so Jeff caught it. Arriving at the shallow end, Jeff found Harry waiting for him. She pointed behind him. Turning, he saw that Akio had indeed found a big wave to ride. And as always, he was doing tricks on his surfboard that no one in their right mind would try.

As the morning continued, the sunlamps overhead gradually heated the water park, which slowly filled up with people. By eleven o'clock, even the Heavy Surf Pool was getting crowded. The three of them decided to sit out a while and sunbathe not far from some artificial palm trees to get dry. Retrieving their things from the locker, they grabbed their lunches, spread out their towels on the fake grass, and sat down.

Digging into his lunch, Jeff enjoyed the feel of the artificial sunlight on his skin. All around them, people shouted happily in the various pools as they surfed, swam, dove, and rode water slides.

"I think," Harry said as she ate, "that we should put Hugh together into two groups of three. Dirk's probably going to target him for a while."

Akio's eyebrows went up. "Two groups?" he asked.

"Mmf," Harry replied, her mouth full of synthpaste. "They can take turns going around with him. That way, he'll never be out alone and the others won't feel too put out. What do you think, Jeff?"

Watching a little boy not far away dump cold water on his sunbathing teenage sister, Jeff shrugged. "Probably best," he answered. "Hugh needs an excuse to get to know more people anyway. He won't make friends if we don't push him some." The little boy dove into a nearby pool in a vain attempt to escape his sister's wrath.

They fell silent a moment while they ate. Then Jeff commented, "I wonder if we're being arrogant by assigning the others in the group to watch out for other kids. No one likes to have their friends picked for them."

Harry shook her head. "No Jeff, I've talked about this with most of the girls and some of the guys. They look to you for leadership and they know they were safer going out in twos and threes. They really don't mind letting you take charge of assigning them into groups. They accept you as our unofficial leader."

"Well then, you two are my unofficial advisors," he replied, smiling.

At noon, the three of them put their clothes back on over their bathing suits, which were now dry. They returned their surfboards, picked up their things, and headed toward the exit.

Making their way to their floor, they retrieved their data pads. Jeff also grabbed his toolbox, and then they rode an elevator to level 3000. Arriving at the maintenance door that led upward to the park dome's maintenance ramps, they sent commands to their robots to come out. When their bots emerged, they took an elevator back down and went to the community center. Every Saturday afternoon, the entire group met together in a room at the center to study. Only about half of them were there when the trio arrived.

"Hi guys," Jeff called out. "Anybody here got 'Introduction to Physics'?" he asked.

One of the guys in the group, Joe Goldman, answered, "Me. I'm done with it. You can have it if you need it. But are you sure you want it? This stuff was so hard I thought my brains were gonna ooze out of my ears."

Joe smiled and tapped some commands into his datapad. Instantly, the book arrived on Jeff's datapad.

Jeff sat down to read and wait for the others. They arrived slowly in groups of twos and threes. As the room filled, Jeff set his datapad down and said, "I'm going around to chat with everyone."

"How come you always do that?" Akio asked.

"I learned a long time ago that the best way to keep the group together is to take time to talk with each person. And I like it."

As Jeff was chatting with the others, he noticed Akio sitting with Kevin Gibson at a table near the back of the room. Unlike the others, they were not studying much. In fact, Akio discovered that if he pounded his fist on the table, he could make it bounce upward a few inches. Kevin quickly copied him. When Kevin suggested that they try pounding the table with their foreheads to see if they could get the same result, Harry stomped over to them, sat on the table with her arms crossed, and glared at them.

"If you two break something," she hissed, "we'll get kicked out of here forever."

Kevin and Akio decided that they really, really needed to study English. Harry continued to glare at them for a while, so Kevin eventually felt that he needed to study with Dane Monson at another table.

When Jeff was finished talking with each member of the group, he went to the table where Akio and Harry were seated. Harry was smiling at him. "What?" he asked.

"Nothing," Harry replied. Then she said, "You."

"What about me?"

She punched him lightly on the arm. "You know."

Puzzled, Jeff asked Akio. "Do you know what she's talking about?" Akio rolled his eyes and went back to the book he was reading on his datapad. Jeff looked back at Harry.

With an exasperated sigh, she said, "You did all this. You got us all together. Thirty-five kids. Thirty-seven now with Hugh and Logan. You should be proud of yourself, Jeff. You've really done a lot for everyone here."

Embarrassed, Jeff looked down at his datapad and mumbled, "I ... I didn't do much."

Still playful, she hit his arm again, a little harder. "Don't say that," she countered. "It was you that got us all together to keep us safe from Dirk. You started the robot fund with your own money. Now we all have robots to take care of our gardens in the farms because of you."

Still mumbling, Jeff said, "Everyone puts money into the robot fund. Not just me."

"Yes, but you started it. Akio and I wouldn't have robots or farms without you. When the others came into the group, we put money in like you did so they could get robots too. Now they do the same thing."

"It's not that big of a deal."

Harry punched his arm once more, harder.

"Ow!"

"Oh, that didn't hurt," she scowled. Jeff just clutched the sore spot on his arm.

"You should be proud," she repeated, clearly growing more agitated. "Everyone buys used and broken toy robots and you fix them and make them do things that no one ever thought they could do. Anyone else would think they're just cheap junk. Without the software you write, we could never get them to do chores on the farm. Our farm money gets us better books and lessons. Jeff, everyone here has a chance at getting into a good high school and maybe a good college because of you. This was all your idea. You should be proud."

Jeff was shocked. It never occurred to him that she thought these things. "It's just easier if we work together," he told her. "It's no big deal."

Instantly, he regretted saying that again. Harry raised her small fist to punch his arm, but he slid his chair away and covered his upper arm with his other hand. Any further discussion was stopped by the arrival of Madison Burke at their table.

"Sorry," Madison said as she looked from Harry to Jeff. "Am I interrupting?"

"No," Jeff told her quickly. "What's up?"

Madison held out her catbot. "Can you take a look at this? There's something wrong with the left eye."

"Sure." Jeff reached for his toolbox, which held both parts for their bots and tools to fix them. He always carried the toolbox to the study sessions because everyone in the group brought their robots. It was a good time to fix whatever was broken on them. Most longtime members of the group had learned to fix robots from him, so they helped with the repairs.

Jeff checked the eye and decided it needed replacing. He used a spare from his toolbox. He and Madison chatted as he worked. In about fifteen minutes, he had the catbot working perfectly.

"The new one's blue, so the color doesn't match the other eye," he apologized as he handed the bot back to Madison. "But it works now."

"That's ok," Madison answered, smiling. She tossed her long, brown hair back with her hand. "The blue looks better anyway. I'll save up for another blue one so both eyes will match. Thanks, Jeff."

Irritated, Harry glared after Madison as she went back across the room. "She could have gotten Luke to fix that," she grumbled. "He's sitting right over there next to her."

Jeff was surprised. "I don't mind," he told her. "I'll fix anybody's bot."

Harry fell silent and sullenly went back to her lesson. From across the room, Dane Monson called, "Can anybody help me with Statistics?" Harry looked up and answered, "Yeah, I already went through those lessons." She moved to Dane's table.

As they studied, members of the group came and went. Jeff didn't pay attention until Brittany Jackson burst into the room and shouted, "Have you guys seen what's going on out there?"

"What do you mean?" Harry asked.

"Someone's been attacked over across the courtyard. In the corridor behind the food stands. The paramedics are there now."

A cold knot formed in the pit of Jeff's stomach as he had a terrible thought. "Does anybody know what time Hugh Benson was supposed to come today?"

No one answered.

Jeff and Akio both bolted for the door. Several other group members were closer and got there first, blocking the doorway as they all tried to jam themselves through at the same time. "We can't all go!" Jeff shouted. "Akio and I'll go see." The others let them through.

Bounding out through the lobby, the pair jumped a bench and shot out the automatic double doors of the community center. Outside, a large crowd was gathered across the courtyard next to an ambulance that floated a foot or so above the floor. They reached the edge of the crowd in a moment and tried to push their way through, but no one was moving. The police were keeping everyone back. All the two of them could see was the paramedics' heads as they loaded a stretcher into the back of the ambulance. Its lights and siren came on as it pulled forward. All down the wide corridor, people moved aside as the ambulance floated toward the vehicle elevator near the center of the building.

Jeff and Akio looked at each other helplessly. "I guess we'd better go back," Akio offered, and together they trudged back to the community center. The rest of the group was waiting anxiously in the lobby and looking out through its plastiglass front wall.

Harry had had the sense to bring her datapad. She said, "I tried to call Hugh, but there's no answer. Same with his parents. I'm trying his older sister now. Oh wait, she's answering."

Janice Benson's face appeared on Harry's datapad. Everyone crowded closer to get a look. "Hello?" Janice said. She looked like she had been crying.

"Janice, I'm Harriet Brightway, one of Hugh's friends. Do you know where he is?"

In a trembling voice Janice answered, "He's on his way to the hospital. We're on the elevator up to there now. The emergency doctor's already looked at the paramedic's scans of him. It looks like he's got a bad concussion, some broken ribs, and a broken nose."

"Oh no!" Harry gasped. "Is he going to be alright?"

"The doctor won't say. He wants to examine Hugh himself first."

The image of Janice's face jerked out of the frame. The plump face of a middle-aged woman appeared instead. "You're one of Hubert's new friends? I'm his mother. Do you know who might have attacked him? The paramedics said that whoever did it knocked him out with a blow from behind and then dragged him into the corridor behind the food stands. The attacker dropped him on his face and broke his nose. Then he kicked Hubert again and again in the side and broke several ribs. Who could have been angry enough at him to do such a thing?"

Harry, Jeff, and Akio looked at each other warily. "Mamsen Benson," Harry replied, "can we come talk to you?"

"We?"

"Me and a couple of Hugh's other friends."

"Do you know who did this?"

Jeff moved closer to Harry so that Mamsen Benson would be able to see him. "Mamsen Benson, I'm Jeff Bowman. I think we might have an idea who did this. Can we come see you in person?"

"Yes. Come right away. We're at the Sector Hospital Emergency Room. Please meet us there. And thank you." The datapad went blank.

Jeff hit his head with his fist. "I'm such an IDIOT!" he shouted. "I thought he'd be ok coming here because the community center is on his same floor. We should have picked him up ourselves." He hit his head again.

Harry grabbed his fist. "Jeff, you couldn't have known. We *all* thought it would be ok for him to walk down the corridor alone. If he had just made it across the courtyard, we would have arranged for the others on his floor to go around with him and protect him. He almost made it."

"Almost isn't good enough!" Jeff shouted. "It's 'almost' that got him beat up."

Akio put his hand on Jeff's shoulder. "We gotta go, man. There's no time for this. It's not your fault. If the adults in this place were doing their jobs, we'd *all* be safe. The important thing is to get to the hospital. We *know* who did this. And the faster we tell Hugh's parents, the faster the police will nail him."

For a moment, Jeff couldn't reply. Then, numbly, he nodded.

"I've already brought all our things," Harry said as she held up Jeff's datapad, backpack, and toolbox. She typed a command into his datapad, and his monkeybot skittered toward them. Jeff took his things from her while Dane Monson handed Akio his things. Akio also typed a command into his datapad and his dragonbot bounded up next to him. With her datapad, Harry put her white tigerbot into follow mode. The three of them stowed their datapads into their backpacks and started toward the elevator with their robots dutifully trailing along behind.

"Videomail us when you know how Hugh is," Madison called out as they walked away.

To Jeff, the elevator couldn't move fast enough as they rode upward. Arriving at the hospital's emergency room, they soon found Hugh's family. Hugh's father was talking to a doctor while his mother and sister waited together in the hard plastic seats. They looked up as the trio approached. A distracting image of an annoying young woman gave stupid and obvious kitchen safety tips from a video stream on the wall panel across the room.

Jeff didn't even try to greet them. "Any news?" he asked.

Wiping her tears, Hugh's mother replied, "He's going to be alright, but it's going to take a while to heal. He'll be in the hospital for a few days, and then he can come home. We're going in to see him in a moment. You said you know who did this?"

"We're not sure, Mamsen Benson," Harry responded. "We know that a boy at school named Dirk Highborne has been picking on him. We were going to arrange for our other classmates on his floor to go around with him and keep him safe."

"Why didn't Hubert tell us about this?"

This time Jeff answered, "Dirk Highborne's mother is a vice principal at the school and she's on the Sector Council. She always gets Dirk off whenever he gets in trouble."

"Well," Mamsen Benson announced huffily, "we'll see about that." After a moment she asked, "How long have you known Hubert?"

"Just since he moved up a grade," Harry replied. "He came into our class. But we didn't really get to know him until about a week and a half ago when Dirk started picking on him. It's mostly Jeff and Akio who have been keeping him safe at school since then."

"You helped too," Akio interjected.

Mamsen Benson was moved. "You three have been doing that for Hubert?"

Embarrassed, all three looked down at their feet. "Well," Jeff mumbled, "we've just been hanging around together with him. Dirk won't go after anyone in a group. It's not been any big deal. We just do things together. Hugh's our friend now."

Mamsen Benson couldn't answer; she just cried. Janice put her arm around her mother. Sirsen Benson, who had finished talking to the doctor, walked up to his wife and daughter. "We can go in now," he said. As his wife stood, he put his arm around her also. Together, the Bensons entered the inner part of the hospital through a set of double doors.

For several minutes, Jeff, Akio, and Harry stood looking after them, unable to move or speak. The wall panel's video stream was replaced by the image of a smug doctor telling everyone how good the care was at this hospital. At last Harry said, "I think we'd better go home." Together, they exited the hospital and walked to the nearest elevator.

5

Jeff and Akio stood outside the door of Harry's flat. Jeff rang the doorbell. The door popped open and Harry stepped lightly out. "Ready?" she asked, beaming.

"We've *been* ready," Akio shot back. "It's you we've been waiting for. Can we go now?"

"Of course," replied Harriet. Together, the three of them went down to the floor the Bensons lived on.

They said nothing as they hurried past the scattered groups of people who were drifting along the wide main corridor. A tram floated by, loaded with familiar faces. Glancing at them, Jeff saw by the bags they carried that most of them were headed off to do their weekly shopping. Two men with red hair and a third with white-blond hair gazed at Jeff from the tram. He didn't know why, but they made him feel vaguely uneasy. An image of giant crabs flashed inexplicably through his mind.

Arriving at the Bensons' flat, Jeff pressed the doorbell. Mamsen Benson answered almost immediately.

"Thanks for coming," she greeted them warmly. "Hubert's really been looking forward to your visit. Please come in."

This was the first time Jeff had ever been inside Hugh's flat. He saw that, like many flats on this level, the Benson's place was basically one large room. The kitchen area was along the rear wall. There was also a door there that led to the bathroom. Everyone slept on beds that were lowered from the ceiling. Hugh's bed was the only one down at the moment.

"Hi, guys," Hugh chirped as they approached his bed.

"Oh Hugh," Harry gasped as they approached. Jeff could see why. The entire left side of Hugh's face was swollen, and so was his nose.

"You look awful." Akio told him. "Almost as ugly as Jeff."

"Akio!" Harry snapped. "Be nice."

Hugh and Akio both smiled. "Don't make me laugh," Hugh chuckled. "Seriously. If I laugh, it *really* hurts. Broken ribs stink. If you roll over in your sleep, it feels like someone just stabbed you in the side."

Jeff asked, "Why is your arm in a sling?"

The smile left Hugh's face, "That was the arm he dragged me with. It got pretty badly sprained."

Hugh looked at their worried faces. "It's not as bad as it seems. They gave me a shot that makes me heal fast. I'll be up and around next week."

"I hope Dirk goes to jail for a long time for this," Harry told him.

Mamsen Benson broke in with a hard, cold voice, "He's been let out already."

"WHAT?" all three shouted incredulously.

"There was no proof," Hugh answered. "I didn't see who attacked me. No one else did either. The police are pretty sure it was him, but they had to let him go."

For a moment, no one said anything. Finally, Jeff got out, "I can't believe it."

With great self-control, Mamsen Benson spoke again. "He planned this very carefully. He made sure he could get Hubert from behind. The police think he hit him with a sock filled with something hard. There were sock fibers found in Hubert's hair."

"Didn't anyone find the sock?" Harry asked.

Mamsen Benson shook her head tightly. "I'm afraid not. The Highborne's flat was searched, but there was nothing. So was Dirk's locker at school. He probably dumped it into the nearest garbage chute. By the time the police started searching, it was most likely recycled."

"I can't believe Dirk would do something so violent," Harry said.

Jeff wondered, "Why would Highborne want to just beat you up like this? He usually only beats people up when he wants to steal from them. And then he only hits them until they give him what he wants."

Hugh told him, "He stole my datapad and robot."

"WHAT?" all three yelped again.

"Why would he want your datapad?" Harry asked.

Akio broke in, "Those things are worth *serious* money Outside."

Harry was shocked. "Outside? Nobody goes Outside. It's dangerous."

"I think Highborne probably goes Outside," Akio countered. "It seems to me he's up to something—something that takes money. Whatever it is, Outside is where he can find the right sort of people to buy what he needs. It's like the private eye."

"Huh?" Harry asked.

Jeff explained, "About a month ago Akio saw Highborne using a private eye. You can't get those inside the arcology."

Harry was puzzled. "What's a private eye?"

"It's a simple type of scanner that lets you see what's displayed on other people's datapads," Jeff said. "They're waaaaay illegal. He was using it in school to cheat. When Akio saw it, I wrote a program to make the classroom's network access point emit a signal that burns out private eyes. I gave it to Sirsen Bering and they use it in all the classrooms now. It fried Highborne's private eye. Remember when the smoke alarm went off but they didn't find anything? That was his private eye. He had to have bought that Outside."

"You're right," Mamsen Benson told them. "The police told us the datapad was taken out of the building. It was you who gave them the evidence, Harriet. When you tried to call Hubert on his datapad, the grid located it down near the bottom of the building. He was almost out the door with it by then. Unfortunately all that proves is where the datapad went, not who took it there. And Dirk has an alibi. There are some girls who swear that he was with them the entire time the attack took place."

Harry blurted out bitterly, "Yeah, he's pretty popular with the girls a year older than us. They think he's good looking and they like all the fancy clothes he wears. He tells them he moved here from a few sectors above ours, instead of a few sectors below ours. It doesn't surprise me that they'll lie for him. He knows all the right things to say to girls. I've heard him at it before. I about threw up. Those girls were so stupid to swallow all that garbage."

Neither Jeff nor Akio knew what to say.

Jeff lifted his datapad so Hugh could see it and said, "I wrote you a game to play. Let me know if you like it." He remembered that Hugh's datapad was gone. "Oh, sorry," he mumbled.

Harry broke in. "Can you get a new datapad?"

Hugh nodded. "Because it was stolen, they'll give me another one for free. But it takes a few months."

Harry was shocked. "*Months?*" she asked.

"Yup. My dad says 'The gears of the system grind slowly.' He means that they take a long time to do anything."

"But you'll miss the rest of school," Harry objected.

"Yeah, I won't finish this year. I'll have to do the year over again. But I'll be back in my original grade. Maybe that's better. Moving up caused me nothing but trouble."

Harry spoke for all of them when she said, "Oh, no. Hugh that's terrible! You're one of the smartest guys around. You shouldn't have to be held back." Hugh looked at them sadly and shrugged.

Mamsen Benson turned to Hugh's sister. "Well, Janice. I think it's time we did our errands and let Hubert visit with his friends."

"What errands?" Janice asked blankly. She recoiled at the severe look she got from her mother, and then said, "Oh, yeah. Errands." The two of them left.

"Mom's really glad you three came," Hugh said looking toward the door.

"It's no big deal," Akio told him. "So when do we beat up Highborne?"

"Akio!" Harry objected. But she calmed down when the look on his face said he was joking—probably.

Jeff changed the subject by handing Hugh his datapad. "Wanna try the game I wrote you?"

Hugh gratefully accepted the loan of the datapad and played with his uninjured hand. The four of them continued to chat as he played. After a while, Hugh told them he was tired, so he returned Jeff's datapad and they left so he could rest.

Out in the stark, beige corridor, Jeff said, "We've got to do something to help him."

Akio nodded, "We should buy him another robot when he gets his new datapad."

"I was thinking of more than that," Jeff replied. Harry asked him what he meant, but he wouldn't say anything else.

6

The evening after visiting Hugh, Jeff sat on his bed playing old, old music on his guitar. 'This thing really needs new strings,' Jeff thought.

Suddenly, the doorbell rang—and rang, and rang, and rang. Jeff's dad wasn't home, so Jeff ran to answer the door. By the time he got there, Akio was pounding on it.

"BlackHat attack!" Akio yelled as soon as Jeff opened the door. "I was just hit by a BlackHat attack. It took everything that was on my datapad. Turn off your datapad NOW!"

It took a moment for Jeff to realize what Akio was saying. When he did, he bolted into his bedroom, grabbed his datapad, and slammed his finger on the off switch.

"Who has BlackHat?" Jeff demanded.

"Who do you think?" Akio shot back. "He's after our term projects. Now we know what he wanted all that money for. With the BlackHat program he can hack anyone's datapad in the sector. There's no way we can keep him out except turn off our datapads."

"We need to tell the others," he said urgently.

"No duh. Let's go to Harry's first," Akio replied.

"Go?" Jeff asked, momentarily puzzled. We can just ..." His voice trailed off as he realized the implications of Highborne with a copy of the BlackHat program.

Akio was already shaking his head. "No we can't. We can't turn on our datapads, so we can't call anybody. And neither of us has a gridPhone. We have to *walk* over to everyone's flats. Now."

Without another word, he and Jeff sprinted to Harry's flat. When she came out, they quickly explained the situation.

"He's on the grid right now," Akio told her. "My datapad was just hit a few minutes ago. I'll bet he tries to hit everyone in the group tonight."

Hurriedly, Harry ducked back into her flat and shut off her datapad. When she returned she said, "We have to spread out and tell everyone as fast as we can. We know Dirk's on his datapad right now, so we can each go alone. I'll go tell Ally Wilson. We'll each go tell half the girls. You two each go tell half the boys."

Jeff agreed, "We'll meet at the courtyard in front of the community center when we're done." Akio and Harry nodded and they each went their separate directions.

It took an hour and a half to get everyone warned. When they met in the courtyard, Harry immediately asked Jeff, "What are we going to do? We can't keep our datapads off forever."

"There's only one thing we can do," Jeff answered thoughtfully. "We have to get a copy of the WhiteHat program installed on everyone's datapads. That's the only thing that'll protect them."

"No way," Akio objected. "We don't have that kind of money."

"Yup," Jeff agreed, "you're right. But there might be a way we can get copies for everyone."

Akio asked, "How?"

"We need to see Sirsen Bering. Come on. He lives a level above ours." Jeff strode with determination toward an escalator. Akio and Harry trailed along behind him.

Sirsen Bering was surprised to have three of his students show up at his door. "What's up guys?" he asked them. They quickly explained the situation. "This is serious," he told them. "BlackHat is virtually untraceable. There's no way we could prove Dirk is doing this."

"I don't understand *why* he's doing it," Harriet interjected.

"That's an easy one," Sirsen Bering answered. "You know that Dirk's already been held back a year, don't you?" The three of them nodded. Because Dirk was a year older, he was also larger. That made it easy for him to bully others.

Still speaking to Harry, Sirsen Bering said, "Well, when Dirk was held back, he started beating up other kids for their homework. As he got older, he changed tactics somewhat. Did Jeff and Akio tell you Dirk had a private eye?" She nodded again. "After Jeff's program burned out the private eye, Dirk's grades were nothing but F's. If he doesn't turn it around, he'll be held back again."

Sirsen Bering looked at the three of them gravely and continued, "Dirk wants to get into an apprentice program to be a pilot on a space freighter. I understand he's a rather gifted pilot in the YPA right now. In the apprentice program, he can quit school after this year—*if* he can pass. If he can't, he can't get into the program. He *really* wants into that program. I understand his family's finances are pretty desperate."

"Why?" Jeff asked.

"They've got a Third," he answered.

Harry gasped, "A Third? I thought that was illegal!"

"It wasn't when she was born," Sirsen Bering said. "The Third Prohibition became part of the Reproductive Allowance laws only about five years ago. Mamsen Highborne's third child is six years old. She's divorced and raising all three children on her own. That's why she works both at the school and on the Sector Council."

Sirsen Bering changed the subject abruptly, "In any case, the problem at hand is preventing BlackHat attacks. I can get the Principal to buy WhiteHat for everyone on an educational discount. I'll just tell him that it was me who had the BlackHat attack and he'll agree." Sirsen Bering's eyes widened. "Actually, that might be true. I haven't checked my datapad. If Dirk's attacking all of you, he'll probably come after me as well." He turned back inside the door of his flat. "Honey," he called. "Could you turn off my datapad please? What? Yes, now. It's important. Thanks."

Returning to the trio, Sirsen Bering said, "Just keep your pads turned off tonight. I'll call the Principal on my gridPhone and get this taken care of. Tomorrow, when you get to school, turn on your pads and the WhiteHat software will load automatically from the classroom's network server. And don't worry about your lost data, Akio. The school's network automatically makes a backup of everyone's datapads every day. Just bring it to my office when you arrive. I'll restore all your data. However, everything you've done on your pad since school ended is gone. I can't get it back for you."

"That's ok," Akio told him. "I didn't do any homework today anyway." A sheepish look passed across Akio's face as he realized what he'd just told his teacher. Sirsen Bering shot a disapproving glance at him.

Jeff, Akio, and Harry thanked Sirsen Bering and went home. As they walked, Harry asked "Why would she have a Third? It doesn't make sense."

"It kinda explains a lot," Akio said thoughtfully. "It tells us why he's so desperate for money. You'd think he'd just study though."

Jeff laughed bitterly. "He can't. He doesn't have the education and he's too stupid anyway. Before his mom got a job here he went to school two sectors below us—down where they live. The schools down there are lots worse than ours. He's never had the education to cut it in our school and he doesn't have the brains to catch up. So he cheats. That's been his answer ever since he got here. The only reason he's even *in* our school is 'cause his mom works there."

Arriving at Harry's flat, the two boys said goodnight to her and headed home. Jeff said, "Kinda makes you feel sorry for him, in a way."

"Who? Highborne?" Akio asked, startled. Then he growled, "Any time you start feeling sorry for Highborne, just think of what he did to Hugh." Jeff nodded gravely. Neither of them said anything more. When they arrived at their flats, they went in silently.

7

As Sirsen Bering promised, he was able to restore the contents of Akio's datapad the next morning. However, Akio's datapad wasn't the only one hit by the BlackHat attack. A dozen students had non-functioning datapads when they arrived at school.

"Plug this into your datapad," Sirsen Bering said as he passed a holodrive to each student in turn. The holodrive was a flat rectangle about three inches long and an inch wide, "It has the programs a datapad needs to get itself booted up and back onto the network. After that, your programs and data will be restored automatically."

Jeff's interest perked up when he saw Highborne parade himself up to the front of the room during the morning break. While the other students milled around the class, Jeff slipped up behind Highborne. When he was as close as he could get without being noticed, he heard Sirsen Bering exclaim, "You redid *all* of your assignments that you got F's on? My goodness, how surprising. Yes, Dirk, this is an amazing amount of work to complete in so short a time. And look how *well* it's all done. This essay for instance, your writing style has improved tremendously."

Sirsen Bering seemed to be reading the essay closely. After a moment he told Highborne, "Interesting. This essay is VERY much like one that Corrine Wong was working on before her datapad malfunctioned. She asked me for help with it last week. Hmm. Well, Dirk, not that I'm accusing you of anything, of course not, no ... but you see, whenever I get homework from a student that highly resembles something I've seen another student working on, well, I naturally get a little interested in that. It's probably just my suspicious nature, nothing to do with you. In any case, I have a program that does a statistical analysis of the word usage in a document. You see, no two people use their words exactly alike. Everyone's writing is as distinctive as a fingerprint when you do a statistical analysis on it. It's a wonderful program. I just got it."

He smiled reassuringly at Highborne. Being behind Highborne, Jeff couldn't see the expression on his face. But he could imagine it pretty well. Highborne managed to stammer, "Uh ... oh ... yeah? I ... I didn't know that."

Again, Sirsen Bering smiled at Highborne and said, "Oh yes. It's all very easy to verify who wrote what nowadays. But don't worry. It's just a precaution. I'm sure that the resemblance to Corrine's writing is just a coincidence. A quick analysis will clear things up right away. You have nothing to worry about, Dirk, I'm sure. Oh, there's the bell. Well, break's over. Thank you, Dirk. This is a lot of work you've submitted here. I hope it gets you exactly what you deserve."

Jeff smiled to himself and returned to his seat. As he did, he glanced over and saw Highborne numbly heading for his own desk. 'This is a VERY good day,' Jeff thought.

At lunch, Jeff observed Highborne deep in a discussion with his sister. Just after lunch, Sirsen Bering called Highborne to his office at the front of the class. Through the office window, Jeff could see the two of them talking for a few moments. Highborne looked upset. Sirsen Bering stood and walked out of his office toward the classroom door. Highborne followed. Sirsen Bering was gone for about 15 minutes. He returned without Highborne.

The rest of the day passed quickly. After school, Jeff, Akio, and Harry were about to head home when Madison Burke and Kristin Howard hurried up to Jeff. Grabbing Jeff's arm, Madison burst out, "Jeff! Jeff! You'll never guess what Kristin and I just saw."

"Uh, no Madison, I don't think I can guess," Jeff told her.

"Dirk Highborne was just getting on an elevator with his sister, Danae," Madison said, "and he was asking her for something."

"What did he ask her for?"

Wide-eyed, both Madison and Kristin nodded. "A key," Madison answered solemnly. "An orange key. Like the ones they use for the lockers in the water park."

Madison had Jeff's attention now. "A water park locker key? Why would she be carrying one of those?"

Something Jeff had heard nagged at the back of his mind. Then it came to him. "Mamsen Benson told us that the Highborne's flat and Dirk's school locker were searched by the police. I wonder if they searched Danae's school locker?"

Akio nodded meaningfully. "She probably kept the thing Highborne hit Hugh with in her locker until today. He must have had her move it to a water park locker during lunch when he realized he might get in trouble."

Harry said, "We've got to tell someone, Jeff. If the weapon is in that locker, Dirk could finally go to jail where he belongs."

"You're right," Jeff agreed. "Let's go to the Benson's right now. Madison and Kristin, thanks a lot. It was great that the two of you noticed what was going on."

Kristin smiled at Jeff's praise, but Madison looked as if she would burst with happiness. "You're *very* welcome, Jeff," she told him shyly. Harry turned bright pink.

Within minutes, they arrived at the Benson's. Mamsen Benson answered the door and the three of them explained what Madison and Kristin had seen.

"I don't know, kids," she said doubtfully. "It may be nothing at all. Still, it's worth looking into. I'll let the police know and we'll see what they do about it."

They said their goodbyes to Mamsen Benson and walked home. That evening, Jeff got a conference call with Akio and Harry from Janice Benson. He touched an icon on his datapad, and their faces each appeared in a little window.

"My mom asked me to call you three and let you know. You were right. It *was* a key for a locker in the water park. When the police searched it, they found one new sock and some rocks from the park on top of the building. The police say that it's not definite proof."

Akio asked, "Did they arrest Highborne? That's what *I* want to know."

Janice nodded, "They sure did. The prosecutor said that she isn't 100 percent sure she can get a conviction, but the circumstantial evidence is very strong. At the very least, the whole family will get kicked out of the building because he stole rocks from the park."

"That's great!" Akio shouted.

Jeff agreed, "Living Outside is almost as bad as going to jail. At least it is in my opinion."

"Well," Janice told them, "Dirk is being prosecuted. He's sitting in jail right now. His mom can't afford the bail money. Oh, and he's also been kicked out of our school. He was caught with a copy of the BlackHat program on his datapad."

Jeff thanked Janice for the news, and they hung up. 'Today is a REALLY, REALLY good day,' he thought as he got ready for bed.

8

Jeff wiped sweat from his face and did his best to make buffalo noises. The buffalo skin and head disguise that he wore was getting hot in the unrelenting prairie sun. Slipping an arrow into his bow, Jeff tried to edge nearer to a large bull. His disguise enabled him to get close, but he was so close now that the buffalo was getting suspicious. It pawed the ground aggressively and made grunting noises.

The broad blue sky whispered a gentle breeze across the sea of grass. In the distance, low, rolling hills were the only witnesses to the scene taking place among the buffalo.

Through the eyeholes in his disguise, Jeff could see his dad, hidden under another buffalo head and skin, moving in as well. Two members of the tribe they were hunting with approached slowly from the other side in their disguises.

In the moccasins Jeff was wearing, his feet made little noise as he warily closed in on the bull. The light tan of his buffalo-skin trousers made his legs blend in with the dry, late summer grass.

Jeff grew excited. He wanted to get the first arrow in. But the bull was growing more anxious. He sniffed the air warily and made angry snorts. Putting his head down, the thunderous creature charged directly at Jeff.

Not waiting any longer, Jeff threw off his disguise and let his arrow fly. He dodged as the giant bull ran past him. At nearly the same instant, the hunters from the tribe came out from under their disguises, roared out a loud yell, and let loose their arrows. Following their continued shouting, the bull turned toward the running hunters as they took off in two different directions through the tall grass. At that moment, Kent appeared from under his disguise and fired his arrow into the bull's haunches. It stumbled, trying to turn.

With a bellow of rage, the giant buffalo tried to charge Kent. But by the time it did, Jeff and the two hunters had each shot another arrow. The bull was badly hurt, but it still barreled toward Kent. As the bull passed him, Jeff fired an arrow into its rear leg. The hunters each put an arrow into its neck. The bull staggered, enabling Kent to jump out of its way.

The hunters moved in for the kill. The mighty creature stumbled and then dropped heavily on its side. Jeff approached the buffalo's head and stood gazing at it. He could see it move its eye and look directly at him. Then a glazed look passed across its features. It was dead.

A cool wind finally wafted across the prairie. The two hunters began a chant to the buffalo's spirit. They thanked it for all it provided them with. As they did, Jeff's dog Boomer, ran up to him barking. Jeff wasn't sure whether the ancient Native Americans had dogs. But he always wanted one, so he asked the artificial reality pod operator to put a dog into the program.

Jeff petted Boomer and watched as the hunters cut the buffalo open. To Jeff, it was pretty gross.

"That was great!" shouted Kent as he approached Jeff. "You got the first arrow in." He thumped Jeff on the back approvingly.

"Thanks," Jeff answered.

Others from the tribe gathered around, helping the two hunters carve up the bull. Jeff and Kent stayed out of the way and watched.

After a while, Kent went off with some of the other men to kill more buffalo. Jeff decided to follow the river back to the village and hang out with some of the other guys his age. Boomer trailed along after him, nipping at his heels.

By evening, the tribe had killed three buffalos. They brought everything that they could use from the animal back to the village. That night, there was a celebration. Sitting by a fire, Kent and Jeff feasted on buffalo meat.

"This is what *real* food tastes like," Kent commented as he ate heartily. Jeff had to admit, it was better than anything he'd ever had. After the meal, they sat back and watched the men of the tribe dance. Eventually, Kent looked at Jeff and said, "Jeff. There's something I need to talk to you about."

"Yeah? What's that?"

"You know what the Reproductive Allowance laws are about, don't you?" Kent asked carefully.

Embarrassed, Jeff replied, "Of course I do. They taught us all about that in school in sixth grade. All adults are allowed to have one child to replace them when they die. A couple has an allowance of two children, one for each adult."

"Well, there's a little more to it than that." Kent hesitated. "You know that no one who's unmarried should do anything that might lead to an Unallowed child, right?"

Jeff shrugged. "Yeah, but so what? I'm too young to date or anything. No one can date until they're 16. That's in the laws."

Kent nodded. "That's right. Girls under 16 can't have boyfriends and boys under 16 can't have girlfriends. Children can only be born to married couples. That's best for the children, best for the parents, and best for everyone else too. The Earth's way too crowded these days to allow for anything else."

"Of course," Jeff agreed. "But why are you bringing this up? It's not like I have a girlfriend or anything. I don't even *know* a girl that would *want* to be my girlfriend."

Kent looked surprised. "Well ..." he said slowly. "You, Akio, and Harriet are all 14 now. And the three of you spend a lot of time together. Harriet is growing into a very pretty young woman."

"Harry?" Jeff shook his head, "Naw, Dad. You've got it all wrong. Harry is just one of the guys. I know she's grown her hair out and all. But even with the long hair, she still does all the guy stuff me and Akio like. She does the girl stuff with her sister."

"Jeff, I think there's a lot about girls you don't know. Harriet is changing. Girls change sooner then boys. I can tell you for sure that it won't be much longer until she won't want to be 'just one of the guys' any more. From now on, you've got to be sure that you're never alone with her. It could get you kids into real trouble with the Sector Council."

"No worries Dad," Jeff assured him. "We always go around with the three of us together. That's the way it's always been since kindergarten."

"Well good," said Kent, clearly relieved. After a moment's pause, he said, "There is one more thing I need to talk to you about."

"Yeah? What?"

"Well, it's been a long time since your mother died. And you know I've been dating," Kent explained.

Jeff nodded.

"Well, I've been dating someone in particular for a while now. Her name is Porsche. And I want you to meet her. You think you'd like to do that?"

"Sure Dad. I think that'd be fine."

Kent smiled. "Good. I'll invite her over to dinner this coming Sunday." Satisfied, he turned back to watch the dancing.

9

The week started well. With Highborne in jail, there was no need to move around in groups any more. But Jeff, Harry, and Akio stayed together as always. Jeff noticed that most of the kids in the group still went around together in their assigned partnerships of twos and threes. He realized that the group they had formed was about more than protection, farming, and studying to get into better schools. Even with Highborne gone, everyone in the group still had strong friendships with the others.

On Tuesday evening, the group held a special meeting in the Mountains of Mars chatworld. Together, they decided to buy two very important gifts for Hugh. On Wednesday evening, the entire group, with the exception of Logan Gibson, went to the Benson's to present it to him.

When he answered the doorbell, Sirsen Benson was shocked to see thirty-five 14-year-olds standing outside his door. The flat was too small for everyone to enter, so Harry, Jeff, Akio, Madison Burke, and Ally Wilson went in. The others stayed out in the corridor and watched through the doorway.

"Hi, Hugh," Harry said as they approached his bed. "You look better." It was true. Much of the swelling had gone down in his face, and his arm was already out of the sling.

Hugh beamed. "The shot they gave me is really helping. Even my ribs don't hurt that much."

"Uh, Hugh," Jeff began, "we all got together and decided to buy you a couple of things. We wanted to help out. Everyone put in some money." But he didn't say, "I really had to lean on some of the group to get them to chip in." He thought it, but he didn't say it.

"Anyway, here's the first present." Jeff put a large box into Hugh's lap. When Hugh opened it, he found a brand new dogbot. Hugh's mother gasped. "How *wonderful!* Thank you kids. Hubert was extremely upset to lose his robot. He really was attached to it."

Hugh looked meaningfully at Jeff. 'Of course he was attached to it,' thought Jeff. 'Without a robot, he can't have a garden on the farm. And without a garden, there's no money for the lessons and stuff he needs to get into a decent school.'

Jeff just smiled at Hugh and said, "There's one more present we got you." Akio gave him another, smaller box. Hugh was stunned when he opened it.

"A datapad!"

All the kids in the corridor yelled, "SURPRISE!"

"Now you can stay in school," Harry told him. "You won't have to be held back."

"How could you kids afford something like this?" Sirsen Benson demanded abruptly. His wife interrupted immediately. "George, don't be so harsh with the children. What he means to say is thank you. But this is *so* expensive."

Jeff replied, "We all chipped in."

More gently, Sirsen Benson said, "It must have cost you all everything you had."

The kids were growing embarrassed. "Well," Jeff mumbled, "we had to do *something*."

In an explosion of grateful tears, Mamsen Benson threw her arms around Jeff and hugged him. Before he could say or do anything, she released him and hugged Akio. Akio reddened. Still sobbing, Mamsen Benson hugged each of the girls in turn. None of them knew what to say.

Hugh's father shook hands with all five of them. Mamsen Benson frantically burst out with, "Something to eat. You must all stay for something to eat." Jeff saw the panicked look on Sirsen Benson's face. There was no way the Bensons could afford to feed thirty-five teenagers.

"Uh, that's ok, Mamsen Benson." Jeff told her, "We really have to be getting home. But thanks anyway. Bye, Hugh. Get better soon."

When they were out in the corridor and the Bensons had closed the door, Madison Burke put her hand on Jeff's arm and quietly said, "That was a really good idea you had, Jeff. It was a really good thing to do." The others nodded their agreement.

"Thanks, everyone," he replied. "I'm sorry it took so much money. But with the new source of compost Hugh found for us, I really think we can make it up by the end of the year." Some of the group looked more convinced than others, but everyone muttered their agreement. They each said their goodbyes and walked toward home.

10

After school on Friday, Jeff sat on a bench near the school's entrance waiting for Harry and Akio before starting for home. Madison Burke skittered to him hastily and blurted out, "Dirk Highborne is out of jail."

"WHAT?"

Madison recoiled. Jeff immediately got control of himself and apologized, "Sorry, Madison. What do you mean, Highborne's out of jail?"

"A girl I know, Kate Jennings, has a sister in the same class as Dirk's sister. Kate's sister heard Dirk's sister talking to a friend. Dirk's mother got him out by promising to colonize. They have to leave Earth forever."

"Forever? You're sure?"

Madison nodded.

"I wonder what Hugh's parents will say about that."

Madison smiled proudly. "I already talked to his sister Janice. She says they wouldn't let Dirk out unless her parents agreed. Until his family leaves Earth, Dirk has to wear an ankle bracelet that sends a signal to the grid. He can't take it off or he'll go back to jail. He has to stay in his flat. The only time he can leave is if his mother gets special permission from the police. He can't even access the grid or use a datapad."

"At least we don't have to worry about him bothering us. Thanks for telling me, Madison." Her whole face lit up at his words.

Madison hesitated, and then said shyly, "Jeff, Kristin and I were wondering. Would you and Akio like to go to the water park with us sometime?"

Jeff couldn't have been more surprised if he had been run over by a hovercar. Wide-eyed, he finally replied, "I ... I don't think that's allowed until we're 16, Madison."

She looked hurt. "But you go with Harry all the time, don't you?"

"That's different," he countered. Anger passed over Madison's face, so he quickly added, " ... because there's two guys and one girl. Two guys and two girls will get us in trouble with the Sector Council. They'll say it's a double date."

Madison brightened. "Well then, maybe just you could go with Kristin and me."

Near panic, Jeff couldn't think of anything to say. He was spared from having to answer by the arrival of Harry and Akio. When Madison saw them approach, she said coyly, "Well, we can talk again later. See you Jeff." She fluttered her fingers in a small wave, flipped her hair back, and walked away.

"What was that about?" Harry demanded. Jeff told her and Akio about Highborne. He left out the part about Madison asking him out.

"I can't believe he got off again," Harry complained.

"He didn't exactly get off," Jeff said. "He's basically locked up in his flat without anything to do. He'll probably be tearing his hair out by the time he leaves Earth."

Akio nodded. "And he'll be gone forever. As long as he doesn't get near the New Tokyo system, I'll be happy."

Jeff felt a stab of sadness at the reminder that Akio was leaving Earth too. They only had two more weeks until school let out, and then he would be gone.

Akio must have realized how Jeff was feeling because he changed the subject quickly. "What are we going to do tomorrow morning before the group meeting?" he asked.

Jeff tried to shake off his feelings of sadness. "How about baseball?" he said to Akio.

"I'd rather surf."

Harry broke in, "Not SURFING again! I want to do something that's fun for *all* of us."

"Surf-ing, Surf-ing!" Akio shouted.

"Baseball!" Jeff shot back.

"Surf-ing, Surf-ing!"

"OUCH!" they both shouted together as Harry hit them each on the upper arm. They stared at her, startled.

Harry's hands were still balled into tight fists. She planted them firmly on her hips, furrowed her eyebrows, and tightened her lips. There was a moment's pause.

'Uh-oh,' Jeff thought. 'We're dead.'

Jeff towered over Harry, who was barely over five feet. But right at that moment, Jeff would have been less afraid of a 2000-pound Nestorian porcuhog with all of its quills extended and its fangs snapping.

Through clenched teeth, Harry said slowly, quietly, and deliberately, "You ... two ... are ... pigs."

Jeff's brain seemed frozen. Kids streamed by babbling happily, unaware of the drama that was unfolding.

"Wha ... we ... why ... what?" Jeff asked. "We ... how ... uh ..."

When nothing else came out of Jeff, Akio asked, "Huh?"

"Did you two not notice that I'm a girl?"

Silence. A tram pulled away from the school, taking a full load of chattering students with it.

"Well?" Harry demanded at last.

Akio looked as if he wouldn't say anything for all the money in the world, so finally Jeff stammered, "Um, y ... yes, we noticed that."

"Did it ever occur to you that girls like to do different things than guys?"

Silence again. Harry folded her arms and turned away.

Jeff sent a pleading look to Akio, but he was still refusing to say anything. At last Jeff got out, "If you want to do something different, why didn't you say so? Ouch!" Jeff rubbed his upper arm where she hit him again.

"I say so all the time!" Harry shouted. "You two never listen and you always outvote me." She folded her arms again and turned back around.

"We ... we're sorry. We didn't mean to," Jeff said carefully. "We thought you liked stuff like baseball. You were the one who taught baseball to us."

"We were 10 then, Jeff."

"Well, what do you want to do Saturday?"

Harry turned her head slightly and in a glowering voice said, "Nothing."

Akio burst out, "NOTHING? All that and you want to do NOTHING?"

Harry's head bowed now. "You two wouldn't do it anyway," she growled quietly.

Feeling like he was seeing a light at the end of a long, dark tunnel, Jeff quickly said, "Sure we would. It's your turn to pick. Whatever you want to do, we'll do. Won't we Akio?" Jeff nodded vigorously.

Akio followed Jeff's lead and nodded too. "Sure," he said. "Anything. You pick."

Harry turned partway around toward them. "Really?" she asked hesitantly.

"Sure, you bet, absolutely," both boys replied enthusiastically. "What do you want to do?"

As she turned around to face them fully, Harry timidly smiled and said, "Dancing."

Jeff looked at Akio. Akio looked at Jeff. They burst out laughing.

"OW!" they both yelped and rubbed their upper arms as Harry hit them and turned her back again.

"I hate you both," she hissed quietly. "You're pigs."

Thinking fast, Jeff told her, "We're sorry, Harry. We thought you were joking. We'd get in trouble with the Sector Council if we danced. You can't do that until you're 16. And what girls would want to dance with us anyway? We don't know how to dance."

Silence.

"So we thought you were joking," Jeff added lamely. "We didn't mean to hurt your feelings. We're really sorry." Behind Harry's back, Jeff hit Akio's shoulder and then pointed to Harry.

"Yeah, sorry," Akio said. Jeff rolled his eyes.

Silence again. Then very quietly, Harry said, "You could learn to dance. And you wouldn't get in trouble."

Jeff wasn't quite sure he liked this line of conversation. The look on Akio's face told him that Akio was *quite* sure he didn't like this line of conversation. "H ... how?"

Turning partially toward them, Harry explained, "My cousin works at a dance studio nine sectors up. She says you can dance at the studio without getting in trouble if you're 14 or older. They have a special thing in their business license that makes it ok. She can give you a lesson in swing dancing in an hour, then you can dance."

"What's swing dancing?"

Harry smiled, "It's an old, old way of dancing, but it's making a comeback. It's really popular in all the upper sectors. Everybody's doing it. It's really fun."

Jeff asked, "Won't it cost money?"

Turning to face them fully, Harry answered, "My cousin'll give us the lesson for free and make it so we won't have to pay the fee for dancing in the main dance hall. You just have to pay for the clothing rental."

"The what?"

"Well you can't go in just regular clothes," Harry told them in an almost disgusted voice. "You have to dress up."

Akio objected, "We don't have clothes to dress up in."

Heaving a sigh, Harry replied, "That's why you rent clothes at the studio."

Jeff looked at Akio. Akio looked at Jeff. Neither was happy. Suddenly, Jeff realized there was a problem. Trying to hide his happiness, he told Harry, "We can't rent clothes. We don't have any money left. We used it all for Hugh's robot and datapad."

Harry was amazed. "You don't have *any* money left? You spent it *all*?" They both nodded. "Why?" she demanded.

Jeff told her, "There wouldn't have been enough otherwise. And Hugh *really* needed a robot and datapad. Besides, we couldn't ask everyone else to kick in if we were holding back." Akio nodded his agreement.

Harry's face softened. Her eyes got watery. Jeff wondered if he had said the wrong thing. But then she sighed and with a gentle smile said, "Just when I think you two are the most thoughtless pigs in the universe, you go and do something like that. Well, Ally and I still have some money left. We'll pay for your clothing rentals."

"Ally? Ally Wilson?" Akio asked, confused.

"Yes," Harry replied. "You're dancing with Ally."

"Why?"

Harry's hands went to her hips again. "Akio, sometimes you amaze me."

"Huh?"

Jeff broke in, "She likes you, dude."

"NO WAY!"

"She likes you, dude," Jeff repeated.

"Since when?"

"Since we were 12."

"No way. And you knew?"

"Everyone knows but you. Get a clue."

Akio was at a loss for words. He stood there with a stunned expression until Jeff asked, "How could you not know? She convinced her dad to let you take karate and sword fighting in his gym for free didn't she?"

"It's not called sword fighting, it's called *kendo*. And it's not called a gym either. It's a *dojo*."

Jeff cut him off, "Yeah but she got him to give you free lessons didn't she?"

"Well, yeah but ..."

"You've been going up there for two years haven't you? So you two are together every Monday night, aren't you?"

"Well, yeah but ..."

"She didn't ask for me or Harry to have free lessons did she?"

"Well, no but ..."

"Do you know *anyone* else from down here that has been asked to take free lessons at their fancy *dojo*? That thing's five sectors up."

"Well, no but ..."

Akio looked at Jeff. Akio looked at Harry. "She *really* likes me? Why didn't she tell me?"

Harry heaved an exasperated sigh and threw up her hands. "Well *I'm* telling you," she said. "Ally likes you and cries all the time because you're leaving. You're going to dance with her and make her happy. You're going to be nice to her and make sure she has fun or, so help me Akio Miyamoto, I'll break your neck."

"You sound like my mother when you say that."

"Your mother is a very sensible woman."

Akio admitted that Harry had a point. Jeff could see that Akio didn't know what else to say. But finally, he got out, "Are you sure you *really* want us to dance, Harry? Ouch! Harry, could you stop hitting me please?"

"Could you stop calling me Harry please?"

'Oh no,' Jeff thought warily. 'What now?'

"Harry is your name. What else am I supposed to call you?" Akio demanded.

"My ... name ... is ... HARRIET ... you ... idiot! Every year since we were 12, I've asked you two on my birthday to stop calling me Harry and start calling me Harriet. You remember for one or two days, then you call me Harry again. I ... am ... *Harriet*. I ... am ... a ... GIRL."

Jeff jumped in with, "Sorry, Harriet. We won't call you Harry any more." To Akio he asked, "Right?" Akio nodded fearfully and rubbed his arm. Harriet finally seemed happy.

"I'll send you both the address of the dance studio when we get home," Harriet instructed. "Ally and I will meet you there at 7:30 tomorrow morning. You can get changed and start the lesson about 8." She smiled and patted their upper arms both at once, not seeming to notice them cringe. "It'll be fun. Shall we go home now?"

"Uh, Akio and I will see you later," Jeff told her. "We need to go up and get our robots. I have some work to do on them before we go to YPA."

"Ok," Harriet said brightly. "I'll see you both tomorrow at the dance studio. Bye." She turned and pranced happily down the corridor.

When he was sure Harriet was far enough away so his words wouldn't be heard, Jeff heaved a relieved sigh and said, "Wow."

Akio nodded. They both looked after her as she continued down the corridor. "I feel like I was just hit by a hurricane," Jeff commented.

"Yeah," Akio agreed. "A hurricane." He appeared to think for a moment before asking, "What's a hurricane?"

Ignoring the question, Jeff told him, "You know, my dad warned me this would happen. He told me someday she wouldn't want to be one of the guys any more. I didn't believe him."

"He *knew*?" Akio asked, astounded. "How?"

"Beats me," Jeff answered, shrugging. "My dad's old—nearly forty-one. He knows all about girls and stuff."

Akio wondered out loud, "So what do we do?"

Jeff said simply, "She wants to be treated like a girl, so we treat her like a girl. She's our best friend and she's always been really good to us. We owe the same to her."

"No, I meant what do we do about tomorrow?"

"There's only one thing we can do."

"You don't mean ..."

Jeff nodded. Far down the corridor, they saw Harriet turn as she got into an elevator. She glanced back at them and waved. They returned her wave.

Akio gulped, "So we're gonna ..."

Again, Jeff nodded and then said grimly, "Dance."

11

Jeff and Akio stepped warily off the elevator and made their way toward the dance studio, which was in a row of businesses along one of the sector's main corridors. Music spilled out of the clothing shop next to the elevator. Young mothers strolled happily along as their small children peered in all of the shop windows. A hovertram passed noisily by as Jeff and Akio stood staring blankly at the front doors of the dance studio.

Since he had first gotten out of bed, Jeff's stomach had seemed to be tied in knots. 'No reason to be nervous,' he told himself. 'It's just Harry and Ally.' But he knew that wasn't true. Harry wasn't Harry anymore. She was Harriet now and that made him very nervous.

Glancing at Akio, Jeff could see that his hands were shaking. Akio noticed Jeff's glance and stuffed his hands in his pockets. Normally, Akio's hair jutted in all directions. Today it looked as if it were trying to escape his head.

The studio doors slid open with a snake-like hiss as they entered. The studio had a large, cold entry area, called a foyer, and long hallways that stretched away in multiple directions. The white, hospital-like walls of the foyer and hallways had windows that gave them a view of large rooms covered with mirrors. Inside the mirrored rooms, people were practicing a variety of dances. Jeff recognized some of the dance types. To his right, he could see a group learning ballet. In the room next to that, a bunch of guys and girls were tap dancing.

"This doesn't look good," Akio whispered as they stood at one of the windows and watched. Jeff nodded.

"Jeff! Akio! Here we are." They both turned to see Harriet and Ally coming toward them down a hall. Behind the two girls was a young red-haired woman that looked a lot like Harriet. As the three of them approached, Harriet introduced the woman as her cousin Savannah. Jeff managed a "Hello" and a "Nice to meet you" but Akio was silent.

Savannah smiled at them and commented, "You boys look like you're marching to your doom. Relax. This will be fun."

"Uh, yeah, uh." Jeff was embarrassed. He wanted to say something more intelligent than that, but his mouth didn't seem to be working. Harriet and Ally appeared irritated.

Savannah put one arm reassuringly around Jeff's shoulders and another around Akio's. "Come on boys. Let's get you into some nice clothes. Then we'll show you some simple swing dancing steps, ok?"

Jeff didn't even try to speak. He just nodded. Zombie-like, Akio also nodded woodenly. As Savannah gently pushed them forward, they thudded slowly down a foreboding hall. About halfway down, there was a booth set in the wall that they could walk into. Inside, a bored middle-aged woman stood behind a counter. The booth contained racks of clothes. Shelves and drawers were set into the rear wall.

"Miss Lee," Savannah addressed the woman behind the counter, "we need complete outfits for these young gentlemen. This one is Mr. Bowman, let's put him in navy blue. And this handsome young man is Mr. Miyamoto, we'll put him in black. Miss Brightway and Miss Wilson, what colors will you wear?"

"Sky blue, please," Harriet replied. Ally answered, "White."

Miss Lee called a young assistant. The two of them rapidly retrieved the clothes and laid them out in four neat piles. Harriet and Ally paid the clothing rental fee and then turned to Jeff and Akio. "Pick up your clothes," Harriet ordered. Wide-eyed, both boys silently took their piles from the counter.

Savannah pointed down a side hallway that ran next to the booth. "The changing rooms are down there. Gentlemen on the left, ladies on the right."

Akio burst out, "Why did you call her 'Miss'? What does 'Miss' mean?"

Savannah smiled and explained, "A long time ago, women who weren't married were called 'Miss' instead of Mamsen. Married women were called Missus. These days we use 'Mamsen' for both married and single women. But here in the dance studio, you say 'Miss' and then the last name when you address women or girls. It doesn't matter if they're married or not. We say 'Mr.' instead of Sirsen when we address a boy or man."

"Why?"

"It's just the tradition in dance studios," Savannah replied. "It's a way of behaving like ladies and gentlemen. And it's nice, don't you think?"

Akio shrugged and shifted his gaze absently to the floor. He and Jeff went into the changing rooms. Before long, they both emerged. Both had on their slacks, shirts, and socks, but that was it. Savannah was nowhere to be found.

"These shoes have strings on them," Akio complained.

"I know," Jeff agreed. "How are we supposed to put them on without Velcro?"

At that moment, Savannah floated gracefully back down the hall to the changing rooms. "Are you having some trouble gentlemen?" she asked, smiling. They both nodded silently.

"Let's start by putting the shoes on your feet. These are laces," she told them as she knelt down in front of Jeff. "I'll tie them for you. Don't be embarrassed. Even most adults can't tie shoelaces these days." She finished Jeff's shoes and then tied Akio's.

Next, Savannah tied their neckties and asked them to put on their vests. Akio held his vest up as if it had been dead for a few days. "It looks like part of it's missing," he told her.

Savannah laughed lightly and explained, "You're right, it does. Most of the back isn't there. The vest has a front, an adjustable strip of material that goes behind your neck, and another that goes behind your back at your waist." She held the vest up so Akio could slip into it. Jeff put his on himself.

Akio commented, "It has two rows of buttons."

Again, Savannah smiled. "The holes for the first row are inside the vest. They don't show through. You button the second row of buttons here in this row of buttonholes that shows. We call it a double-breasted vest. It's the style right now."

Since Akio was asking all the questions, Jeff silently held up his hands, letting his sleeves flop forward. Akio nodded and said, "Our sleeves are too long."

Before Savannah could answer, Ally and Harriet emerged from the women's dressing room. Both girls were in their dresses and had their hair up. Looking at Harriet made Jeff *much* more nervous. He'd never seen her in a dress before, and this particular dress made her look *very* good. 'And her hair is so different,' Jeff thought. Harriet's long, curly red hair was immaculately arranged. She didn't seem to have a strand out of place. Everything about her was strange and familiar at the same time. Her whole face seemed to shine with a brightness he'd never noticed. She just glowed.

'Were Harriet's eyes *always* that green?' Jeff wondered. Suddenly, he grew *very, very* nervous.

Ally paused before Akio and seemed to expect something to happen. Akio stood for a moment gaping at her. Finally, he caught on and said, "You look really good."

Instantly, Jeff realized Harriet was looking at him as well. "You look great too," he told her hastily. She beamed at him. Jeff felt his insides go all mushy.

"Are you having trouble with your cufflinks?" Harriet asked Jeff.

"My what?" Jeff asked.

"Cufflinks, cufflinks," Harriet snapped, impatiently. "Haven't you ever heard of cufflinks before? They're for your sleeves."

Savannah nodded and told the boys, "You fold your cuffs back like this." She gently took hold of one of Akio's cuffs and folded it back on itself. "You see this here?" she asked pointing to what looked like a buttonhole in the cuff. "You put your cufflink through here. You'll find them in the right pocket of your vests," Savannah explained.

Irritated, Harriet broke in. "Here, let me."

Before Jeff could act, Harriet plunged her hand into his right vest pocket and pulled out the two cufflinks. She grabbed his sleeve cuff and inserted a cufflink into the hole in his left sleeve. As she finished his right sleeve, Jeff glanced over at Akio. With a happy glow on her face, Ally was silently putting his cufflinks on him as well. 'I hope I don't look as embarrassed as he does,' thought Jeff.

Savannah said, "Thank you for your help ladies. Don't they look like proper gentlemen now?" Both girls nodded admiringly. Jeff, on the other hand, thought he looked like something from another planet.

"Gentlemen," Savannah continued, "please accompany your partners to the lesson room."

"Huh?" they both asked in unison.

Harriet heaved a huge sigh, "You two are hopeless." She faced Jeff. "She means you're supposed to offer your arm to me when we walk anywhere." Harriet moved beside him. "Bend your elbow," she commanded. Jeff did as he was told. With a small sigh of relief, Harriet took hold of his arm just above his elbow. "Ok, now we're ready to go."

Harriet noticed that Akio hadn't moved. "Akio! You too. Bend your elbow." He silently obeyed, and Ally took his arm. Harriet smiled and said, "We're ready Miss James."

"You call your cousin Miss James?" Akio asked.

"It's good manners in the dance studio. And don't you forget it."

Savannah instructed, "Mr. Bowman, Mr. Miyamoto, please ask your partners to accompany you this way."

"Um," Jeff began as he held out a hand in the direction Savannah indicated, "Miss Brightway, would you please accompany me this way?" Harriet looked up and beamed at him again. This time Jeff's heart did a backflip.

As Jeff and Harriet followed Savannah down the hallway, Jeff heard Akio asking Ally to accompany him.

When the five of them reached a small room whose walls were mostly covered with mirrors, Savannah glanced at a band on her wrist.

'That's a databand,' Jeff realized instantly. Like an old-style wristwatch, the databand had a small, thick, brightly-colored disk on it. However, instead of keeping track of time, the disk was a powerful computer with a camera and a holographic projector. Jeff thought, 'She must be getting paid well if she can afford one of those.'

Jeff had never seen a databand up close. He knew that it was a far more powerful and modern computer than his datapad. Savannah's databand constantly used its camera to check and see if she was looking at it. Every databand recognized the unique pattern in its owner's iris, the colored part of the human eye, so Savannah didn't even need to log on. The databand just activated itself whenever she looked at it directly.

As Jeff watched wonderingly, the databand's holographic projector displayed a 3D set of interface controls in the air above its colorful disk. Savannah selected one icon or menu item after another. The databand's camera watched to see which interface controls she put her index finger through. When she did, it reacted to her selections. Savannah jabbed her finger at one final control, and music began playing from some speakers floating near the ceiling.

"There," Savannah said, "now we'll learn some basic swing dancing. Alright, gentlemen, stand facing your partners. Now hold up your left hand and she'll put her right hand in it. Then you put your right hand under her left arm, around her, and place it gently on the middle of her back right between her shoulder blades."

Shocked, Akio gasped, "You mean we dance *together*? With our arms around *each other*? I didn't think people did that anymore."

"Yes they do," Savannah answered patiently. "It's very popular. Please give it a try, I promise these young ladies don't bite." Akio reddened.

Savannah continued, "Very good, Mr. Bowman. Mr. Miyamoto, you have to stand much closer to your partner than that. Take one giant step forward." Akio stepped closer to Ally. "Yes, that's better. Now give her your left hand. Correct. Put your right arm around her. Yes, that's it. Now everyone keep your heads up and shoulders back."

In a very short time, Savannah taught them a simple dance step. Jeff picked it up rapidly, but he had to concentrate and continually mutter, "Left, right, back-step, left, right, back-step."

Before half an hour had passed, Jeff and Akio not only mastered the swing step, they also learned some tricks like twirling the girls around. By the time the first hour ended, Jeff began to think dancing wasn't so hard to do after all.

After the lesson, the girls went to the ladies room, briefly leaving Jeff and Akio to themselves.

Jeff told Akio, "I thought this was going to be really weird, but it's not so bad."

"It *is* really weird," Akio countered, "but in a kinda good way. I guess we gotta go in that big room there to dance next." He pointed to a large room near them that was crowded with dancers. After a moment, he asked, "Do you think they're having a good time?"

"Who? The girls? Beats me."

"I hope Ally's having a good time. Harry will kill me if she doesn't."

"Probably," Jeff agreed, then he commented, "Have you noticed? They seem to float when they're dancing or walking with us. I was thinking earlier that it's like Harry's a whole different person in here. Ally too."

Akio nodded his agreement and turned to watch another classroom of dancers. "Hey!" he exclaimed suddenly. "That's Dirk Highborne!"

It was true. Gazing through the classroom window, Jeff could see Dirk Highborne teaching a dancing class. He was dancing with an extremely attractive girl a few years older than himself.

Savannah strolled by, so Jeff asked about Dirk. "Why yes," she answered, "that's Dirk. He's a very talented dancer. Do you know him?"

"Yeah," Jeff responded. "So he works here?"

"Yes, he does. We had to get special permission from the Sector Council to allow it because he's only fifteen and a half. Normally you have to be sixteen to have a job. But they let us because we're so short-handed. There are so few people around who know the old dances that are becoming popular again."

"Does Harriet know Dirk works here?"

Puzzled, Savannah told them, "I don't think so. Harriet is usually here on Tuesdays and Saturdays. Dirk comes on Mondays, Wednesdays, and Fridays after school. He's just filling in for another teacher today. I didn't think Harriet would know Dirk anyway. He lives a few sectors above the studio." Savannah smiled and moved along the hallway.

"What a liar," Akio commented venomously. "Telling everyone he lives above here instead of below us."

Jeff muttered, "Now I guess we know where he gets all the money he spends on those clothes he wears. Too bad he can't seem to hang onto any of it. If he could, maybe he wouldn't have beat up Hugh. I wonder how he got permission from the police to leave his apartment?"

"That mother of his," hissed Akio in reply. "With her around, he can get away with almost anything."

Their conversation was interrupted by the return of Harriet and Ally. As they approached, Jeff whispered to Akio, "Today has to be about Harriet and Ally. Let's not tell them we saw Dirk Highborne." Akio nodded.

As the girls stepped up next to them, Jeff and Akio offered their arms. Together, the four of them went to the main dance hall. The theme for the morning in the main dance hall was swing dancing, so the music was one swing tune after another. Jeff was surprised at how quickly the time passed.

At noon, they returned to the dressing rooms to put their own clothes back on. Jeff and Harriet got changed first and sat in the large foyer at the entrance waiting for Akio and Ally.

"So tell the truth," challenged Harriet, "Dancing wasn't so bad, was it?"

Jeff shook his head. "No, it wasn't. Once I got the hang of it, it was kinda fun."

"Are you glad you came?"

"Sure," Jeff told her, shrugging. "I guess. We could do this again sometime, if you want." Jeff was surprised how happy that made Harriet.

"There's Akio and Ally," Harriet said, pointing down the hall. As Akio came toward them, Jeff could see that he had an odd expression, but he didn't ask about it in front of the girls. When they got outside the studio, Harriet turned to Jeff and Akio and told them, "Ally and I have some errands to do before the study session, so we'll meet you at the community center."

"Ok," Jeff said. "We'll see you down there."

"Um," Harriet said hesitantly.

"Yeah?"

"We really had a good time. Thanks guys."

"Sure. We had a good time too." Jeff replied. Akio just nodded.

Jeff and Akio watched as Harriet and Ally left. After a moment, Jeff told Akio, "I don't think they had any errands to do. I think they just wanted to talk about us." Akio nodded.

"What's with you?" Jeff asked.

"What do you mean?"

"You had a weird look on your face when you came out of the dressing rooms. And you haven't said a word since then."

Akio paused, then explained, "She kissed me."

"What? Who? Where? Ally *kissed* you? Right on the lips?"

"Yup."

"What did you do?"

Akio shrugged. "Nothing, really. It happened so fast. She told me she was sorry I was leaving and I said me too. She said she'd miss me and then asked if I'd miss her. I didn't know what else to say, so I said I would. Then she kissed me and cried and kind of cuddled up to me. She asked me if I'd remember her forever. I told her I would, then she made me promise to never forget her. I was starting to wonder if she thought I was some kind of idiot with memory problems."

"What did you do?"

"What could I do? I promised just like she wanted me to. Then she cried a little more and kissed me again. Then she wiped her face and we came out. It all happened so fast."

"So what was it like?"

"What, getting kissed?"

"Yeah."

Akio shrugged again, "Ok, I guess. Kinda wet. But kinda nice."

"Wow, dude." Jeff admired. "*Nobody* gets kissed before they're 16."

Akio didn't seem to want to talk about it any more. "Let's go get our datapads and stuff. We need to hurry or we'll be late." It wasn't true, but Jeff let it go.

"Ok," he agreed. "Let's go." They headed toward the nearest elevator.

It wasn't long before they reached the community center. The study session went like most others until Jeff stepped out into the lobby to get a drink of water from the drinking fountain. After he got his drink, Jeff straightened up and turned around. He was startled to find Madison Burke standing close behind him and looking upset.

Stepping even closer, Madison wrung her hands. "Jeff," she said, her lower lip quavering. "Jeff, I'm leaving."

"You're going home early? Well, that's ok. I guess we'll see you tomorrow at the baseball game."

Madison blinked rapidly, and then looked up at Jeff with what suddenly seemed to be the hugest and brownest eyes he had ever seen. Tears streamed down her cheeks. She shook her head. "No, I mean we're all leaving. My family. We're colonizing. We're going to live on the San Bernardino Shipping Station in the California system. It's one of the farthest Alliance systems from Earth. We leave in two weeks, on the day before Akio leaves."

'Why is she saying this to just me?' he wondered silently. 'Shouldn't she be telling everyone?'

Before Jeff could say anything, Madison grabbed him and kissed him. "Remember me, Jeff. Please don't forget me. I'll always remember all you did for me," she sobbed.

Jeff thought, 'I don't believe this is happening.' Out loud, he replied, "Of course Madison. I could never forget you."

Abruptly, Madison burst into tears again, and ran into the women's bathroom. For a moment, Jeff was in a daze. Then he realized that Akio was standing next to the door to the study room. He came over to Jeff.

"You saw?" Jeff asked.

"Yup," Akio answered. "I saw. You're lucky no one else was around. You two could have gotten into real trouble kissing right out here in the lobby."

Jeff realized he was right. It could have been a real problem for both of them. "But what was that all about?"

Akio laughed. "She likes you, dude."

"NO WAY!"

"She likes you, dude," Akio repeated, obviously enjoying himself.

"Since when?"

"Since we were 12."

"No way. And you knew?"

"Everyone knows but you. Get a clue dude."

When Jeff could finally think properly, he said, "I wonder what Harry will say about this."

"Nothing. You're not going to tell her," Akio commanded.

"Why?"

"Just trust me, dude. Don't tell her."

"Ok," Jeff gave in. "I won't. You know what? I'm too weirded out to study any more. Let's get our stuff and go surfing. There's still some time before we have to be back for dinner."

"Sounds good to me," Akio said. They re-entered the study room, told the others they were leaving, and headed home to change. As they walked, Jeff told Akio, "This is a *really* strange day. I hope tomorrow is different."

"It's gotta be," Akio said. "Things couldn't get weirder."

"You're probably right," Jeff agreed.

12

On Sunday morning, most of the study group met at the baseball park to play softball together. The whole way down to the baseball park, Jeff and Akio did everything they could to avoid talking about the dancing on the previous day. But Jeff couldn't stop thinking about how different Harriet looked in her sleek, powder-blue dress, and how warm and soft she felt in his arms.

The group gathered on the simulated dirt of the infield and chose teams. There were enough players for two games at once. As always, Jeff, Harriet, and Akio were on the same team. Ally Wilson made sure she was on their team as well, which made Akio redden a little at first.

Harriet took her usual position as pitcher with Akio as catcher. Jeff generally liked shortstop, but Kevin Gibson wanted to play that position so Jeff took center field. Ally played first base.

After playing a few hours, they ate a late lunch together on the bleachers. As everyone was pulling out their food, Madison Burke noticed that Jeff was eating plain vegetable synthpaste. "Ew," she commented, "do you like eating that all by itself?"

"Naw," he replied, "but I'm out of money until my next crop comes in."

Harriet, who was sitting on the next bleacher above Jeff's, put her hand on his shoulder and told Madison, "He spent everything he had on Hugh's robot and datapad."

Jeff didn't know whether he was more embarrassed by Harriet's hand on his shoulder or by her telling everyone why he didn't have any money. "It's no big deal," he muttered. "Vegetables are supposed to be good for you anyways. I heard that somewhere."

With more than a little ceremony, Madison took a container out of her backpack, opened it, and put a plastic spoon in the food it held. With the appearance of someone galloping to the rescue, Madison grandly handed the container to Jeff. "You can't eat that synthpaste with nothing else. Here have my strawberries. They're from my part of the farm. I squished them up to make them look like synthpaste so no one would know."

"Uh, thanks Madison," Jeff accepted awkwardly but gratefully. As he took the container, he felt Harriet's grip tighten on his shoulder. He pretended he didn't notice.

"Hey everyone!" Madison called out to the others perched around her in the bleachers. "Jeff spent *all* of his money to help Hugh. Can you believe that? Now he has nothing for lunch but green bean synthpaste. Who wants to share with him?" Instantly, the other members of the group offered food.

"I'm ok," Jeff objected, self-consciously. "It's no big deal. Besides, Akio spent all his money too." But the only effect his words had was to cause them to shower gifts of food on Akio as well. Ally slid onto the bleacher next to Akio and gave him some applesauce, smiling shyly. Akio looked like he was about to have a heart attack.

As the food was passed to Jeff and Akio, Harriet's grip on Jeff's shoulder became so tight he felt like she was going to rip his arm off. He looked up at her questioningly. She noticed his gaze, released his shoulder, and turned away red with embarrassment. Or anger. Jeff wasn't sure which.

After lunch, most of the guys returned to the field to play baseball, while most of the girls seemed to prefer frisbee. The games continued until nearly dinnertime, when the members of the group said their goodbyes and left for their homes.

Jeff arrived at his flat to find his dad standing just inside the front door, but facing inside. "I think he forgot you're coming. He's playing baseball with his friends," he heard his father say. "So he doesn't have his datapad. I'll run down to the park and get him." Jeff couldn't see who he was talking to because Kent blocked his view.

At that moment, Kent turned and noticed Jeff standing behind him. "There you are," Kent said as he turned toward Jeff. "I was just going to go get you. Did you forget who you're meeting today?" Kent moved aside, smiling. "Jeff, this is Porsche Highborne. I told you I've been dating her lately and she came to have dinner and to get to know you. This is her son, Dirk, and her daughters, Danae and Denise."

Jeff stood frozen in horror, not believing what he was seeing.

"Jeff?" Kent said as his smile faded. "Be polite and say hello."

Without thinking Jeff pointed at Porsche Highborne and shot back, "You didn't tell me it was her!"

"What's wrong Jeff? You should know Porsche. She works at your school."

"You just ... you just said Porsche. You didn't say Highborne. I didn't know Mamsen Highborne's first name. No one calls her by that."

"Oh," Kent put his hand reassuringly on Jeff's shoulder and said, "Well, I guess I understand why you're surprised. It doesn't matter. Let's sit down to dinner and get to know each other."

Feeling like a cornered animal, Jeff took a step back and pointed at Dirk. "He's not supposed to be out of his flat! The police will get him."

Dirk, who had been moping sullenly by his mother's side until then, turned toward Jeff angrily and demanded, "How did you know that?"

Jeff shot back, "Everyone knows. You're going back to jail where you belong."

Horrified, Kent broke in, "Stop talking like that Jeff! No one's going to jail. Dirk has permission to be here tonight. It's all a misunderstanding anyway. Porsche's cleared it all up."

"MISUNDERSTANDING!" Jeff shouted. "You've got to be kidding! He beat Hugh Benson to a pulp and then stole his datapad and robot and took them Outside and sold them. He bought a copy of BlackHat while he was out there and hacked our datapads and took our homework and term projects."

Pouncing like a mother tiger, Porsche Highborne shouted furiously, "That's utterly ridiculous! My son has never been Outside. And he was with friends the morning that boy got beat up."

Jeff stood with his arms straight down at his sides and his fists tight. "That's a lie and you know it," he hissed. "He was caught red-handed with the ..."

Kent commanded, "Jeff! Don't you dare call Porsche a liar."

" ... BlackHat program on his datapad," Jeff finished. "He was caught turning in other people's homework. And the only reason you got him out of jail was because you promised to drag his sorry butt off this planet forever."

Kent exploded into motion. Grabbing Jeff by the shirt, he pinned his son against the wall. "WHAT DO YOU THINK YOU'RE DOING?" he screamed in Jeff's face. "What do you think you're doing?" he repeated, more controlled this time. He released Jeff.

"Don't you know who that is?" Jeff demanded, pointing to Dirk. "How could you not know? I told you when I was eight that I got in a fight with Dirk Highborne."

Kent was beyond furious. "Is that what this is about? A fight when you were eight? You're in real trouble Jeff."

Jeff was stubbornly undeterred. "That's not what this is about. Ever since then he's been beating up kids for their homework and money."

"That's not true," Porsche Highborne tried to interrupt.

"How many times has he been to the police and principal's office for fighting?" Jeff shot back. "How many? And you get him off every time. Thirty-seven kids, including Hugh. He's even beat up girls. He steals and he lies and you get him off. Every time! And none of the adults stop him." Jeff shook his index finger at his dad. "You've never stopped him. Never. I had to do it myself."

"What's that supposed to mean?" hissed Porsche. "What do you mean you stopped him?"

Jeff looked at his dad. Kent seemed not to know whether to intervene or let Jeff talk. Jeff glanced at Porsche's daughters. The younger one was hiding behind the older one and holding her tightly. Dirk glared at him fiercely.

Jeff took a deep breath. More calmly he said, "I formed a group. We protected each other. Dirk's such a huge wuss that he won't go after anyone in a group. He won't go near anyone who might be able to fight back. So everyone had partners. We all stayed together and watched out for each other every single day for the last six years. Six years!"

No one said a word, so Jeff continued, "And when he couldn't beat anyone up, he got a private eye to see what was on everyone else's datapad. But I wrote a program that burns out private eyes and gave it to the school. So when his private eye burned out he stole Hugh's robot, but I got it back." Shaking with rage, Dirk turned a deep shade of purple and took a step forward. Porsche grabbed his shoulder with her claw-like hand and pulled him back. Jeff kept going. "And so he beat up Hugh and stole his stuff and sold it Outside to buy a copy of BlackHat."

Porsche hissed, "That ... is ... enough!"

"It's proven!" Jeff shouted at her. "The police caught him with the sock and rocks in the water park locker. They caught him with the BlackHat program. They caught him! It's not some *misunderstanding*!" Jeff shook with rage.

Dirk looked at his mother and said, "It was him. He must have framed me. It was all him." Porsche suddenly looked viciously pleased.

Six years of pent-up anger exploded within Jeff. He leaped across the small room, landed on Dirk, and began pounding him on the head. "LIAR!" he screamed, completely out of control.

"LIAR!" He shouted as he pummeled Dirk's head, "THIS IS FOR HUGH! THIS IS FOR HUGH!"

Large hands pulled Jeff off of Dirk and threw him across the room. Like a limp puppet, he hit the wall with a thud and crumpled on the floor. Jeff couldn't move; his father had never done *anything* like this before. Kent towered in front of him, blocking his view of the others. He jabbed his index finger into Jeff's face. In a low growl he said, "You ... get ... control ... of ... yourself. Now."

Jeff picked himself up from the floor and took a few deep breaths. He backed away from his father.

Kent began, "Whatever problems you and Dirk have had in the past are over now. You hear me? Over!"

Jeff's clenched fists burned for another chance to pummel Dirk.

Kent spread his hands and moved aside so Jeff could see the others. "Let's all just calm down. I understand that you two have had some problems. Ok? I understand. But you need to learn to get along."

"Why?" Jeff asked sullenly. "He's leaving Earth."

Kent paused. "I know. We're going too. You see Porsche and I are getting married next weekend ..."

"WHAT?" Jeff screamed.

" ... and we're all colonizing on the planet Boulder in the Colorado system in two weeks," Kent finished.

Jeff couldn't move. He couldn't speak. He couldn't think. His heart felt like it would pound its way out of his chest. He stared at Kent wide-eyed.

Kent just looked back and said, "Jeff, I know this is sudden for you, but it's sudden for us too. We just made the decision this week. You and I have been alone for a long time. Now we can have a whole family." Kent waved his hand toward Porsche Highborne and her children. "You'll see."

Kent smiled and told Jeff soothingly, "Don't worry, this is a great opportunity. Your uncle Clark and I are buying a ship repair business from a guy who's retiring. With the money we get from that, we think we can buy our own ship in five years. Our own ship Jeff! Not a very big one, but enough to start a shipping company out there in the colonies. Uncle Clark will be the captain. Dirk can pilot. You can be the engineer. Think, Jeff, think! Eventually you'll be captain yourself."

"Why should he be captain?" Porsche interrupted. "He should run the repair business. Dirk can be captain. He's got a higher-level pilot's license."

Kent turned to Porsche. "He will be," he said reassuringly. "We'll be able to buy more than one ship eventually. Dirk will have a ship of his own too. Don't worry." But Porsche shot a poisonous look at Jeff that sent ice through his veins. Not noticing, Kent continued, "Now let's just calm down and have something to eat."

Dazed, Jeff was still unable to speak. Kent reached out and put his hand on Jeff's shoulder. Everything seemed to move in slow motion.

"I know this is a lot to take in," Kent told him. "But it will be alright. You'll see. Now sit down. Come on, sit down at the table. Get to know your new mother."

In almost a whisper Jeff rasped, "My mother's dead." No one moved or spoke.

Jeff's heartbeat thundered in his ears. Without a word, Jeff turned and threw himself out of the room as fast as he could. He ran hard. His feet slammed the floor. A couple got off an elevator a short way down the corridor in front of him. Jeff dove through the door before it closed and pounded his hand on the button panel. The elevator slid upward.

13

Jeff sat on a bench staring at the fish drifting below his feet. The large orange Japanese carp swam lazily by, ignoring the people above them. Jeff remembered the times he came here as a little boy. Back then, he always wondered why the fish didn't hear the people walking on the clear floor panels over their heads. Now he knew that the clear floor tiles were so thick that they muffled all the noise of the busy shoppers.

It occurred to Jeff to wonder how long he had been sitting there. 'I don't even remember how I got here,' he thought.

Blearily, he gazed around. The shops scattered around him were closing, the people trickling home. The lights were dimming to simulate late evening. Jeff stared back down at the fish.

After a long, long time, someone came and sat next to him on the bench. Then someone else sat on the other side of him. He didn't look up. A hand slipped into his, a warm, small hand.

"Jeff," Harriet quavered. "Jeff, everyone is looking for you."

Wordlessly, Jeff looked at Harriet on his right, and then at Akio on his left. Still feeling like he was in a dream, he asked, "How did you find me?"

Harriet said, "Your mother used to bring us all here to see the fish when we were little. You ran away from your uncle's place when you found out your mother died. This is where we found you." She paused, and then asked, "Are you all right?"

Somehow, her question couldn't connect itself to him. For a while, Jeff stared at the fish in a detached haze. At last, he said, "My dad helped build this just before he went into the Space Corps. Some rich guy died and left his money to pay for it. My mom used to bring me here every Sunday to see the fish. Real live fish. Dad never comes here. I think he's forgotten about it."

Jeff noticed that Harriet's hand was still in his. He let go. "Don't do that," he warned her. "I don't want you to get in trouble." Her hand slid away, leaving his heart feeling even emptier than before.

The three of them were silent for a long time. The fish swam contentedly under their feet. The music of the stores and the twittering of happy shoppers flowed away like a receding tide.

At last, Harriet spoke again. "Jeff, your dad told us about him and Porsche Highborne. He … he told us about colonizing too." Jeff gazed at Harriet. She was crying silently, but he couldn't make himself reach out to her. He wanted to make her feel better, but it seemed as if there was a wall between him and everyone else.

"Jeff," Akio said. "I have my datapad with me. We called your dad before we sat down. I asked him if you could stay with my family for a few days."

Harriet wiped her tear-covered face and advised, "We should go now Jeff. It's getting late. The police will know we're not from this sector because we don't have nice clothes like the people here. They don't like kids from the lower sectors hanging around here until late. We'll get in trouble."

"Let's go," Akio agreed. They stood, but Jeff couldn't move. Harriet grasped Jeff's hand and pulled. He stood. Akio put his arm around Jeff's shoulders and gently pushed him forward. Robotically, Jeff plodded along. Without a word, he let them lead him to Akio's flat.

14

Jeff plodded down the corridor at school. Harriet and Akio appeared on either side of him.

Worried, Harriet asked, "Are you ok Jeff?"

"No."

"You seem worse today. What happened?"

"My dad said that I have to be in the wedding party. He said I have to put on a suit and stand in line. You shake everyone's hand and tell them how wonderful it all is. They take pictures and stuff." Jeff paused, and then told Harriet, "I told him no. We had a fight in the corridor. Everyone was looking. A policewoman came. My dad said I'm doing it whether I want to or not. Then he went into our place."

"It might not be that bad, Jeff," Harriet told him hopefully.

Jeff ignored her comment. "You know, he hasn't asked me when I'm coming back to our flat." Harriet and Akio silently glanced at each other.

As they got on an elevator, Akio informed Jeff, "My dad asked your dad if you could come live with us when we go to the New Tokyo system. He went over late last night when he thought we were all asleep. When he came back, I heard him talking to my mom."

"I know," Jeff answered. "I heard them too. My dad said no. But tell your dad thanks. It means a lot to me that your parents wanted me to be in your family."

The three walked the rest of the way home in silence.

15

Jeff, wearing a rented suit, stood just inside the door of the wedding chapel with Akio and Harriet.

Harriet said worriedly, "Jeff, you look like a zombie. You've got to find a way to snap out of this."

Jeff cast a wary look toward the front of the chapel where his father was talking with his uncle Clark as they buttoned the vests of their suits and put on their jackets. Dirk, also in a suit, sat dejectedly in a chair off to the side.

Harriet was being persistent. "Have you thought about what you're going to do?"

"Do?" Jeff asked. "What do you mean, do? There's nothing I can do. They're getting married."

"I know, but so what? There's still got to be something you can do to make things come out right."

"Why would you say that?" he asked.

"Ever since I've known you, you've always been able to find a way forward for yourself no matter what. It was that way when your mother died. And when Dirk made our lives miserable, you found a way out. You always do. And you're always happier when you take action."

For a moment, Jeff pondered her words silently. He watched his uncle talk with the minister while his father made Dirk take off his jacket. Dirk had his vest on wrong, so Kent showed him how to put it on properly.

Jeff felt like his insides would explode. Harriet hovered protectively next to him. "Jeff," she said, "your hands are shaking. Are you ok?"

Turning, he gazed directly into Harriet's eyes. Jeff told her firmly, "You're right. There *is* something I can do—leave." Without another word, he marched out the chapel. Caught completely off guard, Akio and Harriet stood stunned for a moment and then trailed after him.

Jeff gazed around the plaza, wondering where he would go next. His father had paid for an expensive wedding in a chapel two sectors above theirs. Unlike their Sector, fake trees in ornamental pots lined the street. People rode by on sleek, modern hovertrams instead of the old, rickety trams that plied the corridors on his level. Some people even had their own hovercarts and hovercycles.

Gazing at the unfamiliar scene, the world seemed to close in around Jeff. But the people and the traffic flowed by heedlessly.

Akio approached him from behind and asked, "Are you really going to ditch the wedding? Won't your dad kill you?"

Jeff nodded. "Probably. But whatever he does, it won't be as bad as what his wonderful new wife will do."

"You'd better not do this Jeff," Harriet warned. "It will only make things worse."

"You're probably right," he told her. "You usually are. But this once, I'm not going to listen to you."

Flustered, Harriet asked, "Where will you go then?"

Before he could answer, Akio announced, "To the zoo."

"He can't go to the zoo," Harriet objected. "They book reservations for a day at the zoo a year in advance. And how could he ever afford a ticket?"

"I have four right here," Akio told her as he pulled them from his pocket.

"Akio," Harriet asked, "How in the universe did you ever get those?"

"My family has reservations. Mom made them last year. Dad gave the tickets to me and told me that Mom and him don't need to go to the zoo. He wanted me to take you, Jeff, right after the wedding. He said you'd need something good to happen. He figured we'd want to take Harriet too, so he gave me all the tickets. But we have to take my little brother. He'll have a meltdown if he doesn't get to go. Sorry."

Amazed, Jeff asked, "Your parents did that for me?"

Akio nodded, "My mom says you're like one of her own sons. This was her idea."

For the first time in days, Jeff smiled. "Go get your brother," he told Akio. Akio smiled too. Without a word, he slipped back through the huge double doors of the chapel. In moments, he returned with Akifumi, his 10-year-old brother. As they approached, Jeff asked Akifumi, "Are you ready to go to the zoo?"

Akifumi lit up, "Now?" he squeaked. "Sure. Let's go!" Before anyone could stop him, he zipped toward the nearest elevator. After a surprised moment, Akio, Jeff, and Harriet trotted after him, trying to catch up.

A while later, the four of them were more than fifteen hundred floors higher in the building. They approached the entrance of the zoo. Jeff saw that there was no line; hardly anyone was around. 'I guess that's because it's so early,' he thought. Jeff, still wearing his rented suit, felt like he really stuck out, but he didn't let it bother him too much.

As soon as they got inside, Akifumi shouted, "I want to see the tigers!" Before he could launch himself in the direction of the tiger enclosures, Akio grabbed the back of his shirt. "You have to stay with us, Akifumi. Mom said. You can't run around on your own."

"I want to see the tigers!"

Jeff actually laughed. "I think we'd better get over to those tigers fast. His head is going to explode if we don't."

"I hope it does," Akio replied, still hanging onto the back of his brother's shirt.

After spending about twenty minutes in front of the tiger exhibit, they wondered what to see next. "Monkeys! We gotta see the monkeys!" Akifumi shouted repeatedly.

Along the way, Harriet made them take a detour past the birdcages. Each bird exhibit, which was about the size of a large closet, contained a few birds of different species. Fascinated, Akifumi wanted to linger in front of each one. It was difficult to get him to move on. Eventually, Jeff, Akio, and Harriet got several cages ahead of him.

Harriet told Jeff, "You look more like your usual self. I'm glad."

"Yeah," he agreed. "I feel better. I know ditching my father's wedding was a pretty bad thing to do, but there was no way I could stay there."

Their conversation was interrupted by an odd voice from behind them. They turned and looked back at Akifumi, who was standing frozen in front of a cage they had passed moments before. They heard a high-pitched voice saying, "Hello," to Akifumi. Akifumi stared intently at one of the birds.

"Hello," the bird said again. "I'm a mynah bird. Pretty, pretty bird. Hahahahahahahaha."

Akifumi cast his gaze around wildly until he saw Akio. His eyes seemed about to pop out of his head and his mouth worked up and down as he pointed at the bird. After a few moments, he was able to get out, "Akio!" in a hushed voice. "Akio, this bird is talking to me. What do I do?"

"Nothing," Akio told him. "That's a mynah bird. It talks."

"Can I talk to it?"

"You can if you want, but it won't do any good. They just repeat the sounds they hear. They don't understand the words."

The mynah bird interrupted by belting out, "Hello! Hello! Hello! Hello!" as loud as it could. It was nearly half an hour before they got Akifumi away from the mynah bird's cage.

When they finally arrived at the primate house, they found that the apes and monkeys were active and very loud. Even so, it was hard to tell who was more excited, the animals or Akifumi. He darted around the exhibit, calling to the various creatures and imitating their sounds.

After viewing the gorillas and chimpanzees, the three of them sat on a bench in front of a huge exhibit containing many types of small primates. Akifumi, who seemed glued to the clear plastic front of the enclosure, continued to chatter to the animals.

After a while, Harriet asked Jeff, "Is your father really going to buy you a ship?"

"It's not for me," he answered. "It's for a shipping company he wants to set up. Uncle Clark will be the captain first. When he retires, Dad and Clark want to make me captain. They say you can make more money than in the Space Corps."

"When you're captain, do you think you'll come back to Earth?"

"I don't know. They want to get a Firefly. It's a small freighter about 350 feet long. It would take about a half year to get from the Colorado system clear to Earth in a ship that small."

Harriet sat in thoughtful silence. Then, very quietly, she asked, "So you're never coming back?"

"I don't know, Harriet. I just don't know."

"You have to come back someday."

"Why?" Jeff asked, but Harriet wouldn't answer. Without warning, Akio burst out with, "She likes you dude."

"Who?"

Akio pointed both index fingers at Harriet, who sat looking down at the ground with her arms folded.

"That's not funny Akio," Jeff scolded.

"She likes you, dude," Akio repeated, nodding. Harriet seemed to turn to stone.

"Harriet," Jeff asked gently, "is that true?"

Quietly, she answered, "Of course it's true, you idiot. How could you not know?"

Akio agreed. "She's right. Don't you remember what she said to you the morning Hugh got beat up? And what about the dancing? And she always cuts your hair for you."

Tenderly, Jeff asked, "How long have you felt this way?"

Akio rolled his eyes and answered for her, "Since forever."

Jeff waited, watching Harriet, who was still looking downward. After a silence she said, "Do you remember the first day of kindergarten? I didn't know anyone because we'd just moved into this arcology. I tried to play dodgeball with the first graders and they knocked me down with the balls? You came and helped me up and chased them off even though some of them were bigger than you. Then you and Akio said you'd play with me and be my friends."

"Since then?" She just nodded.

Jeff looked back at Akio. "You knew?"

Rolling his eyes again, Akio told him, "Everyone knows but you. Get a clue, dude."

Jeff could see Harriet's eyes fill with tears. "I'm not going to cry," she told herself, but it didn't work. She turned to Jeff and told him, "You're MY guy. You're THE guy. I went home that day and told my mom I was going to marry you. I've never changed my mind. You were supposed to stay here with me. You were supposed to be here on my 16th birthday. You were going to throw me a big surprise party."

"I was?"

"Yes, you were. It was going to be *huge*. The best party any girl ever had. And you were going to dance with me. And when everyone else went home, you were going to kiss me right outside my front door and not care who saw because we'd be 16 and we could do that without getting in trouble."

Akio made a snorting noise. "If you two are going to start talking about kissing, I'm taking Akifumi to see the kangaroos." He got up, poked his brother and ordered, "We're leaving. There's some kangaroos that want us to come look at them."

"Really?" Akifumi asked. He bolted for the exit. Akio rolled his eyes one last time and ran after his brother.

For a while Harriet and Jeff sat in silence. After a time, Jeff said, "I'm not going to be here on your 16th birthday."

"I know," Harriet sighed sadly.

"You have to get the kiss now."

Startled, Harriet turned her face up to Jeff's. "We can't do that, someone might see."

"No one's going to see but the monkeys. And I made them promise not to tell."

Through her tears, Harriet laughed sadly and said, "My first kiss isn't supposed to be in the monkey house at the zoo. That's not romantic. Look, all the monkeys are staring at us."

"Let them stare," Jeff said as he slid closer to her and took her in his arms. Softly, he caressed her cheek and then kissed her.

At that moment, they heard the laughing of small children as they ran toward the entrance of the primate house. Jeff pulled back, stood, and offered his hand to Harriet. She took it and he helped her stand. Before anyone else could see, he let go of her hand, and the two of them left the primate house. As they did, Harriet wiped away her tears.

"I'll always remember that, Harriet."

Harriet laughed a melancholy little laugh and said, "So will the monkeys."

Jeff chuckled too.

Around noon, the four of them went to a cafe in the zoo and had lunch using money that Akio's parents gave him. To Jeff, the rest of the day seemed to pass like a good dream. It was nearly ten o'clock that night when they arrived at Akio's flat with Akio carrying Akifumi on his back.

"He's sound asleep," Harriet told Akio quietly. "He's had a big day. I've never seen a little kid get so excited. I had a good time too. Thank you for taking me Akio."

Not wanting to wake his brother, Akio just nodded and smiled. He entered the flat. Jeff and Harriet stood, glancing at each other awkwardly.

"I can't kiss you again," he told her. "Someone might see." Silently, she nodded and stared up at him with amazing green eyes. As he had the day they danced, Jeff melted inside.

"Goodnight Harriet. I promise you that if there's any way I can come back to Earth, I will."

Harriet smiled and said, "You'd better. Because if you don't, I'll come after you and track you down no matter where in the universe you go."

Smiling, Jeff agreed, "You would, too." With a dazzlingly sweet but disconsolate smile and a wave, Harriet left.

Jeff turned to go into Akio's flat, but then hesitated. He gazed a moment at the door to his own flat. Squaring his shoulders, he marched in. Everything was quiet.

"Of course," Jeff said out loud to no one. "They're off on their honeymoon." Going into his room, Jeff noticed that there was a message on his datapad. He picked it up. The message was from his father.

A long time later, Jeff returned to Akio's flat. As he entered, Akio asked, "Were you and Harry out there all this time?"

Jeff shook his head.

Akio could see that there was something wrong. "What?" he demanded. "What happened?"

With the tightness of a guitar string about to snap, Jeff explained, "I went over to my flat. There was a message from my dad on my datapad."

"Was he mad?"

"Yeah. There was lots of yelling. A fair amount of name calling. It was pretty brutal. I deleted it."

Jeff didn't realize Akio's mother was in the room until she stepped up next to him and put her arm around his shoulders.

"I'm sorry," she consoled Jeff. "I'm so very sorry son." She hugged him tightly as tears welled in her eyes.

Part 2

WATCH THAT FIRST STEP

"Leaving our comfort zone is never easy. Learning to live a new way is always hard. But sometimes, we must leave the world we know to see that world for exactly what it is. The same is true of ourselves. We often need to get outside what's comfortable to see ourselves for what we really are." *Thoughts on Life*, Hugh Benson, p. 257.

16

"995 Express to Orlando, Florida now arriving on platform 12. 995 Express to Orlando, Florida now arriving on platform 12."

Jeff piled himself on a bench at the end of the breezy skytrain platform with Akio and his family. He absently watched the train float into the station on the 1500th floor of the arcology. The force field over the opening, which kept air from flooding out, shimmered and buzzed as the train moved through it.

A group of happy vacationers ambled toward the bluish-grey train as it drew up to the platform and thunked open its doors. A young girl laughingly pointed at Jeff's trunk as she passed by and said to another girl, "Look, wheels." The two giggled and scooted toward the doors. Their own trunks floated behind them a couple feet off of the floor, following obediently. Jeff's trunk lay at his feet as he held onto its handle.

'I haven't seen Dad in days,' Jeff thought, gazing blankly at his feet. He mulled emptily on the fact that after the wedding, Kent and Porsche went to the Rim Hotel for their honeymoon, which overlooked part of the park on top of the arcology and also had an outside view of the city. 'He never took my mom there,' Jeff thought bitterly as he watched the skytrain whoosh away from the platform. 'There wasn't enough money.'

But now there was money. Jeff's father and uncle sold their flats to buy the spaceship repair business on the planet Boulder. The sale of Porsche's flat was paying for all their tickets out to the Colorado system. 'But he had enough left over for a honeymoon for his new wife,' Jeff thought as he felt ice creep through his insides.

On the day Kent returned, he dropped Jeff's trunk off at the Miyamoto's flat while Jeff was out. Akio's mother told him, "Your father said that everything you're taking has to fit in this trunk and your backpack. They won't allow anything else on the ship."

Jeff went to their flat to pack his stuff the next day. He found all of his things piled in a corner in the main room. Going into his bedroom, he saw that his bed had new bedding on it. There was also an open suitcase sitting on the bed. It contained a woman's clothes. Jeff realized that his dad and Porsche had moved into his room. With anger burning inside him, Jeff packed his things. He couldn't find his guitar, so he packed everything else he could into the trunk. Before he left the flat, he put his monkeybot and datapad in his backpack. For the last time, he walked out his home.

As Jeff thought about that day, his face twisted into a bitter grimace. He struggled not to be angry. 'Getting mad again won't do any good,' he thought. 'It'll only make things worse.'

It would have been much easier to let himself be mad. When he emailed his father asking about his guitar, he got a reply that said:

> I sold it. It's too big to take with us. The money is in your account.

That was all. He'd had no other communication with his dad since then.

Another train whisked in from the sky and came to a stop. Two women with white-blond hair seemed to be staring at Jeff from the other end of the platform. They quickly looked away when he glanced in their direction. For some reason, they made Jeff feel even more depressed.

To make himself feel better, he put his hand into his coat pocket and fingered the pocket watch Harriet gave him. The day before, the group threw a surprise party at the community center for him, Akio, and Madison Burke. After the party was over, Madison went straight home to pick up her stuff. She was leaving that afternoon. Jeff, Akio, and Harriet lingered for a while at the community center. That was when she gave him the watch with her picture on its face.

"I like this," he told her. "You're in 3D. How did you get your picture on it?"

"You can get them specially made a couple of sectors up," she replied awkwardly. "It plays music too. I downloaded some guitar songs that you like." She hugged him tightly for a long moment. Then Harriet hugged Akio as well.

Harriet had promised them she wouldn't come to see them off. Jeff preferred to just leave. But when Jeff left Akio's flat that day, he heard a small voice behind him say quietly, "Goodbye Jeff." He turned around just in time to see Harriet ducking down a side corridor, crying. He stood staring after her until Akio's mother gently said, "It's time to go Jeff." He walked with the Miyamotos to the train platform.

As Jeff sat waiting, he saw Kent descend the escalator with Porsche and her kids. He watched them park themselves on a bench at the other end of the platform. Kent didn't look over at Jeff. 'I guess he's still pretty mad about the wedding,' Jeff thought.

"Maybe you should go over there with your Dad," suggested Mamsen Miyamoto.

Jeff shook his head. "I don't think he wants me to. I think he'd rather I stay with you until we get to the spaceport." Akio's mother glanced sadly at her husband, who nodded silently.

After a while, their train arrived. Jeff wheeled his trunk as he followed Akio's family into the last car. As he did, he saw Kent, Porsche, and her kids get into the first car. When the doors closed, the train pulled out of the arcology and into the clear, blue sky. Dirty grey-brown clouds hung over the city far below. Jeff watched the huge building fall rapidly behind him.

Leaving didn't seem real. He couldn't even believe he was Outside.

The train wound its way through the many arcologies scattered across the seemingly endless city. In minutes, the only world he had ever known was hidden behind all the other arcologies. His home was gone.

The spaceport was on the other side of the state, but the train moved so fast that they arrived in only an hour. As they drew close to it, the train descended. It startled Jeff when the train plunged into an underground tunnel. 'That's right,' he thought to himself, 'Akio's dad said that the train station is under the spaceport.'

The skytrain slowed to a stop and the doors opened. Jeff yanked his trunk as he followed along behind the Miyamotos. In the huge domed train station, the Miyamotos came to a stop not far from Jeff's dad. Kent had his back to them as he talked with Porsche.

"We have to leave you here son," Sirsen Miyamoto said to Jeff. "This is where you go with your family." He extended his hand. Numbly, Jeff shook it. "Goodbye Jeff."

"Goodbye. And thanks for everything. Especially thanks for not getting mad when Akio and I tried to teach Akifumi to fly with plastic wings. I was really sorry about the broken arm."

Sirsen Miyamoto smiled and chuckled. "You were 10 then Jeff. And I knew that was Akio's idea anyway."

Jeff turned to Mamsen Miyamoto and saw that she was crying. "Goodbye," he said to her as he put out his hand for her to shake. Ignoring his hand, she grabbed him in a tight hug. Tenderly he whispered, "You've been like a mother to me. Thank you for taking care of me after my mom died. Thanks for teaching me to cook and stuff." Jeff hesitated and then said, "I ... I love you Mom."

Releasing him, she looked up into his eyes. "Goodbye my son. I love you, too. Grow up into a fine, handsome man. Then you come back here and marry Harriet. You know she loves you." Jeff nodded. "And then you come to the planet Yokohama and see your little Japanese mama-*san*." He nodded again.

Jeff faced Akio. He surprised himself by abruptly hugging his friend. He wasn't embarrassed to be hugging another guy. He told Akio, "You're my brother," and then he let go.

Akifumi clamped his arms around Jeff's waist. "Bye Jeff. If you come see us, I'll give you a fish."

Jeff laughed and said, "Thanks, Akifumi. I like fish."

Jeff smiled at Akio and his family one last time. Then turning away from them, he grabbed the handle of his trunk and made his way toward Kent, Porsche, and her children.

17

"Welcome to Spaceport Security," the computer said. "Please insert your ticket in the blue slot and state your full name."

Jeff shoved his plastic card-like ticket into the slot. "Jefferson Joshua Bowman," he told the machine. A line of red light passed over him from head to toe. "Security clearance granted," it said as it spat his ticket back out at him. He grabbed it and put it in his pocket. "Please proceed to gate S3811," the computer directed. The clear plastic doors slid open to let him through.

As Jeff came out of the bleak security area, he saw his father waiting. Dirk was standing beside Kent. Porsche and her girls weren't through security yet. Kent waved for Jeff to join him.

"Come over to the side for a second," Kent instructed, guiding both boys off to the side of the corridor. As he did, Porsche and Dirk's sisters emerged from the security area and approached them.

"Look you guys," Kent began as Porsche came up beside him. "I know the two of you boys have had some problems. This is where it ends. Beginning today, we're starting a new life. It's time to let the past be the past. From now on, I want you two to forget all that's gone on between you and just move forward. I'm asking you both to behave like adults rather than kids. All I ask is that you be decent to each other. We can all make a good life together if you two will just act like men and let things go. I want you to start by shaking hands."

When neither boy moved, Kent said, "I mean it guys, I want you to shake hands."

After a moment's hesitation, Jeff stuck out his hand. Dirk looked like someone had asked him to kiss a Nestorian porcuhog on the lips. But his mother commanded, "Dirk. Do what you're told."

With a grimace of pure revulsion, Dirk grabbed Jeff's hand, shook once, and quickly let go. Kent smiled. "You see. That didn't kill either of you. Now let's go get on the shuttle to Lunar Central Station." He led the way toward the gate as Jeff and the others followed.

At the gate, they found some unoccupied seats to plop into while they waited to board their shuttle. The chair was cold and hard, and it was just the perfect shape to ensure it was uncomfortable.

Kent sat next to Jeff. He told Jeff brightly, "You know, you're lucky. I didn't get to go into space until after you were born. You're on your first space voyage at 14." Kent stared off at nothing, lost in thought. "I remember it like it was yesterday," he said. "It was one of the best days of my entire life."

Jeff didn't share Kent's enthusiasm. He was leaving behind everything and everyone that were important to him. It would be years before he saw Harriet again. The thought made his heart go dead inside him. And losing Akio and the Miyamotos made Jeff feel completely adrift in the universe. 'I wish none of this was happening,' he thought.

After a tedious hour, they boarded the shuttle. As they entered the spacecraft, Jeff saw that the seats were grouped into three sections separated by two aisles. Each section contained six seats. "Our seats are in the middle section," Kent told them.

Jeff's seat was on the far aisle. Entering the row, he made his way there. After stowing his backpack under his seat, he plopped down. Porsche's youngest daughter sat next to him, with her older sister on her other side. Dirk came next, then Porsche, and finally Kent.

Kent said to the kids. "You can watch the launch from the ship's cameras on your datapads." Jeff got his datapad so he could watch.

It took another half an hour for the shuttle to be loaded and cleared for takeoff. The captain came on the ship's intercom. "This is your captain, Alex Bell, speaking. You are currently aboard Jupiter Space Lines flight 1331 to Lunar Central Station. If your travel plans today do not include going to the Moon, now would be a good time to get off." Some of the passengers chuckled. After a little more of the pilot's banter (his jokes didn't improve), the flight attendants closed the doors and the walkways withdrew from the shuttle. They were ready to go.

Jeff could tell immediately when power hit the engines. From all around him, he could hear a gentle hum like a large choir of men with heroically deep voices singing a soft, gentle "Aaaah." The large spacecraft wafted upward like a feather carried on a breeze. As it rose, it picked up speed. The ground dropped away swiftly. As they rose, the clear blueness of the sky slipped into the deep blackness of space. Jeff's datapad showed the bright blue Earth below them and the shining stars above. The humming faded to silence.

The wonder of what was happening around Jeff pulled him out of his depression at last. Jeff's eyes stayed glued to his datapad. He saw the shuttle approach a large group of structures in orbit.

'Ah,' he thought, 'That's the Biodome Belt.'

The silver domes stretched across the blackness of space above the ship and arched off into the distance. Each of the structures had a flat circular base that was covered by a huge dome like the one on top of the arcology, but larger. The space between the base and the dome was filled with air and made habitable. Growing up, Jeff had often looked at pictures of people who were wealthy enough to afford these huge, private habitats. It wasn't uncommon for biodomes to have trees, rivers, lakes, and many kinds of animals. A famous singer that Harriet liked kept a horse ranch in her biodome.

The Earth rapidly fell behind them as they broke orbit and launched toward the Moon. But after an hour and a half, Jeff grew bored. A flight attendant came around with some food.

"Is there anything to do on this flight?" he asked the stewardess who gave him his lunch.

"Yes," she replied. "If you log onto the ship's network, you can play all of the latest games during the flight. There's also a wide selection of music to listen to and 3D video programs to watch. In fact, our 3V service offers 1000 channels and a selection of 1,000,000 movies and shows that are playable on demand. If you want, you can get information about this flight by selecting the 'Travel' icon when you log on. Is your family colonizing?" Jeff nodded. "Well you can use the 'Travel' icon to get information on your entire trip. Just hold your ticket up to your datapad's camera so it can see the ID of each ship you're going to ride on. It'll tell you about each ship and their flight paths."

Jeff realized he knew almost nothing about their trip. His uncle Clark had told him that it would take five months to get to the Colorado system. Other than that, he was completely in the dark. He'd been too wrapped up in the turmoil of leaving. "Thanks," he told the stewardess.

Logging onto the ship's network, Jeff immediately looked up the flight he was on to see what information he could get. The flight was a little more than twelve hours long. At the end, they would dock at Lunar Central Station, which orbited the Moon. The network informed him that Lunar Central Station was the primary departure point for all ships leaving near-Earth space. According to the information on the ship's network, Lunar Central was nearly sixteen miles long.

At Lunar Central, they would board a freighter that also took passengers. The freighter's name was the Edmund Ellsworth. Jeff pulled up a live view of the Ellsworth, which was currently docked at Lunar Central Station. He could only see part of the huge vessel, so he switched to a 3D model of the ship that he downloaded.

The Ellsworth was a Leviathan-class megafreighter that was built around a central cylinder. The huge cylinder was a mile long and 420 feet in diameter. Attached to the rear of the cylinder were three large spheres containing the ship's huge gravity mirrors. Behind the group of mirror modules was a chunky structure that housed the powerful fusion generators and main engineering. Tanks for fuel, water, and air were crowded all along the ship's central cylinder. In addition, there were long rectangular blocks that were the ship's holds. Inside them, the ship carried thousands and thousands of tons of cargo. According to the network, one of the cargo holds had been converted into cabins for passengers. The Ellsworth could carry as many as 800 people at a time.

As Jeff looked through the data on the Ellsworth, Porsche's youngest daughter, Denise, peered over at his datapad. Watching him rotate the 3D model of the Ellsworth, she turned to her sister, pointed at Jeff's datapad, and whispered cautiously, "What's that?"

He turned to her and said, "That's the ship we're riding to the Colorado system. It'll take us to the planet Boulder."

Obviously frightened, Denise stared at Jeff.

"What's the matter?" he asked. She shifted in her seat, moved away from Jeff, and clung to her older sister's arm. Her older sister, Danae, answered for her, "She's just surprised, that's all."

"Why?"

Danae and Denise glanced at each other, puzzled. To Jeff, Danae explained, "No one talks to Thirds."

Jeff sat and regarded them for a moment, thinking of what to say. Then he looked straight into Denise's eyes and said, "I talk to Thirds."

Denise was speechless. She looked up at Danae for reassurance. Danae shrugged, so Denise turned to Jeff. In a very, very small voice she asked, "Really?"

Jeff smiled. "Sure," he told her.

Dirk and Porsche acted as if they hadn't heard the conversation. But Jeff's father turned toward them and corrected Denise. "You're not a Third any more Denise. You mother has a

Reproductive Allowance of two children because your father gave up his allowance when he and your mother divorced. I got my first wife's Reproductive Allowance when she died. So I have an allowance of two children, but she and I only had one son. Between the two of us, we have an allowance for four children. That means you're not a Third any more. You're an Allowed Child."

Shyly, Denise leaned her head back on Danae's arm. Looking up at Danae, she asked in a whisper, "What's his name?"

Jeff smiled as Denise pointed at him. In an exaggerated whisper he answered, "My name is Jeff." The girls giggled.

Jeff held his datapad so the two girls could see it. Pointing to the ship it displayed, he said, "This is the Ellsworth. We'll be staying in cabins in this section here." He pointed to a long, rectangular block that was held to the main cylinder of the ship by a latticework of beams. "There'll be about 800 people in it. These round things back here are the gravity mirrors. There are three more here at the front. They make the ship go. This here at the very front is where the crew lives and where they steer the ship."

Hesitantly, Denise asked Jeff, "Sirsen Jeff, do you know a lot about space ships?"

"Some," he told her. "And you don't have to call me Sirsen. Just Jeff is ok. I was going to go to the Academy and be an engineer on a big spaceship."

"Don't you want to go any more, Sirsen Jeff?"

Tightness gripped Jeff's insides as he replied, "I want to go, but I'm not. Not any more."

Kent broke in again, "You'll still be an engineer, Jeff. Maybe even a captain. It won't be in the Space Corps, but you'll still do well."

Jeff's eyes dropped to his plate. At that moment, he had no appetite. But he forced himself to eat his meal.

18

The twelve hours it took to get to Lunar Central Station seemed to drag on forever. Jeff played a lot of games on his datapad. It was nice to have access to so many new games for once. He also watched some shows with Porsche's daughters. Their datapads were packed in their trunks, so he let them use his to play games while he slept for about two hours. When he awoke, the shuttle was drawing close to the Moon.

Spellbound, Jeff watched their approach on his datapad. Living in an arcology, he seldom saw the sky. When he did see the Moon during his evening visits to the domed park at the arcology's top, it was barely visible. The many artificial structures and satellites in orbit around the Earth made it nearly impossible to see anything beyond the atmosphere.

Space was blacker than he ever thought possible. The Moon looked like a bright, circular island in a dark and infinite black ocean. Across the Moon's face were the bright lights of its many cities. Jeff looked toward one of the ship's large windows to his right. He could see the vast depths of space sprinkled with diamond-like stars.

Danae, who seemed to have warmed up to Jeff, followed his gaze. She commented, "There are so many stars. I never would have believed it. How could there be so many stars?"

Jeff smiled and answered, "It's amazing, isn't it? It's too bad we can't see this from Earth."

One of the flight attendants announced that they would be docking at Lunar Central Station in a few minutes. "A robot porter and a luggage cart will be at the gate waiting with your bags. Please exit directly to the waiting area and let the robots find you. You do not have to search for them. If you encounter any difficulty, please see one of the attendants at the gate." As she spoke, the ship docked. "We are now at Lunar Central Station. Thank you for flying Jupiter Space Lines. We hope to see you again soon." The doors opened automatically, and the passengers began making their way off the ship.

Lunar Central Station was big. On the opposite side of the large waiting area he entered, Jeff could see robots standing at the controls of luggage carts. He heard a voice speak near his dad that sounded as if it came from thin air.

"Sirsen and Mamsen Bowman?" it asked. "Please follow the green arrows on the floor that contain your surname. They'll lead you to your luggage cart." All six of them trailed along after the arrows. Jeff glanced around to see other groups of people following arrows toward their own carts.

"Welcome, Sirsen and Mamsen Bowman, to Lunar Central Station," greeted the robot driving their luggage cart. "Welcome Dirk, Danae, Denise, and Jeff. I hope your trip was pleasant." It waved its hand fluidly toward the seats behind it. "As you can see, your luggage is ready to go. Please be seated and I will take you to your connecting flight."

Wordlessly, they sat on the bench-style seats behind the robot. "Thank you. If everyone is ready, we will now proceed." The cart moved away from the gate. Soon it was weaving in and out of the flood of other carts, each filled with travelers.

"If you like, we can stop at any of the many fine restaurants available here in the spaceport," the robot told them, "Currently, Lunar Central Station time is 4:21 p.m. on June 26th, 2715. According to your schedule, you also have time for a thirty minute stop at our state-of-the-art artificial reality suite. All of the latest AR programs are available."

The robot continued to rattle on, but Jeff tuned it out as he watched the scenery flow by. Lunar Central was really a city unto itself. It seemed every available inch of the spaceport was filled with businesses of all kinds.

As they slowed down to turn a corner, they were suddenly confronted by a huge monster the size of an ambulance. It was a jumble of claws and dagger-like spines. The creature noticed them immediately and leaped toward the cart. Its gigantic jaws opened to reveal several rows of razor-sharp teeth. Jeff and his entire family recoiled and Dirk screamed. Just before the monster reached them, a man ran up behind it and shot it with a ray gun. Pieces of the monster splattered in all directions. 3D text hovered over the man's head. It read:

Creature Kill 4
Now Available In All Spaceport AR Suites
Play Today. Get Them Before They Get You.

"It's just a stupid holographic ad for a game," Kent told them, irritated. "What idiot thought that something like that was a good idea? They could give someone a heart attack!"

The cart sped on. Jeff could see 3D holographic ads everywhere. He momentarily wondered why there weren't ads like this in the arcology. 'Maybe they realized we didn't have money down where we lived.'

Kent instructed the robot, "Let's stop at that cafe. We want to get something to eat." The robot complied by pulling the cart to a stop in front of the restaurant and everyone got out.

In the entrance to the cafe, they saw a large display that contained the menu. The 3D image of a young man greeted them as soon as they walked in. "Welcome to the Sumptuous Synthpaste Corporation's Sunny Sandwich Cafe, Sirsen and Mamsen Bowman. It's nice to see you. And you've brought, Jeff, Dirk, Danae, and Denise. Hi, kids. Everyone please place your orders with me, and your sandwiches and drinks will be ready by the time you reach the pick-up station on your left. What will you all have today?"

Jeff was surprised the cafe's computer knew their names. It was a little unsettling. He was last to place his order. After he did, the 3D image said, "Thank you for your order. Either Sirsen or Mamsen Bowman can say 'Yes' when you hear the beep to authorize the payment for your meals."

When the beep sounded, Kent uttered a distinct, "Yes."

"Thank you. Your payment has been received. Please proceed to the pick-up station on your left. We hope you enjoy your meals."

They gathered their food at the pick-up station and sat down at one of the cafe's tables to eat. Immediately, Denise told Danae, "I have to go to the bathroom."

"There's one right next door to the cafe," Kent said to Porsche. But Porsche didn't move. Instead, Danae stood up, took Denise by the hand, and led her toward the restroom.

Jeff took a bite of his sandwich. The synthetic bread wasn't bad. Neither was the synthpaste meat and cheese. 'At least it's better than the stuff we had back home,' he thought. 'They didn't even *try* to make that look like real food. It was all just blocks of synthpaste.'

Munching his sandwich, Jeff watched the steady stream of carts go by carrying passengers and luggage. The passengers wore styles that were nothing like what he had seen in the arcology. He glanced down at his own plain clothing.

There were *lots* of robots. Spaceport service robots of all kinds went by, intent on their various tasks. Travelers passed by with personal robots in tow. Seeing the differences between the worlds inside and outside the arcology, Jeff realized what a backwater place he'd been growing up in. It was a little intimidating.

Jeff noticed a cart slow down with three red-haired men and one man that was white-blond. They seemed to look at him as they passed. He wondered uneasily about it and shrugged it off.

Denise and Danae returned and started in on their food. It didn't take long for all of them to finish eating. As they reboarded the cart, the robot said, "I hope you enjoyed your meal. Shall I take you to your departing ship now?"

"Yes," was Kent's curt reply. The cart accelerated again.

It didn't take them long to get to their ship. As soon as they did, the robot told them, "Please go on inside. I'll bring your luggage in directly. And thank you for riding with QuickCarts Automated Porters. We hope to have the opportunity to serve you again sometime."

They followed Kent to the gate where a man in a blue uniform stood. Jeff wondered why he wore a circular band around his head. The small triangles that ran along its top edge made it look almost like a king's crown. "Kent Bowman?" the man asked. Kent nodded. "You have six in your party. Four kids? How'd that happen? None of my business I suppose."

"This is a second marriage for both of us," Kent explained.

The man nodded and said, "Ah, I see. Well you and your wife are in cabin 25. The kids are in 26. You purchased your synthpaste supplies through us, so they're already loaded. The porterbot will load your bags, so you're all set. I'm John Anderwell, the passenger liaison. If you need anything, contact me using one of the communication panels. I assume you read the material we sent you?" Kent nodded. "Well, the first passenger association meeting is in an hour. Adults only. They'll be setting up classes for the kids, so you'll probably want to get yours signed up right away."

Immediately, Dirk asserted belligerently, "Classes? *I'm* not doing school."

"Mamsen," Sirsen Anderwell interrupted, gazing at Porsche. "When we say that something is ship's policy, that means that those who don't comply are put off the ship. If your son is put off, the entire family goes. You signed the agreement we sent you."

"Of course, of course," Porsche reassured him. She shot a scathing look at Dirk, making him cringe. "We're just married, and in the rush of the wedding and colonizing, we haven't had a chance to talk with the kids about this yet. We'll make sure they understand all of the ship's rules and follow them. Dirk, you'll be doing school just like everyone else."

Dirk scowled and fell silent.

"Great," Sirsen Anderwell replied, but he didn't appear to mean it. "Well, I hope your transit with us will be pleasant. I see your porterbot has already entered the ship with some of your trunks. So we'll see you at the meeting in about an hour. That's 7 p.m. ship's time. Our clock is not the same as Lunar Central's."

Together, they entered the tube that connected the ship to the station and followed it into the passenger section of the Edmund Ellsworth. They found their cabins easily.

"You kids go ahead into your cabin and get yourselves settled," Kent instructed. "We'll get our stuff put away and go to the meeting. When we get back, we'll have a talk about how things will go on the ship." He and Porsche entered their cabin.

When Jeff went into cabin 26, he saw that it was about the size of the main room of his flat back in the arcology. There was a communications panel next to the door. The beds were set into recesses in the wall. On the left side was a large bed that was obviously made for two people. On the right were two bunks, one above the other. 'This cabin is designed for a regular family,' Jeff thought. 'The big bed for the parents, and the two bunks for their two kids.'

At the back of the cabin hung a thick plastic curtain that could slide down the middle of the room to divide it in two. On either side of the curtain was a door. Jeff walked back and opened the right one first. It was a bathroom. Behind the other door was a room about the same size as the bathroom. It was stacked to the ceiling with boxes.

'Yuk,' Jeff thought, reading the box labels. 'Ready-to-eat synthpaste. You don't even have to cook it. This must be the food for the four of us for the entire trip.'

From behind him, Jeff heard Dirk declare, "This is *my* bed." He turned to see Dirk flopping onto the largest bed. Danae and Denise stood in the doorway. Danae eyed the bunks.

"Dirk," she said in a cautious monotone, "there are four of us and three beds. That means two of us have to sleep together. The bunks are too small for Denise and me to sleep in one of them. That means you have to take one of the bunks on that side."

"I said this is *my* bed," Dirk growled. Denise moved behind Danae.

Danae stood her ground. "Dirk, we can go ask Mom and Sirsen Bowman ... Kent about it if you want. But you know what they're going to say. And this room has a curtain in it. One side for boys and one for girls. That's what they're going to say." She waited.

Dirk ignored her.

"Fine," Danae said calmly. "I'll go next door and ask."

The robot porter entered the cabin with their trunks. "Where would you like these?" it asked.

Before anyone else could answer, Danae commanded it, "Put Dirk's bag over there on the top bunk. Jeff, do you mind taking the bottom?"

Jeff saw that Dirk's face was turning a bright shade of red. "No," replied Jeff, answering as calmly as Danae. "I don't mind the bottom bunk at all." He instructed the robot, "My trunk goes in that space behind the bottom bunk. Danae and Denise's go over there where the big bed is." The robot moved to obey.

"I'll be going next door," Danae said, taking a step toward the door. Dirk popped up off the bed, standing with his fists clenched. When the robot finished stowing Dirk's trunk, he stomped across the room to the bunks, and clamored up the ladder that was set into the wall next to the beds. He plopped himself onto the upper bunk and hit a button in the wall. A sliding door swooshed across the opening to his bunk, completely enclosing it into a private little space.

The robot put the rest of the trunks away and left. Danae went to the back of the cabin and pulled the big curtain forward until the room was neatly divided in half.

Jeff stood where he was for a moment and then thought, 'Wow. Tense. Is this what it's going to be like for the next five months?' He called out to Danae through the curtain, "I'm going to look around. I'll be back in a while."

No answer. Jeff left the cabin.

Wandering in no particular direction, Jeff eventually found the large open common area. It was carpeted with fake grass and sparsely decorated. The walls were displays. Some of them showed images of famous works of art. Others showed external video of the ship being loaded.

Jeff gazed at a video feed. Large containers guided by Lunar Central's cargobots were being stowed into the cargo bays through huge doors that opened to the vacuum of space. Turning his attention to his immediate surroundings, Jeff saw that the adults, and many of the kids, were already starting to gather there in the commons. Around the edges of the commons were public restrooms, a workout room, a doctor's office, and an artificial reality suite. Jeff made a beeline for the AR suite.

As soon as the double doors of the AR suite slid open, a computer-generated 3D image of a young man appeared on one of the wall panels and spoke to Jeff. "Welcome, Jefferson Bowman. The AR suite is not currently in operation," it informed him. "AR services will be reactivated in thirty minutes. The AR suite will be offline during departure. Departure is in two hours and forty-five minutes. Would you like to reserve a time to enjoy our services later?"

"Um, I don't have any money."

"Begging your pardon Sirsen, but the AR suite is free to passengers. However, you are limited to two hours per day per person. Would you like to reserve a time to enjoy our services later?"

"Sure," Jeff answered immediately. "When is the next available time?"

"The next available time is in thirty minutes. Would you like to make a reservation?"

"Yes."

"How many AR pods would you like to reserve?"

"One," Jeff told the computer. Then he saw a communications panel in the wall and had a thought. "Wait, I need to make a call before I answer that." He activated the communications panel and said, "Danae Highborne." After a short pause, Danae's face appeared in the panel. "Hello?" she said.

"Danae, this is Jeff. I've found an AR suite. They've got some pods available in half an hour. Do you guys want to come? It's free."

Before Danae could answer, Jeff heard Dirk's voice call out, "Like I'd go *anywhere* with *you*!"

Danae scowled over her shoulder and answered, "Denise and I want to come."

"Ok, I'll reserve three pods. Ever been to the beach?" Danae shook her head. "I'll pick a good beach program, if that's ok." She nodded. Jeff signed off.

"Computer," he called. "I want to reserve three AR pods for the next available time slot."

The computer replied, "Three pods have been reserved in the name of Jefferson Bowman. Please select a program."

"Do you have any beach programs?"

"An enhanced simulation of Sunset Bay on the island of Hukilau located on planet Maui in the Hawaii system is our most popular beach program. Would you like to try it?"

"Yeah, that sounds good."

"Your time begins at 6:30 p.m. exactly. Please be prompt. If you are more than five minutes late, your reservation will be canceled. Thank you for allowing us to make your stay more pleasant." Jeff left.

There wasn't much more to see. Other than the commons, the entire passenger module was made up of identical corridors lined with what Jeff assumed were identical cabins.

At 6:25 p.m., Jeff returned to cabin 26 to pick up Danae and Denise. Dirk was still sulking behind the door to his bunk. Danae didn't seem inclined to try and get him to come along, so Jeff didn't make the effort either. They left the cabin and went to the AR suite.

"Welcome, Jeff Bowman, Danae Highborne, and Denise Highborne," the computer greeted them as they entered the AR suite. "Artificial reality services are now back online. Your pods are ready for use." Three large cylinders slid out from the rear wall. A clear door on top of each cylinder opened. "Please enter your pods now."

The white AR pods were lined inside with pale blue padding. Jeff climbed into the leftmost pod. Denise still stood near the suite's front door, staring at the pods.

"It's ok," he told her. You just lay down inside. It's like taking a nap, but you get to have a really fun dream." Danae tugged her hand and Denise moved cautiously forward. When Denise was inside her pod, she closed her eyes and seemed to instantly fall asleep. The door to her pod closed. Danae peered at her through the pod's clear plastic door. When she was satisfied that Denise was ok, she got into her own pod.

Jeff was glad he chose the program he did. The tropical, sandy beach they were standing on sloped gently down to a large bay. The waves lapped soothingly on the shore. Jeff was dressed in a plain blue bathing suit. Denise and Danae, who were standing next to him looking around, were dressed in simple pink.

"Hi kids," called a voice from behind them. They turned to see a young woman in a booth on the grass above the beach. "Come on up here if you need any beach equipment, food, or you want to change your bathing suits."

Jeff didn't much like the look of his swimsuit, so he strode toward the booth. Danae and Denise followed, holding hands. "Can I get a different suit?" he asked the woman.

Instantly, a selection of boy's bathing suits appeared on racks behind the woman in the booth. "Sure," she answered cheerfully. "What would you like?"

"That one," he said, pointing to a suit that seemed to have been through an explosion in a paint factory. "The one on the top rack that's mostly neon green."

"There you are," the woman said brightly. "Anything else?"

Jeff was confused. He expected the woman to hand him the suit. But a little gasp from behind him made him look around. Looking over his shoulder, Jeff saw that Danae and Denise were staring at him. He looked down at himself to discover that he was wearing the new bathing suit. It looked good on him.

"Me too, me too!" Denise chirped, jumping excitedly up and down. Racks of suits for girls appeared on the back wall of the booth. Drawing near to the counter, Denise picked a purple suit. It instantly appeared on her. For the first time, Jeff saw Danae smile as she too approached the booth. "I'll have the red and pink one down there," she indicated. Her smile grew when she found herself wearing the suit she selected.

"What else do you have?" Jeff asked the woman in the booth.

"Almost anything," was the answer. "We've got surfboards, boogie boards, hoversurfing boards, waterskimmer boots, all types of boats, kites, pails with shovels, swim fins, food, fish food, and lots more."

Jeff told her. "I want a surfboard. A short board please." A rack of short surfboards materialized behind the woman. Jeff chose a purple one with yellow lightning painted on it. "Where's the best surfing?" he asked.

"Beginners should stay near the shore. The waves get larger the farther away you get. Our waves today are two feet high near the shore and increasing in size to 12 feet near the mouth of the bay."

Jeff looked at Danae. "Do you two mind if I go way out and surf on my own? I can stick around here if you want me to."

Danae shook her head. "I want to see you surf."

"Well, I'm not that great," he said. "My friends Akio and Harriet are better." Jeff instantly wished he hadn't mentioned Akio and Harriet. He felt a stab of loneliness as he realized that they were a quarter of a million miles away.

Danae could see what he was feeling. "I guess you miss them," she consoled.

"Yup."

Denise, who had let go of Danae's hand and was now standing knee deep in the warm, clear water, broke into the conversation. "Sirsen Jeff, thank you for bringing us."

Throwing off his sadness, Jeff smiled and said, "You're welcome. It's more fun when there's more of us anyway." He grabbed his surfboard and trotted toward the water.

Paddling out near the mouth of the bay, Jeff reached the heavy surf. Casting a glance back at the long beach that wrapped around the long inlet, he could see the tiny figures of Danae and Denise playing in about knee-deep water. Denise noticed him looking and waved at him. He waved back.

Jeff turned toward the large, perfectly-curled waves that came in at regular intervals from the deep blue ocean. He took the next one that came to him. Moving immediately into the cascading tube of the large swell, Jeff did his best to make his surfboard bob and dance in a way that would make Akio proud. Unfortunately, he cut into the wave a little too sharply and was sucked up over its top and slammed downward in a spectacular wipeout. Akio always used to call that "going over the falls."

When Jeff popped back up to the surface, he was coughing out water. He looked toward the shore, hoping that Denise and Danae hadn't seen how lame his surfing was. They were standing together holding hands and staring out toward him. Embarrassed, he waved at them to let them know he was ok. They waved back.

Jeff turned again to the incoming surf and caught wave after wave. After an hour of surfing, Jeff paddled back to the golden shore. He didn't see Danae and Denise anywhere. Walking up to the shady booth above the beach he asked, "Do you know where those two girls that I came with went to?"

The woman pointed toward a long dock down the beach. "They went on the bubble boats," she answered.

'Bubble boats?' Jeff thought as he turned toward the dock and began walking. 'That sounds good.'

Reaching the floating dock, Jeff went out to the end. A young man stood next to a large, clear sphere. "Would you like to ride a bubble boat?" he asked.

"Uh, sure," Jeff told him. "How do they work?"

The man touched the side of the bubble, and an opening appeared. "Just climb in." Jeff got into the bubble and sat on the cushioned seat.

"Press the joystick to move forward," the man instructed, "The more you press it, the faster you go. Turn left or right by moving the joystick left or right. To go higher or lower in the water, move the slider next to the joystick forward or back. That map on the other side of the joystick shows you where the other bubble boats are. And when you get near other people in bubbles, you can talk to them. They'll hear you just fine."

Touching the side of the sphere again, the man shut the sphere's opening. Cautiously, Jeff pressed the joystick forward. The bubble skimmed lightly across the surface of the water. He moved the slider toward himself. The bubble boat slipped gently under the water.

Within moments, Jeff was guiding the bubble boat skillfully among the schools of fish that darted in and out of the reef. A dolphin rocketed by, beeping and chirping as it chased the fish.

Jeff saw on his map that Denise and Danae were near the mouth of the bay in rather deep water. He reached them quickly. When he did, he found the two of them zipping around among huge coral arches. They laughed and giggled as they chased each other and bumped their bubbles together. Jeff hid his bubble in the reef, waiting. He could tell they weren't paying attention to their maps. Waiting until they were right on top of his position, he rocketed upward from his hiding place in the reef and banged his bubble into both of theirs at once. "HA!" he yelled.

Immediately, Jeff regretted surprising them. Both girls screamed with fear. However, as soon as Denise recognized Jeff, a mischievous grin spread across her face. She slammed her joystick forward, careening her bubble into Jeff's. Jeff smiled again and yelled, "You got me! Bet you can't do it again." Away he sped with Denise giggling in hot pursuit. Recovering herself, Danae joined in, scattering a group of sea turtles as she went.

The two girls rapidly became experts at finding Jeff's bubble and banging it with theirs. He enjoyed their laughter as he tried to avoid their crashes. All too soon, they heard a chime sound and a male voice say, "Your time will end in five minutes. Thank you for using MyWorld Corporation Artificial Reality Pods. We hope to see you again soon." They heard the chime again.

"No, no," Denise wailed. "I want to play."

"Don't worry," Jeff told her. "We can come back."

Reaching the dock, they saw the young man again. He helped them out of their boats.

"How do we leave here?" Danae asked the young man.

"All you have to do is want to leave and you will," he explained.

Danae disappeared. Denise followed right after her. Jeff willed himself to be out of the program, and opened his eyes in his AR pod. The pod's door shooshed open and Jeff climbed out. The two girls were already standing next to him.

"That was fun," he said. "Thanks for going with me." Both girls beamed. "I guess we better get back to our cabins," he advised. "The ship leaves Lunar Central Station in 15 minutes."

At their cabin, the three of them found Kent and Porsche there waiting for them. The dividing curtain was pulled back. Dirk was still in his bunk, but the door was open.

Kent smiled as they entered. "I see you three found the AR suite," he grinned. "What program did you run?"

"We went to the beach," Denise squeaked happily. "It was fun." Porsche arched her eyebrows, clearly surprised. Denise saw her expression and immediately became more subdued.

Kent hadn't noticed. "Good," he said, looking at Jeff. "I'm glad the three of you had a good time together. Maybe next time Dirk will go too." Kent smiled in Dirk's direction. Stony-faced, Dirk let his gaze slither away.

Kent continued, "The ship is about to leave the station. We haven't had a chance to discuss this with you until now, but you know the trip will take five months. It takes three weeks to get out of the Solar System and travel to the hypergate we'll be using. Does everyone know what a hypergate is?"

Silence.

"Jeff, I know that you know this. Explain it please."

Jeff wasn't too pleased to be put on the spot, but he said, "Hypergates make wormholes that are like tunnels through hyperspace."

"And why do we need them?"

"Because nothing in the universe goes faster than light. If we just went through normal space, ships would take years and years just to get to the nearest star. Wormholes are shortcuts through hyperspace—a higher dimension of space. We don't go faster than light, but because we take a shortcut, we get there fast anyway."

"That's right," Kent nodded. "Our first hypergate will take us to the New York system. Once there, it will take a week to get to the gate that goes from New York to the Ohio system. From the Ohio system, we'll be crossing into British space and stopping at the planet New Oxford in the Far Oxford system. That'll take about 2 months. From there, we go to the Nebraska system, and then to the Colorado system."

Kent paused. No one spoke.

"During the trip, there are some rules," Kent informed them. "The most important ones are all kids *must* attend school and *no fighting*. If any of us breaks the rules, the entire family will get kicked off the ship at the next stop. And we don't have the money to buy tickets on another ship. That could mean getting stuck for at least several years somewhere. We all have to just get along and do our best here until we arrive. This is *really* important. Understand?"

The four kids nodded wordlessly.

"If you want to watch the ship leave the station," Kent said, "you can see it on your datapads. The ceilings above your bunks are also displays. Just tell them what you want to see and they'll show it. After you watch the launch, I think all of you kids should go to bed. We've all had a long day." He turned to Porsche, "Don't you agree, Honey?"

Porsche smiled sweetly, nodded, and answered, "Yes, Dear." Jeff felt a little sick. Kent and Porsche went back to their own cabin, holding hands. Jeff got downright nauseous.

Danae herded Denise toward their side of the room. She pulled the curtain back across the middle of the cabin.

Jeff heard Denise's small voice ask, "When will we go to the beach with Sirsen Jeff again?"

He answered for her, "Tomorrow. We can go tomorrow."

Danae said gently, "Come on Little Mouse, it's time for bed."

Denise's voice came again, "Goodnight Sirsen Jeff."

"Goodnight," Jeff answered.

Danae also sent over a cautious, "Goodnight Jeff."

"Goodnight," he said again.

Jeff cast a silent glance in Dirk's direction and decided he'd prefer the privacy of his bunk. He flopped down on his bed and hit the button to close the door that separated it from the rest of the room. After a moment, he heard Dirk close the door of his bunk.

Jeff turned on the display above his bed and connected to the ship's external cameras. The launch was pretty unspectacular. The docking clamps were released, the magnetic seals turned off, and then the ship slid silently away from the space station. That was it. Jeff continued to watch for about an hour. He could see the Moon visibly dwindle in size. The Earth looked like a small blue coin in the sky.

A strong wave of sadness washed over Jeff as he watched his home planet drift away behind him. He wondered how Akio was doing on his way to the planet Yokohama. A tide of memories of Harriet pulled Jeff's mind and heart back toward Earth. He wished they would sweep him back to his home in the arcology—back to his little spot in the Universe.

Jeff pulled out his datapad and called up a picture of his mother and himself. It was something he looked at fairly often, but never when his dad was around. The picture was taken in the shopping plaza with the fish in the floor when he was six. As he gazed at the photo, he wondered if his father ever thought of her.

'Just don't look back,' he thought to himself. 'The best way to handle this is to keep looking forward. Someday I'll come back. Someday I'll see Harriet again. And then I'll go see Akio.'

Jeff turned his datapad off, and pulled out the watch that Harriet had given him. To his surprise, Harriet's picture was dressed in pajamas and cleaning her teeth. Jeff smiled. "Good night Harriet," he said. The image looked out at him with a sonic toothscrubber sticking out of her mouth and replied, "Goo nigh Yeff."

A pang of loneliness stabbed into him. He turned off the light, and went to sleep without bothering to change into his pajamas.

19

Thump, thump, thump.

Jeff woke, confused. It took a moment to remember where he was.

Thump, thump, thump. "Jeff, are you awake?" It was his father's voice. "Jeff? It's time to get up."

Jeff touched the button that opened the door to his bunk.

"Morning, Jeff," Kent greeted him. "It's 7:00 a.m. and you need to start getting ready for school. The other kids are already up and have eaten. It's your turn in the shower."

"Mff," was Jeff's only reply. Blearily, he unlocked his trunk and got his clothes for the day.

Jeff was sure he'd only slept minutes instead of hours. He nodded to his father and dug into his trunk for a change of clothes. Then he wobbled toward the bathroom. Just before he entered, he inserted his dirty clothes into a drawer in the wall next to the bathroom door. When he was done with his shower, he opened the drawer again to retrieve his clothes, which were now clean and pressed. He put them into his trunk and locked it.

Jeff saw a small table that was folded down from one wall. A bowl of synthpaste was sitting on it.

"That bowl is yours, Jeff."

"Huh?" Looking around, Jeff saw Danae observing him.

"That one's yours," she repeated tentatively.

"Uh, thanks," he mumbled, wishing he could get his brain working. He sat down in a hoverchair and ate the synthpaste.

"Kent said that our class list has already been sent to our datapads," Danae told him.

After eating, Jeff felt a bit better. He retrieved his datapad from his bunk and turned it on. Sitting on the edge of his bed, he examined the class list.

'Astronomy,' he thought. 'I guess it makes sense, since we're on a spaceship. But why did it have to be first thing in the morning?'

After Astronomy was Robotics, taught by his dad. Robotics was followed by math, English, and then lunch. In the afternoon, he had a study period, History ('ugh!' he thought), and finally

Japanese ('Nice. Thanks Dad.'). All in all, it seemed like a pretty good schedule.

Jeff glanced up to find Denise standing in front of him, just staring. He made a silly face, and her giggle lit up her features.

"We're going to school, Sirsen Jeff. Do you like school?"

"It's ok," he answered. "It's something to do while we're on the ship."

"Danae said we're going back to the beach today," Denise said.

Jeff looked at Danae, eyebrows arched. She nodded and told him, "I called the AR suite and reserved time for all three of us for right after school. Do you still want to go?"

"Sure," he said. He looked around. "Where's Dirk?"

Danae stiffened and her face went blank. "He got up at 6:00 and went to the AR suite. Mother just went to get him. Classes start in just a few minutes."

"Shall we go?" Jeff asked.

Smiling, Danae nodded. She retrieved her datapad from her bed and told one of the chairs, "Follow me." Denise grabbed her datapad, ran for the door, and shouted, "Let's goooo!"

'I wish I could get that excited about school,' Jeff thought.

Before Denise could get very far, Danae told another chair, "Follow her." It zipped away after her.

Jeff went with Denise and Danae to Denise's first class, his chair following after him. After getting her settled, he and Danae each went to their classes.

The morning passed uneventfully. At noon, Jeff returned to cabin 26 for lunch. Dirk was already there, pigging out on a bowl of pizza-flavored synthpaste. Jeff took the tube from the table, filled his own bowl, and ate. He finished just as Denise and Danae returned.

"This blows so bad," Dirk complained when the girls entered. "I can't believe we're going to school for the whole trip. I've already got tons of homework. These people act like it's real school." He rose, grabbed his datapad from the table, and stomped toward his bunk. "It's not *real* school. I hate studying." Climbing into his bed, he turned on his datapad and shut the bunk's door.

Danae prepared meals for herself and Denise. Jeff stretched out on his bed to do some homework. "How were your classes?" Jeff asked the girls.

Denise yelled, "Fun! Fun! Fun! My teachers are nice. Everyone's nice. They talk to me and I have a friend. Her name is Bethany. She's my second friend."

"Second friend? What do you mean? Who's your first friend?"

"You are, Sirsen Jeff. You're my very first friend."

"Didn't you have friends back on Earth?"

Surprised, Denise answered, "No one talks to Thirds."

Unbelieving, Jeff asked Danae, "You mean I'm the very first friend she's ever had in her entire life?"

She nodded wordlessly. "Not even her teachers talked to her that much," Danae said quietly. "Only when they had to. It was always just the two of us."

"Then why does she like school so much?"

"She likes the programs you get to use in school."

"Just the programs? Not the people?" he asked.

Danae nodded somberly and replied, "Just the programs."

"But now I have lots of friends," Denise interrupted. "Sirsen Jeff is my friend and Bethany is my friend."

Gently, he agreed, "Yeah, that's right. You and me are friends." Denise seemed about to explode with happiness. Jeff flashed a grin at her and then started his math homework.

When the lunch period was over, Denise and Danae left for their next classes. Moments later, Dirk grumpily thumped his way off to class. Jeff enjoyed the quiet of his study period. He got his math done, and most of his English.

After his study period, Jeff got himself off to History and Japanese. Jeff's Japanese class was taught by a young couple, the Suzukis. They were just married and on the way to the colonies to start their life together. But they made Jeff miss Akio and his family. Even though class was fun, he left feeling depressed.

Dropping off his datapad in his cabin, Jeff walked to the AR suite. Denise and Danae were there waiting for him. As soon as they were back on the beach, Denise ran to the water and started splashing. Danae followed after her. The three of them played together for about an hour.

As it turned out, neither of the girls knew how to swim. So for the second hour, Jeff gave them swimming lessons.

"You don't have to do this," Danae objected. "The lady in the booth says that the program has a swimming teacher. You can go surf if you want to. We don't mind."

"That's ok," Jeff said. "This is fun too."

When the second hour was done, the three of them returned to cabin 26.

"We have to go next door," Dirk told them as soon as they entered. "They want to have dinner together. Bring chairs. I don't know *what* the big deal is. We've never had dinner together before."

"My dad and I *always* have dinner together," Jeff stated. Dirk scowled, commanded his chair to follow him, and left. Jeff, Denise and Danae rounded up their chairs and went to the other cabin.

The meal together was tense at first. They didn't quite fit around the small fold-out table, so Jeff sat behind the others.

"How was the first day of school?" Kent asked.

Silence. Then Denise whispered loudly to Danae, "Are we supposed to talk?"

Kent, in an exaggerated whisper answered, "Yes." Remembering himself doing the same thing on the shuttle to Lunar Central Station, Jeff thought, 'Whoa. I never realized I was so much like Dad.'

Kent's exchange with Denise had a thawing effect on everyone in the room. Soon conversation flowed easily. Denise chattered nearly endlessly about her new friend Bethany. Jeff and Danae both described the events of the day. Still sulking, Dirk made no effort to talk.

At school, Bethany had invited Denise to her cabin after dinner. So when the meal was finished, Danae took Denise for the visit. Jeff went back to his bunk to do his homework. Dirk stayed behind in cabin 25.

A short time later, Kent came into cabin 26. Porsche and Dirk followed him in. When Jeff saw the look on his dad's face, he asked, "Something wrong, Dad?"

"Well, son," Kent answered slowly, "I hope not. You see Dirk says he noticed when he came back from school that the door to the food closet was open. When he looked in he found that one of the boxes was mostly empty."

Concerned, Jeff questioned, "You think someone came in here and stole our food?"

Kent shook his head, "The door won't let anyone into the closet but us without our permission, so no one could break in and steal something. Dirk mentioned that your study period is after lunch."

"So?"

"Well, it's just that you were in here alone."

"Are you saying you think *I* took the food? How do you know *Dirk* didn't take it? He was here alone after school while we were in the AR suite."

Kent shrugged. "Well, that's true, but Dirk said ..."

"DIRK said! You believe him more than me? I DIDN'T TAKE ANY FOOD!"

Kent's voice was almost a quiet growl. "Jeff, don't scream at me. I'm not accusing you of anything. I'm just trying to find out what happened here. I want you and Dirk to both open your trunks."

"Fine," Jeff shot back. "Fine with me." Without hesitation, he marched to his bunk, reached across it, and jerked his trunk open. Inside were several tubes of synthpaste. He froze, unable to believe what he saw. Pointing to the synthpaste, he turned to his father, "Dad ... I don't know how that stuff got in there. I didn't put it there."

Sympathetically, Kent asked, "Was your trunk always locked? Was there ever a time when you left it open when you were out of the room?"

"I ... I don't know," Jeff stammered. "I thought it was locked."

Standing behind Kent and Porsche, Dirk smirked at Jeff. Jeff pointed to Dirk, "He did it. He put it there to get me in trouble."

"How could he unlock your trunk, Jeff?"

"I don't know, but he's done stuff like that before. Remember he was kicked out of school for that BlackHat attack. He may have some sort of lock-picking device he bought."

Kent turned and glanced toward Porsche. "I think the most likely explanation is the one we should go with," she advised Kent.

"What possible reason could I have to steal food?" Jeff demanded. "There's absolutely no reason for it!"

"What reason would Dirk have to put food in your trunk?" Porsche demanded back at him.

"Because he's still mad at me for getting him caught in the BlackHat attack and for telling the police about his locker in the water park. That's what got him kicked off Earth."

"Absolute nonsense!" Porsche asserted indignantly. "You took the food and you're trying to blame Dirk just like you always have. Dirk never did *any* of those things. It was you."

"Oh, *sure*," Jeff retorted. "*I* beat up my own friend and *I* put the BlackHat program on Dirk's datapad and *I* put the sock and rocks in a water park locker and *I* put the key in Dirk's pocket. SURE! THAT SOUNDS REASONABLE TO ME!"

Kent intervened. "STOP SCREAMING! Just stop screaming. We'll get this worked out."

Porsche put her hand on Kent's shoulder. "Maybe," she began, "maybe it isn't such a good idea for Jeff to come to Boulder with us. I was looking at information about the Albany Transfer Station in the New York system. There's a good apprenticeship program for spaceship engineers there. It's four years. Maybe Jeff could enter that and join us when he's done. It seems to be a very reputable program."

Kent looked from her to Jeff. Porsche glanced at Dirk, who was now standing next to her. Just for the briefest moment, Jeff saw a tiny smile cross her face. Dirk saw it too. His smirk got *much* bigger. Jeff realized they were in this together.

Horrified, Jeff asked his dad, "You'd really do that? You'd dump me off at the first station we dock at?"

"Well, Jeff ..."

"You WOULD, wouldn't you? You're going to throw me away like a piece of garbage!"

"Jeff, don't be so dramatic. No one's throwing you away. It's just that ..."

"HOW COULD YOU DO THIS? How could you just go off and leave me like this? Why didn't you just leave me in the arcology where I was happy?"

"Jeff, calm down."

"Calm down? Calm down? You're gonna leave me somewhere in space where I don't know one single person and you want me to *calm down*? I can't believe you'd do this! But I guess you got yourself a new wife and a new family so you don't need me anymore."

"That's not true."

"Yes it is. You've forgotten all about my mother, and now you want to dump me in space and forget about me too."

"Jeff, I'm just trying to do what's best for you."

"If that were true we'd still be on Earth. If that were true you wouldn't have married *her*!"

"That's ENOUGH!" Kent exploded. "I won't listen to any more of this!" He heaved a long, slow breath, trying to calm himself down. Then he said, "Jeff, I'm really disappointed. Just when it seemed like you were settling in and we were starting to be a family, this happens. It's made me realize that I might have been wrong to bring you along. I think if this apprenticeship program turns out to be good, maybe we should think about putting you into it."

A cold stab went through Jeff's insides. He stood, fists clenched, glaring at his father. Dirk was smiling broadly. Jeff had never seen him this happy. Porsche's smile was barely suppressed.

Feeling like he was being smothered, Jeff turned and ran out the cabin door. Behind him, he heard Kent yell, "Come back here! There's nowhere to run to. Just come back."

Jeff didn't care. He dashed away until he got to the front of the passenger module. There he found a door labeled "Restricted Area: Authorized Crewmembers Only." Jeff slammed his palm on the scanner panel that opened the door. The panel flashed red. The door was locked.

Glancing around anxiously, Jeff whipped his Swiss ultra knife out of his pocket. Folding out a magnetic decoupler, he feverishly attempted to pull off the plating around the panel. No luck. He tried it with a circuit drill. Still no good. With a mounting fear of being caught, he tried a morphic magnoclamp. This time, he got the panel off and hastily examined the circuitry in the doorframe. Quickly finding what he was looking for, he did his best to steady his shaking hands as he unfolded a knife blade and shorted two connections. The door slid open and he plunged through.

Jeff was now in the ship's main section. It was the long cylinder that ran nearly the entire length of the vessel. But if he stood long in the corridor, a crewmember would come along and find him. He needed to get out of sight fast.

A short way down the corridor, Jeff saw a hatch for a maintenance tunnel. He sprinted wildly to it, tore it open, and crawled inside. The narrow vertical tunnel had a ladder inside. He paused momentarily and wondered, 'Which is best? Up or down?'

Far down the corridor, Jeff thought he heard footsteps. He scrambled inside the tunnel and jerked the hatch shut. He looked down, then up. "I'll go up," he mumbled.

Climbing as rapidly as he could, Jeff found another maintenance tunnel that ran horizontally and crawled into it. He followed it for what seemed like hundreds of yards. In the dim light of the tunnel, he could see a wide spot up ahead. Desperately, he scooted himself along until he got there.

This section of the tunnel opened out to a maze of pipes that snaked among support beams. Jeff grabbed onto one of the beams then heaved himself up into the network of pipes. As he ascended, he spied a recess behind a large pipe that was just big enough for him to slide into and lie down. Jeff collapsed into the recess, panting.

Jeff lay in the nearly dark nook for a long time, just glad to be hidden away. At last he said, "I've got to get off this ship. I've got to find a way home." But he knew he couldn't go back to the arcology. 'There's nothing to go back to,' he thought. 'There's no one there that could take me in.' But he still wanted to go back. Harriet was there. "I've got to find a way off this ship," he said again.

Thrashing in his mind over what to do, Jeff felt like a small animal caught in a giant trap. Outside was nothing but an empty vacuum. There was nowhere to go and no way to get there. But if he stayed on the ship, he'd be dumped by his father at a space station that was impossibly far away from everyone and everything he knew. After a long, long time, he thought, 'This is hopeless. There's nothing I can do.'

Tears welled in Jeff's eyes and streamed down the sides of his head. He turned himself over and lay in a heap on his stomach. He couldn't stop the tears, but he stifled the sobs that wanted to escape from inside him.

Time passed. Eventually the tears stopped flowing. Jeff felt like his insides had been squeezed out. He lay in the near darkness completely without hope. 'I'm so tired,' he thought. 'Tired right down to the bone. I can't fight them. He's just going to dump me. I'll be stuck on some space station the rest of my life. I'll never see Harriet or Akio again. I wish I was dead.'

Exhausted, Jeff drifted into a deep sleep.

20

Jeff awoke. It was very cold. He didn't know how much time had passed. Feeling empty, he had no desire to move. But it kept getting colder and colder. He didn't understand it. The cold soon got so biting that he knew he couldn't stay where he was. Moving like a puppet made of lead, he dragged himself from the recess he was hiding in and lifted himself onto the pipe that ran in front of it.

Jeff's breath formed puffy little clouds in front of his face. Being from the temperature-controlled world of the arcology, he'd never seen anything like it. His ears and nose started to hurt with the cold. 'I need to get out of here,' he thought.

Climbing back down to the access tunnel, Jeff looked back and forth along its length. "Which way now?" he asked himself. As if in answer, a door over the tunnel in the direction of the passenger module slid closed. "Ok," Jeff said, "I guess it's forward, not back." He crawled toward the front of the ship.

As Jeff crept through each section of the tunnel, a door slid closed behind him. By the time the third one had shut itself behind him, Jeff thought, 'This is just plain creepy.' He thought of the horror shows he and Akio had watched together over the years. There always seemed to be someone in them crawling through a tunnel like this in some ship somewhere deep in space. At the end of the tunnel, there was usually an alien monster with *lots* of teeth and a big appetite.

Jeff cringed. 'That's silly,' he thought. 'Don't get yourself worked up over nothing.' Another door slid closed behind him.

The tunnel ended at a junction. The junction was a large round room where several tunnels came together. Ladders were attached to the walls to provide access to the various passageways. Jeff paused at the junction, looking at all the other tunnels.

"Hmm," he mumbled. "Which way now?"

The doors on the lowest tunnels all closed. 'Oh man,' he thought. 'That's not good.' The doors on all of the tunnels at his level, except the tunnel he was sitting in, closed. Panicked, Jeff leapt onto the nearest ladder. The door on the tunnel he just climbed out of slid closed.

Jeff scurried up the ladder as fast as he could. The doors on all of the passages except one closed. Jeff retrieved his Swiss ultra knife from his pocket. He folded out a flashlight and shined it down the only remaining tunnel. It was long and dark.

Suddenly, a sprinkler above Jeff shot water in every direction. Jeff clamored into the tunnel to get out of the shower. As soon as he was inside, the door closed behind him.

His fear was so strong he could taste it now. Slowly, he edged through the narrow tube, shining his light as he went. He shivered violently. The cold was beginning to numb his hands and face. Being wet only made it worse. His knees hurt from all the crawling.

Feeling desperate, Jeff came to another junction. All of the doors to the other tubes were closed. In the side of the junction, near the bottom, was a hatch. It looked just like the one he had first used to enter the maintenance tunnels. 'Probably leads back out into the main corridor,' he thought. 'But I don't want to go there.' Jeff sat in the entrance, not daring to go into the junction.

A loud hissing sound blasted from behind Jeff, making him jump. His heart racing, he turned around and shined his light back down the tunnel. Far behind him, a white gas was shooting into the tube from some nozzles in the walls. The gas stopped. Another blast of the gas shot into the tunnel, this time it was closer. It turned off. A third blast exploded right behind him. Jeff scrambled out onto the nearest ladder. The door closed behind him.

From the top of the junction, water began to fall. Jeff dropped down the ladder as fast as he dared. He grabbed the handle of the hatch and yanked it open. In a flash, Jeff was out into the corridor. He collapsed on the floor, shivering and panting.

Feet. There were feet in front of him. Jeff looked up. A man in his twenties grinned down at Jeff.

"You like our fire control systems?" the man asked. He chuckled. Then he laughed a large, full laugh.

"You ... you did that on purpose," Jeff gasped.

The man's smile got broader. "You better believe it. I don't climb through those tunnels. I send a bot if I need anything done in there." He laughed again.

Jeff sat up and ran his numb hands over his face. Then he laughed too, relieved. "You know," he chuckled, "I kept thinking of all those horror movies you see about guys on ships. You know, with the aliens with all the teeth."

The man hooted and cackled so hard he doubled over. "I bet you was expecting me to eat your face," he guffawed.

"Something like that."

Extending a friendly hand, the man said, "Come on. Chief Connors wants to see you."

Jeff took the man's hand and let him help him to his feet. "Who?"

"Chief Connors. He's the Chief of Engineering on this ship. And my name is José, José Martinez." He shook Jeff's hand. "Come on," José instructed. "The Chief's waiting."

Realization swept over Jeff. He remembered Sirsen Anderwell's warning about passengers who violated the rules. 'They're going to kick me off the ship,' he thought. 'They're going to kick us all off.'

José noticed Jeff's sudden reluctance. "Don't worry," he told Jeff. "The Chief isn't that bad. In fact, he's a nice guy. I'll bet he hasn't eaten anyone in almost a month." José whooped at his own joke. Jeff didn't think it was funny.

The two of them walked a long time through the sterile, tube-like, corridor. They moved continuously toward the rear of the ship. Every now and then, crewmembers passed them. They each eyed Jeff curiously as he dripped and shivered behind José.

They eventually reached main engineering. To Jeff, it was a technological wonderland. He was so fascinated with everything that he almost forgot how much trouble he was in. José took him to a door labeled, "Darius Connors." Under that were the words, "Chief of Engineering." Jeff stood before the door, eyeing it warily. José knocked and the door slid open.

"Martinez," said a full, quiet voice from inside. "It's about time. I see you've been testing the fire control system. Go get him a blanket before he gets hypothermia."

Chief Connors rose from behind his desk. He was a tall, muscular man of African descent. Jeff was instantly awed by him. He had a look of comfortable authority and was clearly used to being in charge. Jeff knew he was in the presence of a man who was not to be trifled with.

Jeff noticed that Chief Connors had a band around his forehead like the one Sirsen Anderwell wore. Indicating a chair in front of the desk, Chief Connors invited, "Sit down, Jeff. I'm glad you're finally here."

Jeff sat. "You ... you know my name?"

Resuming his seat, Chief Connors replied, "Oh, yes. I had a good, long talk with your father and mother."

A sudden hardness inside Jeff made him say very quietly, "She's not my mother."

Surprisingly, the Chief was not mad. "No," he replied. "No I don't guess she's any kind of a mother to you at all."

Jeff shot a startled look at Chief Connors.

Chief Connors asked, "Do you know that your father and I were in the Academy together? Your uncle was there, too. The three of us got into a lot of trouble together in the wild days of our youth." The Chief smiled. He seemed momentarily lost in old memories. "There weren't many engineers like your father. I've never seen anyone rise as fast to Senior Engineer as he did."

The Chief's attention returned to Jeff. "You know," he explained, "If anyone else's son had crawled into a maintenance tunnel, the entire family would have been put off the ship as soon as possible." He saw the fearful expression on Jeff's face and chuckled. "You don't need to worry. I'm actually quite impressed by you. I never would have believed any 14-year-old boy could get that door open with nothing but a Swiss ultra knife. I'm amazed that you could read the circuits well enough to figure out which connections to short out to bypass the lock. No other passenger has ever made it into that corridor. Mind you, nearly every trip we get some kid who tries. One thing, though; you didn't bypass the door's sensors. They notified us immediately when you got it open."

A knock sounded at the door. The Chief called, "Come in." José entered, handed Jeff a blanket, and left. Jeff wrapped the blanket around himself like a protective shield. The blanket emitted a toasty warmth on its own. He felt immediately better.

The Chief smiled and continued, "When I found out whose son you were, I went to see your father right away. I knew your mother, too—your real mother. It's been years since I'd seen them. Many years. In fact, the last time I saw your parents, they had a brand new baby boy. So, you see we have, in fact, met before. But I think you were too busy drinking your bottle to notice me."

Jeff reddened. Chief Connors' laugh was rich and deep. "Well here you are after all these years. You've turned into an exceptionally talented future engineer. And that's why I wanted to talk with you this morning."

"Morning?" Jeff asked.

Nodding, the Chief told him, "Yes, you were in the maintenance tunnels all night. It's just after 9 a.m. now."

Jeff was silent. Chief Connors said, "Jeff, I had a long talk with your father about you. I understand why you don't get along with his new wife." To Jeff's questioning look, the Chief answered, "Yes, yes I do. I meet a lot of people in my many travels. I've been all

121

over human space and I've met others just like her. I can spot her kind a million miles away." He paused, and in a low voice told Jeff, "In fact, my father was very much like her. It's probably one of the reasons I never had a family of my own."

For just a moment, Jeff saw a look of deep sadness and regret pass across the Chief's face. It was gone quickly. Chief Connors continued, "I was very dismayed to find out that Kent was not going to keep you with him. The apprenticeship program he wanted to put you in would not have taken you far in life. It was very disappointing indeed that he was considering enrolling you."

Jeff shrugged, "It doesn't matter. He has his new family. He doesn't need me anymore."

Chief Connors' deep voice resonated gently, "That's not true. He needs you very much. In fact, he needs you more than either of you realize. But we can't let him stick you in a second-rate apprenticeship program just because his pretty, young wife wants to get rid of you. Instead, I want to ask you if you'll consider an apprenticeship right here on the Ellsworth."

Caught by surprise, Jeff could only stammer, "What? On this ship? But, what would my dad say?"

The Chief smiled, "Well, he isn't sure about it himself. But by the time I finished talking with him, he felt rather ashamed of the way he treated you."

Fiercely, Jeff shot back, "I don't believe that."

Nodding gravely, Chief Connors agreed, "I can see why you say that. But, you see, what you don't know is that one of my engineers was doing some maintenance in the passenger module yesterday."

Jeff's eyebrows shot up questioningly.

"Oh, yes," the Chief said, "It's true. And she was approached by your father's new wife. Porsche is her name, isn't it?" Jeff nodded. "Well Porsche said that her son was having problems with the lock on his trunk and would my engineer please take a look at it and see if she could open it for him, that's what she asked."

After a pause, the Chief asked, "Do you know which trunk it was?"

"I think I might," Jeff answered. "Was it the one next to the bottom bunk?"

"Yes. Yes it was. The only person in the room was Porsche's son. He gushed his thanks at my engineer until she almost became sick. She didn't like that boy much at all. The way he kept looking at her. She's a rather attractive young woman, you see."

"What did my dad say when you told him that?"

"He expressed his regrets at his treatment of you. He demanded an explanation of his wife. She informed him that she only told my engineer what her son had told her and that it was all her son's fault. She chastised her son most severely. He looked very humble and repentant. It was all a nice performance that your father, unfortunately, believed."

"Why doesn't that surprise me?"

"Yes, well in any case, your father is quite anxious to make amends with you. He's no longer sure he wants to send you away. I, on the other hand, would be very happy for you to join our crew. I've already cleared it with Captain Vorless."

"Listen," Chief Connors continued, "You don't have to make any decisions today. Let me propose something. When we arrived at Earth a week ago, three of my engineers left to purchase their own ship so I'm very short-handed. Let me offer you a temporary job as an engineer-in-training until we arrive at the Colorado system. Then, you can decide if you want to stay on and do a full-fledged apprenticeship. What do you say? You've already met your roommate, José. Although his sense of humor leaves a little to be desired, he's really quite a nice fellow."

"What does my dad say about it?"

"He's willing to let you live and work with us until we get to the planet Boulder. After that, he can't say. I get the impression he is now feeling like he can make you part of his new family." Chief Connors looked questioningly at Jeff.

"I kinda don't see that happening. *She* wants to get rid of me."

"Well, don't worry about it now. You have five months to think it over. You can make your decision when we reach Boulder. So I take it you'll accept the temporary job?"

Squaring his shoulders, Jeff answered, "Yeah. Yes, Sirsen. I think I will. I think it's best. Best for me and probably best for them."

"That's a very mature and insightful thing to say for a young man of your age, Jeff. I congratulate you on your new appointment. I'll have your things brought to your new quarters."

At that moment, José knocked at the door. "You wanted to see me, Chief?" he asked when it slid open.

'I wonder how he knew that?' Jeff thought.

The Chief told José, "Yes. Young Sirsen Bowman is joining our engineering staff as an engineer-in-training. He will be rooming with you."

"Yes, Sirsen."

"And Sirsen Martinez, get him into a nice dry uniform as quickly as possible."

"Yes, Sirsen. I'll get him a full set of uniforms issued."

Chief Connors said reassuringly to Jeff, "Go with José. Get yourself a sonic shower and settle in."

"Thank you, Sirsen," Jeff said. "Thank you very much." He turned and followed José out of the Chief's office.

"Come on," José said. "You can shower while I get you dry clothes. Then I'll get Wendy to show you around the ship."

Jeff followed José, still dripping, but now with some hope for the future.

21

"Jeff," José said proudly, "I'd like you to meet Wendy Darnelle, my fiancée. It was Wendy that got all the uniforms for you while you were in the shower." José slipped his arm around Wendy's waist.

"Um, thanks," Jeff said awkwardly to the stunning Wendy. "It's nice to meet you." She pulled off the tight cap she was wearing and let her honey-blond hair fall around her face. Jeff decided that her short, pageboy style suited her. With a radiant smile Wendy put out her hand. Jeff shook it self-consciously.

Turning to José, Jeff said, "Thanks, José, for getting my stuff from the passenger module. I didn't expect all that to happen so fast."

Wendy explained, "When the Chief gives an order, he expects it to happen now, if not sooner. That's a good thing to remember since you're working for him now. By the way, you look good in that uniform."

Turning a little red, Jeff thanked Wendy again.

"José has to get back to Engineering, but I have free time right now," Wendy said. "Why don't I show you around the ship?" Jeff smiled and nodded.

José winked and said, "Just don't steal my girlfriend while you're at it."

Jeff got redder.

Putting an arm around Jeff's shoulders, Wendy told José, "He just might. He's really cute." Jeff was now a nice shade of scarlet.

José laughed and left. Wendy apologized, "Sorry if we embarrassed you, Jeff. José is a real joker. I suppose I'm starting to pick up his sense of humor. Anyway, let's go."

Wendy led the way out of the cabin that was to be Jeff's home for the next five months. "All the crew cabins are on this level," Wendy informed Jeff. "The junior crewmembers are all two to a cabin. The senior crewmembers all have flats up front." She pointed up the corridor.

Arriving at a ladder, they climbed to the next floor up. "There are elevators at the front and back of the crew module," Wendy explained, "but most of us use the ladders. They're usually closer and more convenient."

Jeff just nodded mutely.

"Right," Wendy continued, "The cafeteria is toward the bow on this level." She pointed toward the front of the ship. "My dad's the cook. Breakfast is served from 6 a.m. to 9 a.m. Lunch is 12 p.m. to 2 p.m. and dinner is 6 p.m. to 10 p.m. But there's food available at all hours. So if you're working a night shift, Dad has breakfasts, lunches, and dinners in the stasis freezer that you can just heat up in the ultrawave oven."

"The AR suite is toward aft," Wendy said pointing to the rear. "Right here is the workout room and the dispensary. My mom's the ship's doctor. She's also the ship's vet and runs the farm module."

"A farm?" Jeff asked, astonished. "You have a farm? I'd *really* like to see that."

Wendy agreed and guided him toward the farm module. When they arrived, the door slid open to reveal a brightly lit room. As Jeff scanned his surroundings, he could see that the farm module was as long as the passenger module. The entire space was an explosion of green. Jeff had never seen so many growing plants in his life.

Wendy guided Jeff toward a large section of corn. There they found Wendy's mother checking the plants with a hand-held scanner. Jeff saw that, like Chief Connors, Mamsen Darnelle was wearing a crown-like band around her forehead.

Wendy introduced Jeff and then said, "Jeff, this is my mother, Dr. Darnelle." Turning to her mother, she asked, "Mom, do you think Jeff could have a shift or two here on the farm?"

Dr. Darnelle agreed, "Sure. Do you like growing things Jeff?"

"Sure."

"Have you ever done it before?"

"Well ..." Jeff hesitated. Feeling like he could trust the Darnelles, Jeff told them about the farm he and his friends had created in the arcology. As he described the large garden, Jeff saw an admiring smile spread across Wendy's face.

"That's amazing," she praised. "I can't believe that you could hide a big garden in a building with 6 million people. What did you grow?"

Smiling proudly, Jeff told her, "Well, we couldn't grow anything tall, or they might be spotted from below. So pretty much any fruit or vegetable that grows on a short plant or bush. I had potatoes, carrots, and stuff like that. My friend Akio likes hot food, so he grew chili peppers and stuff. People had lots of different kinds of berries. I grew lots of strawberries 'cause Dad likes them." Jeff's smile faded at the thought of his father.

Dr. Darnelle quickly changed the subject. "How did you learn to grow your plants? It's not always easy to raise food."

Jeff shrugged. "Our datapads have mostly old books that we get for free. Some of the really old ones talk about growing stuff."

"I'm impressed, Jeff. Yes, I'd like to have you help on the farm. Would you like to learn to care for the animals?"

"You have *animals*?" Jeff blurted out, disbelieving.

"Yes, of course," Dr. Darnelle responded. "This is a full working farm. Right now we have fifteen cows, some goats, sheep, rabbits, turkeys, chickens, pigs, and even pheasants. Our farm provides all the food for our crew, plus enough extra to sell whenever we get to the Solar System. They pay a lot for real food there."

"You bet! I'd love to learn how to take care of them."

"Alright. I'll talk with Chief Connors at dinner tonight and arrange it."

She was interrupted by a loud growling from Jeff's stomach. Embarrassed, Jeff told them, "Sorry. I haven't eaten today."

Dr. Darnelle reprimanded her daughter, "He hasn't eaten? Why didn't you take him to the cafeteria first? Your father would have been glad to feed him."

"It's ok," Jeff assured her. "I really wanted to see the farm. Could I see some of the animals before I go?"

Wendy and her mother guided Jeff to the animal pens. To Jeff's surprise, Dr. Darnelle cared for every animal by hand. She didn't use any machines to feed or give water to them. She even milked the cows by hand. "Machines don't care for animals as well as people do," she asserted. "Even if an animal becomes food, which is the way nature works in the wild, it still should have a decent life. I don't see my animals as products." Jeff was impressed.

Saying goodbye to Dr. Darnelle, Jeff and Wendy made their way to the cafeteria. Wendy told Jeff, "Everyone in the crew has at least one shift on the farm a month. They're happy to do it so that they don't have to eat that awful synthpaste. I've only had that stuff once. I can't see how anyone can stand it."

As soon as Jeff and Wendy stepped through the cafeteria doors, they made a beeline for the food counter. "Have anything you want," Wendy offered. "Dad's just putting out lunch. Ooo, curry chicken. And it looks like he made ice cream."

Gazing down the smorgasbord of foods, Jeff was confused by their variety. Most were dishes he had never seen before. To his embarrassment, Wendy had to explain to him how to eat some of them. She giggled when she saw him attempt to cut up his meat. In the end, she did it for him. Jeff couldn't believe how good the ice cream was.

"Careful," Wendy warned him. "You have to eat it slowly or you'll get a headache."

Puzzled, Jeff asked, "A headache? Why?"

"I don't know. That's just the way it is when you eat cold things."

Their conversation was interrupted by beeping. Wendy pulled up her sleeve to reveal a databand. As soon as she looked at it, a small 3D image of Chief Connors appeared in the air above her wrist.

"Wendy, please bring our new engineer to cargo bay 7. I've got a job for him."

"Sure, Chief. He's almost finished with lunch. We'll be on our way in a second." The Chief's image disappeared. Jeff finished eating and let Wendy escort him to cargo bay 7. She dropped him off and headed aft to the engineering module.

Chief Connors greeted Jeff, "The uniform looks good on you, Jeff. How was the cafeteria?"

"Great! You said you have a job for me?"

Nodding, the Chief indicated a huge, haphazard pile of robots at one end of the cargo bay. "You may know that most of Earth's junk gets recycled. However, recycling some things costs more than it's worth. That's where we come in. We've been paid to haul away these old robots. Many of them are lifters for moving cargo, but there are some construction bots, and even personal bots in the pile as well. Your task is to see if any of them can be rebuilt into working robots using parts from unsalvageable bots. The tools are there in those containers along the wall."

Raising a cautionary finger, the Chief warned him, "This task has to be done by the time we reach the Albany Transfer Station in the New York system. Most people in the colonies are there because they lost their jobs to robots, so New York is one of the few colonies where people will buy bots. Any robots we're going to sell must be ready when we reach the New York system. Understand?"

Hesitantly, Jeff nodded. "I've never worked on robots this big before."

"The principles are the same, no matter what the size. I suggest you start with some of the smaller bots that you can handle yourself. That way, when you work on the large bots, you can have the smaller bots move the parts around and hold them for you."

Again Jeff nodded.

"One final thing, Jeff. I've found another qualified engineer to help out part time. He isn't available in the mornings, but he'll be here in the afternoons to work with you on these robots." The heavy doors of the cargo bay slid open. "That must be him now."

In walked Kent Bowman.

Jeff went from surprised to angry in almost the same moment. As Kent approached, Chief Connors told them, "I'm putting the most senior engineer in charge of this work crew."

Kent smiled and replied, "Well, I'll do my best ..."

"I'm sorry," the Chief interrupted. "You've misunderstood. The most senior engineer is the one I hired first. Jeff, you're in charge."

Shocked, Kent fell silent.

"You two must work together as effectively as possible to accomplish this task. This trip must be as profitable as possible. Your work will help make that happen." Without another word, Chief Connors turned and strode purposefully through the cargo bay doors.

Jeff looked angrily at Kent. Kent looked awkwardly at Jeff. He cleared his throat and asked, "Where would you like us to start, Sirsen?"

That caught Jeff off guard. Realizing that both Chief Connors and his dad were seriously placing him in charge, Jeff moved to the heap of battered robots. Pointing to a smaller construction robot, Jeff instructed, "That one, that riveter. That looks like it's in good enough shape to try and fix. You ... you start on that one. I'll go around the other side and see what I can find."

Jeff beat a hasty retreat to the other side of the towering mound. Purposefully avoiding his father's gaze, Jeff found a butler robot and heaved it out of the pile. It was missing a leg. Searching the pile, he found another bot that was similar enough to become a leg donor. He could hear his father pulling apart a robot on the opposite side of the pile. Grabbing the tools he needed, Jeff started wordlessly to work.

22

Jeff spent most of his first day as a crewmember working hard trying to not talk to his father. Kent finished the riveter robot, so Jeff had him start on a small load-lifter bot. Not to be outdone, Jeff put in some extra hours that night to finish the butler robot as fast as he could. After that, he had the bot help him. It retrieved parts from the junk pile, got his tools, and whatever else he needed.

Later, Jeff sat in the cafeteria eating his dinner alone. Wendy and José entered with a few of the teenagers who lived on the ship. As soon as Wendy spotted him, she waved briefly at Jeff and headed straight for him. Arriving at his table, she introduced the others. "Jeff, this is Linmei, Carmen, and Mark. Guys, this is Jeff Bowman. He's the new crewmember I told you about."

Linmei, who looked Chinese, extended her hand. As Jeff shook it, she said, "You must be really good if Chief Connors wanted to hire you. How old are you? Sixteen?"

A bit embarrassed, Jeff replied, "No. I'm just fourteen."

Linmei smiled, "So am I," she told him with a pleasing lightness in her voice. "Do you mind if we sit and eat with you?"

"Sure, it's ok with me."

Smiling even more brightly, Linmei said, "Thanks. We'll just go get our dinners and be right back." All of them except Mark went to get their food.

Sitting across from Jeff, Mark explained, "I already ate with my family. Carmen and I just came along because Linmei wanted to meet you but didn't want to come alone."

"Meet me? How come?"

Mark, who looked about sixteen, chuckled. "You're the new guy. You're her age. She's on the hunt."

"What?"

Laughing now, Mark told him, "We don't get many new people on board—except for the passengers, and usually only the adults see them. So when a new guy comes on board, all the girls go crazy for him. The guys did the same thing when Carmen came on board last year. I was the lucky one. She's my girlfriend now." Pausing, Mark smiled again. "So you can consider yourself fresh meat. Enjoy it while it lasts."

Jeff asked, "Isn't that against the Reproductive Allowance laws?"

Mark shrugged. "Kinda, but things are a little more relaxed here on board the ship. Not much, but enough so you could have a girlfriend if you wanted."

Jeff didn't know what to say, but fortunately, he didn't have to say anything. Linmei, who had already retrieved her food, returned to the table and slid gracefully into the seat next to him. Moments later, Carmen, Wendy, and José came to the table as well.

As she began her meal, Linmei peppered Jeff with questions about himself. Appearing fascinated with his answers, she kept Jeff talking throughout the rest of dinner. At the end of the meal, she asked, "Jeff, we were planning on going to the AR suite after dinner to ride horses. Would you like to come too?"

"Well," Jeff hesitated, "I guess, but I don't know how to ride."

"Don't worry," Linmei volunteered immediately, "we'll show you how."

As they stood to go to the AR suite, José said, "Actually, Wendy and I are going to run a sailing program. I just programmed up a new yacht and I want to see how it handles."

Wendy chimed in, "Yes, but you guys go ahead and ride horses. We just got a new simulation of the ancient moors of England. It's really pretty country to ride through."

Linmei chatted her excitement to Jeff as they walked together, while Mark glanced at them with a knowing smile. He seemed to be enjoying Jeff's discomfort.

At the AR suite, each of them got immediately into a pod. They appeared in a flowering heath that stretched to the horizon in all directions. In the far distance, Jeff could see an area of blue lakes and ponds that reflected the fluffy clouds like mirrors. They looked like pieces of the sky lying on the ground.

Their horses stood next to a nearby pond saddled and ready to go. Jeff was a little hesitant to get up on such a large animal, but with encouragement from the others, he gave it a try. When he was seated in the saddle, Linmei said, "Why don't you slide back and I'll get up and show you how to ride."

Jeff was surprised, but he slid back and let her climb up. Carmen and Mark looked at each other with barely suppressed smiles, mounted their horses, and trotted away.

Linmei matter-of-factly grabbed the reins and explained to Jeff how to use them to guide the large mare. She told him, "Now if you'll hold onto my waist, we'll ride together for a while before you try it on your own."

Awkwardly, Jeff reached his arms around Linmei and held her gingerly. Linmei flashed him a dazzling smile, faced forward, and nudged the horse's sides with her heels. The horse ambled lazily forward. Linmei snuggled closer into Jeff's arms.

For about the next fifteen minutes, Linmei demonstrated how to control the horse. Jeff could hardly concentrate on what she was saying. His mind kept returning to how warm and soft she felt in his arms. At last, Linmei brought the horse to a stop next to her own mount and said, "Ok Jeff, I think that's about all there is to it. I'll hop down now and let you try it on your own." Jeff released her and she dismounted.

Sliding forward into the saddle again, Jeff carefully nudged the horse's sides as Linmei had done. The horse plodded forward. With Linmei's encouragement and instructions, they rode together over the rolling hills.

After an hour and a half of riding, Linmei said, "Oh Jeff, I'm sorry but that's all the time I have tonight. I've got some homework to do."

"Homework? Aren't you done with school?"

She shook her head. "No, we go year round. That way we can take pre-Academy courses."

"Pre-Academy courses? You're going into the Space Corps?"

Shaking her head, Linmei replied, "Probably not. But I'll probably want to live on a ship when I graduate college. Most ships require an Academy education for their crews."

"How can that many people get in?"

"Oh, you don't have to go to the real Academy. You take classes in the Virtual Academy. It's an AR program that the Space Corps started selling a few years ago. We can graduate high school, get an Academy education, and go to college right here on the ship. You can too, now that you're a crewmember." Linmei hopped lightly down from her horse. "Well, bye Jeff. Shall we do this again tomorrow?"

"Uh. Sure. I get off at 6."

"My parents want me to eat dinner with my family tomorrow, so I'll see you about 7?"

"Sure."

She smiled a smile that seemed to make Jeff's heart both leap and stand still at the same time. Waving, she disappeared from the program.

After several dazed minutes, Jeff realized that he was now alone in the program. He willed himself out and opened his eyes in the artificial reality pod. José was waiting for him.

"So, how'd it go with Linmei?" José asked.

Jeff wasn't quite sure what he meant by that, so he answered, "I liked the horses. I never rode them before."

José's smile broadened as he commented, "Well, I'm sure you and Linmei will have a lot of chances to run the program again."

Shrugging, Jeff walked with José toward their quarters. As they walked, they passed a small group of girls about Jeff's age. "Hi, José," they all greeted in unison.

"Hi girls," he replied. "Have you met Jeff Bowman? Say hi to him too."

"Hi Jeff," they said, again in unison.

"Hi," Jeff answered shyly as he and José walked on past the group. They walked about three or four more paces when Jeff was startled by an explosion of giggling behind them. Both he and José turned and glanced over their shoulders. "My grandfather used to call that a gaggle of girls," José told Jeff as they watched the girls laugh their way down the corridor.

Glancing at Jeff, José explained, "They're all daughters of crewmembers. That's the rest of the girls that are close in age to you. Except for one. But you'll probably meet her later."

They continued on toward their quarters.

23

As the week passed, Jeff spent his evenings with Linmei, Mark, and Carmen, or else with Wendy and José. His days were spent silently fixing robots on the opposite side of the pile from his father.

The next robot Jeff worked on was a medium-sized ditch-digger. He fixed it before Kent got the load-lifter working. Jeff was surprised that day when Kent stayed late to work on a domestic butler bot. Trying to keep his lead, Jeff worked extra hard on the small welder bot he was fixing. He was extremely pleased when he got it working before Kent completed the butler bot. Jeff got Kent to start work on a robotic backhoe.

Now that he had a welder bot to help him, Jeff decided to attempt to fix a large demolition robot. Rather than do the work himself, Jeff programmed the ship's computer to control the welder and the butler robot he had fixed previously. Together, the two mechanoids continued the work while he was not there. It was the same technique he used when he controlled his monkeybot with his datapad. Jeff was especially pleased to come in the next morning and find all the welding on the demolition bot's chassis complete. Following instructions from the program Jeff wrote on the ship's main computer, the butler robot had already gathered all the parts he needed to fix the demolition bot. Jeff assembled and repaired it before Kent showed up at lunchtime to start work. Jeff now had four working robots to Kent's three. However, Kent caught up before his shift was over.

The undeclared competition continued through the week with few words exchanged between the two of them. On the seventh day, Chief Connors summoned Jeff to his office at the end of Jeff's shift. When Jeff entered, the Chief leaned forward from behind his desk.

"Jeff," Chief Connors began, "I think I need to explain something to you."

"Sirsen?"

"There's something you have to understand. While you're undergoing your training, you're also being evaluated. Do you know what that means?"

"It means you're seeing if you want to keep me on as a crewmember."

"That's right. You're doing far better than expected on your task of repairing robots. But you're not doing well at all in getting along with your fellow crewmember. I have observed that the two of you do not work together and hardly even talk to one another. You were given this job to do *together*. I expect you two to work out your differences and cooperate. If you do not, you will not succeed when you come to some of the more complex robots in the pile. In particular, there is a medical bot in there that I am very keen to have fixed. It can fetch an extremely good price if properly repaired. I want you and your assistant to work on that one next. Understand?"

Mumbling again, Jeff answered, "Yes, Sirsen." The Chief dismissed him from his office. Jeff hesitated.

"Is there something else?" the Chief asked.

"Yes, Sirsen." Tentatively, Jeff asked, "I've heard that this ship has pre-Academy and Academy training programs in the AR suite."

"Yes, Jeff. That's true. Would you like to start taking classes?"

"Yes, Sirsen!"

"I tell you what," Chief Connors offered, "After we sell the robots at the Albany Transfer Station, I'll allocate some time in your day to take classes. Dr. Darnelle has also been after me to schedule shifts for you on the farm. Are you interested?"

"Sure! I mean, yes Sirsen."

"Do a good job on these robots, Jeff. It will open a lot of doors for you in your future if you become a permanent crewmember."

"Yes, Sirsen."

As Jeff started toward the door, Chief Connors said, "Before you go ..." Jeff paused at the door. "I was talking with your father yesterday," the Chief continued, "and he happened to mention that you play guitar. That's rare these days."

The mention of his guitar brought back a flood of unpleasant memories. With a spasm of sadness, Jeff nodded. "I couldn't bring it with me," he informed the Chief. "Dad ... Dad had to sell it for me."

"Did he tell you I play as well?" Chief Connors asked. Jeff shook his head. The Chief stood and instructed, "Come with me." With Jeff trailing along behind, Chief Connors left engineering and made his way to a cargo bay. As they entered, he told Jeff, "The cargo bays on this ship are filled with cargoes that we are paid to haul. However, *this* cargo bay is reserved for cargoes that the individual crewmembers buy and sell. We all get space in it according to our ranks. Mine is over here."

The Chief picked his way through the crowded bay to a stack of containers on a shelf along one wall. He pulled a container from the bottom shelf and paused. "I sold most of my personal cargo on Earth. But on my last trip I promised a dealer in the Colorado System that I'd sell him some of these. They're very hard to get. He's meeting us at the Loveland Shipping Station to pick them up."

Jerking open the container, the Chief extracted an odd-shaped object and pulled off its plastic wrapping.

"A guitar!" Jeff blurted out excitedly.

Chief Connors smiled. "Indeed it is." He handed the guitar to Jeff.

The guitar was the most wonderful thing Jeff had ever seen. It had two necks; the top one was a six-string and the bottom was a twelve-string. The front was a deep burgundy. The sides faded from burgundy to black, and the smooth, curved back of the instrument was jet black.

"Give it a try," the Chief urged. "It is both acoustic and electric. The controls for the built-in amplifier are here on top." He pointed to some knobs and switches near the neck. The controls were similar to Jeff's old guitar. He turned the amp on. Slinging the strap over his neck, Jeff formed a G cord with his left hand and gently strummed the twelve-string with his right. The sound was rich, warm, and full. "It's tuned," he said, surprised.

"Yes, it's self-tuning," the Chief explained.

"What is this guitar made of anyway?"

"That's wood."

"*Real* wood? You're kidding!"

"A small company out in the Beirut System makes these out of the sunwood trees that grow so plentifully there. Every time we get out to the planet Triopli, I buy as many of these as I can transport. It's extremely profitable." He patted Jeff's shoulder. "Enjoy it Jeff."

Jeff was confused, "What? You mean this is for me?" The Chief nodded. "But Chief ... if it's that expensive ..."

"Don't worry Jeff. I make enough money on these so that it's no problem to give one away occasionally. I'm always glad to encourage a fellow guitarist. Now there are three of us on board."

"There's someone else who plays guitar?"

"There is. And the best way to meet her is to go right now into Junction 35E of the maintenance tubes. That's where I always go when I want to play really loud so I don't bother anyone else."

Jeff stroked the top neck of the guitar, still not believing it was real. "Ok," he replied hesitantly, "I'll go there now. Thanks, Chief. I don't really know what to say. Just thanks."

"You're welcome, Jeff. And now, I have to get back to my maintenance reports." The two of them left the cargo bay and the Chief went aft, toward Engineering. Turning in the opposite direction, Jeff walked along the ship's main corridor. He stopped at a comm panel and used it to leave a message for Linmei that he'd be late to the AR suite. Then he strode along the corridor until he reached the entrance to Junction 35E. Pulling open the hatch, Jeff stepped inside.

The junction was like those Jeff had been in before. Seating himself in an entrance to a maintenance tube, Jeff turned on the guitar and played. At first, he picked and strummed gentle tunes on the twelve-string neck. After a while, however, he wanted to see how well the instrument did with louder music. Turning up the volume, Jeff played some early 22nd century rock music on the six-string neck. After several songs, Jeff swung into an old blues tune.

Suddenly, the entrance hatch banged open, making Jeff jump to his feet. In the entrance stood the oddest-looking girl Jeff had ever seen. She was carrying a guitar that was identical to his—except that it was purple. She was thin and tall, about the same height as Jeff. Her purple hair was streaked with pale blue highlights. It was cut short and spiky on the sides and top, but it was nearly waist length in the back. Her clothes were a wild mix of black, neon blue, and electric pink. The girl, who seemed to be about 16 or 17, stared at him with startled purple eyes.

"Who ... who are you?" the girl stammered.

"I'm Jeff. Jeff Bowman. I work for Chief Connors. He gave me this guitar. I guess he gave you one too."

The girl nodded.

"What's your name?"

Recovering from her surprise, the girl answered, "Barbie. I'm Barbie Tomorrowmoon."

Jeff thought, 'Tomorrowmoon? Wow. What kind of a name is that?' But out loud he said, "The Chief said that you and him play guitars together a lot. Do you want to play some songs with me?"

After a moment's hesitation, a mischievous look passed across Barbie's face and she answered, "Ok. Let's see how good you are." She climbed the rest of the way into the junction and sat in the entrance of a maintenance tube. Knowingly, she eyed Jeff and said, "I know who you are now. You're that Arcology Boy that Little Miss Linmei has her hooks into."

"Arcology Boy? I guess so. But 'hooks?' What do you mean by that?"

Barbie just smiled a knowing smile. "Hooks, baby. Or claws, is more like it. Little Miss Linmei is like a cat—very cute, but don't get her mad or you'll find out just how sharp her claws are. She goes after all the new guys—especially the sweet and innocent ones like you."

Jeff was beginning to get irritated. "Sweet and innocent? What do you mean by that?"

"Oh come on. A sheltered Arcology Boy like you doesn't know squat about the Big Bad Universe. You're perfect for her. She can make you into whatever she wants."

Jeff retorted, "No one's making me into anything. I am what I am. Do you want to play guitars or not? Cause if you're just going to badmouth my friend, you can just get out."

Barbie was taken aback at the sharpness of his words. Jeff instantly felt bad about having said them, but this girl was just being plain rude. A wicked smile spread across Barbie's face. "So you're not so sweet and innocent after all. Frosty. I like a guy with some backbone."

"Frosty? What's that supposed to mean?"

"You *are* a total Arcology Boy. If you say something is frosty, that means it's good. It slithers like a snake. Or you can just say it slithers."

Dumbfounded, Jeff asked, "Boy, what planet are you from? I've never heard *anyone* talk like that."

Instantly, a stony expression fell onto Barbie's face. Guardedly, she replied, "Everyone talks like that outside your arcology. And I'm from Hades."

"What?"

"Hades. The planet Hades, in the Brimstone system. Ever heard of it?"

Jeff thought for a moment and asked, "Isn't that where all the seaboricite comes from?"

Disgusted, Barbie answered, "Yeah. That's where it comes from."

"I heard that's a pretty dangerous place. Aren't they having a civil war?"

Looking as if Jeff had just hit her in the face, Barbie cringed. Then she said, "It's not a war and it's sooo not civil. It's hell; that's what Hades means."

The only words Jeff could find were, "Oh. I'm sorry."

Barbie's stared down at her hands, which were folded on top of her guitar. When she didn't say anything, Jeff asked, "How did you get off-planet? They said on the news it's hard right now."

Not looking up, Barbie replied, "Yeah. It's hard. Because the planet sits in the middle of six stars going around each other, only ships with special shielding can go there. Most of them wouldn't make the trip if seaboricite wasn't so valuable or if you could get it anywhere else. But it's all the heat and plasma that hits the planet from those six stars that makes the seaboricite."

"Did your family go there to mine seaboricite?"

Throwing back her head, Barbie let out a resounding, but bitter laugh. "No, Arcology Boy, they were neo-hippies, like all the original settlers. That's why my hair and eyes are the colors they are and I have such a stupid name." With a mocking sneer, she continued in a fake, little-girl voice, "My mother had *beautiful* ideas about having children that were all the colors of the rainbow." Barbie pasted an exaggerated look of happy innocence across her face for a moment. Then the cynical sneer came back. "She and my father had themselves genetically engineered so that we would turn out this way."

Shocked, Jeff asked, "Isn't that against the law?"

"I *told* you, my parents were neo-hippies. The whole group they went with didn't *care* about the 'stupid rules made up by the crypto-fascist establishment.' They did what they wanted. They 'stuck it to the man' and other stupid things like that. The whole group originally went to Hades to make a commune and turn the place into a paradise. Then seaboricite was discovered and they threw it all away to get rich. Now my parents are rival warlords. My mother has personally shot my father three times. He's been a little nicer, he's only stabbed her once."

"I'm sorry," Jeff said again quietly.

Disgusted, Barbie told him, "Don't worry about it. My older sister Stacey knows how to program computers. She got a job on a freighter after one of their computer people got sliced up in a bar fight. She brought me along. Eventually, we ended up here. It's the first home I ever really had." Shaking her head in apparent disbelief, Barbie mumbled, "I don't know why I'm spilling my guts to you, Arcology Boy. I never tell people this."

Softly, Jeff agreed, "I don't know why either, but I think maybe you needed to tell someone. I don't know much about these things, but I know it helped me to have friends to talk with when my mother died on the Moon."

"What moon?"

"*The* Moon. Earth's Moon. Luna. She and my father went there on vacation. She was killed in a moonbuggy accident. No one knows quite what happened. But she died and my dad was in the hospital for a long time. Then he had to give up his career in the Space Corps to come back to the arcology and take care of me."

Raising her eyes now, Barbie stared as if she was looking deep inside him. Then she said, "So. We're sharing our life stories. I guess that makes us friends."

Jeff smiled. "I guess it does." Strumming his guitar, he asked, "Know anything by Marvin Maylor?"

"Marvin the Martian Maniac? Of course."

Jeff immediately began strumming loudly. Smiling, Barbie joined in without hesitation. They spent the next couple of hours banging out the best and loudest music Jeff knew. They played so long that Jeff's fingers started to hurt. He pulled out his pocket watch. Harriet's smiling image on the front said, "Hi, Jeff. It's 9:34 p.m. Hope you're having a good evening." The time flashed itself twice under her face.

"Who's *that*?" Barbie asked, staring at the watch.

"She's my friend. She gave me the watch when I left Earth."

Barbie cast him a sly look.

Jeff changed the subject. "I'm hungry, wanna go get dinner?"

"Yeah," Barbie agreed.

Jeff followed Barbie out of the maintenance junction. Carrying their guitars, they walked to the cafeteria. Dinner was done, but there was still some warm food out for those with late work shifts. Jeff and Barbie helped themselves and sat down to eat. Linmei appeared when they were just finishing up.

Eyeing Barbie warily, Linmei asked, "Jeff, where were you? I waited at the AR suite for you."

Surprised, Jeff queried, "Didn't you get my message? I said I'd be late."

"I ... I didn't think it would be *this* late. I was hoping we could go riding again." Coldly, she continued, "I see you've met Barbie."

"Yeah, Chief Connors gave me a guitar. Barbie has one too. We played some old, old songs."

Linmei nodded. "I heard. The noise echoed through the entire central section of the ship. It always does."

Jeff turned to Barbie, "Always?"

Nodding, Barbie informed him, "The Chief and me play guitars in that junction a lot. The crew generally clears the area when we do." She seemed pleased by that.

Stiffly, Linmei interjected, "Oh. I see. I guess you'll be playing guitars with Barbie in the evenings from now on."

Jeff shrugged, "I dunno. I like riding horses too. I was wondering if we could get Mark and Carmen and some of the others together to ride tomorrow." Turning to Barbie he said, "We could all go together. Do you ride too?"

Stonily, Barbie answered, "I don't know how."

"That's ok, Linmei taught me. She and I can teach you."

At Jeff's words, Linmei looked as if someone had just poured a bucket of Nestorian porcuhog spit into her hair. Seeing her expression, Barbie smiled a wicked smile. "Sure. That would be great," she replied suddenly cheerful.

Linmei glared witheringly at Jeff. If looks could kill, Jeff realized that he would be nothing but smoke at that moment. Retreat seemed the best option. He pulled out his watch. Harriet's image said, "Hi, Jeff. It's 10:30 p.m. exactly." The image waved and smiled.

"I have an early shift tomorrow so ..."

"Who's that?" Linmei interrupted.

Before he could reply, Barbie shot back, "His girlfriend back home. She gave him that."

"Is that true?" demanded Linmei, tight fury mounting in her face.

Suddenly wishing he was anywhere else in the universe, Jeff cautiously answered, "Yes. Her name's Harriet."

Jeff felt as if the room got about 50 degrees colder as Linmei said, "I see. I thought you and I ..." She left her sentence unfinished.

"You and I are friends, Linmei. Just like Barbie and I."

"But that girl Harriet is more than a friend?"

Jeff didn't like her prying. Bristling, he replied stiffly, "Yes, Linmei, she's my girlfriend. We've known each other since we were in kindergarten."

"I see," Linmei said again. Before he could say anything more, she turned on her heels and marched out of the cafeteria. Barbie burst into such a fit of laughing that Jeff thought she would choke.

"It's not funny," he told her.

Still laughing, Barbie disagreed. "It is. It was the best thing I've ever seen in my life. Jeff, you're the first guy that Linmei has wanted that she hasn't gotten. No guy *ever* puts her in her place. I would have paid all the money this ship can carry to see that."

Quietly, Jeff said, "Barbie, she's my friend. I didn't mean to hurt her feelings."

Abruptly, Barbie stopped laughing, fixed him with a wide-eyed stare, and then exploded in hilarity again. "You *are* sweet and innocent, Arcology Boy. *Nobody's* THAT nice."

Sighing, Jeff stood. "I think I'd better go. I have an early shift tomorrow."

"I'm sorry," she said, still laughing. "Look, I really am interested in learning to ride. Do you really want to teach me tomorrow?"

"Yeah, I'll teach you. But somehow I don't think Linmei and the others will be showing up."

"The Arcology Boy catches on at last. See you tomorrow, then." Barbie picked up her guitar and left. Jeff grabbed his guitar from the table and returned to his quarters.

24

Jeff started the videomail recorder on his datapad.

"Hi, Harriet. I got all of your vmails. I'm sorry it took me so long to answer. I didn't mean to make you cry. It's just that a lot has happened here."

Jeff paused, and then described the events that led up to him running away and becoming a temporary member of the crew. "They've offered me a permanent job here on board if I do well in the evaluation period. I don't know what to do. My future could be really good here. The Chief Engineer, Chief Connors, even gave me a guitar. It's really frosty. That means it's good. People talk a lot different outside the arcology."

"All of the senior crewmembers on this ship wear datacrowns. Have you ever heard of them? I never had. We're pretty out of things in our part of the arcology. A datacrown is like a datapad, only it talks directly to your brain. You can send mail, control machines, and get information just by thinking about it. It's totally frosty. If I join the crew permanently and stay long enough to get on the senior staff, I could get one too. The Chief says they're really expensive, but they're worth it because they put all the knowledge you can afford right into your head. No studying."

"Anyway, the Chief says that tomorrow I have to try to work better with my dad. I'm not sure how that's going to happen. It's hard, Harriet. I wish you were here. And Akio. I wish the three of us were together again."

"It's nearly 11:30. I'm going to end this mail. But I'll send another tomorrow. Bye, Harriet. I miss you."

Jeff stopped the recorder and sent the videomail. The ship was already outside the Solar System, but that wouldn't stop Jeff's letter from reaching its destination. The letter would automatically be transmitted from ship to ship and from planet to planet as it wended its way toward Earth. Harriet probably wouldn't receive it for two days.

After glancing again at Harriet's smiling face on his watch, Jeff sighed and went to bed.

25

Linmei wasn't nearly as mad the next day. But she also wasn't nearly as friendly as she had previously been. "I think you're right, Jeff," she told him distantly at lunch. "I think we should be friends. Are you still going riding with the Demongirl?"

"Demongirl? You mean Barbie? Yes Linmei, she's my friend. And she wants to learn to ride. I'm going to teach her what you taught me. Why do you hate her so much?"

"I don't know. She's just so weird."

Jeff told Linmei, "To me, she doesn't seem so weird. She's been through a lot of hard things in her life. So have I. After all she's been through, it's really not very frosty of you to give her all kinds of grief."

"Frosty? Jeff, now you're starting to talk like her! No one uses that kind of slang any more."

"She made it sound like everyone talks that way. What do I know? I'm just a dumb hick Arcology Boy."

"No. No, you're not. You're nice. Alright, I suppose I can lay off Barbie," Linmei said. "If," she added hastily, "she'll start being nice to me."

"Good. I've got to go. My lunch hour is almost over and I've got to get back to fixing robots." Jeff returned his tray so it could be washed, and then left.

Kent arrived just as Jeff got to the cargo bay. Squaring his shoulders, Jeff instructed, "Chief Connors wants us to work together on this medical bot. Its neural processor matrix has burned out. I don't know how we can even start to fix that. Without a brain, the bot's no good."

Almost gingerly, Kent pointed toward a large robot at the back of the pile. "That bot over there is used to do advanced repairs on luxury space liners while they're traveling. It uses almost the same neural processor matrix as the medical bot. But it's no good without the medical bot's programming."

Still a little skittish, Jeff said hesitantly, "The medical bot's memory unit is still good. It's the processor matrix that's dead. The software is probably still there, so I guess that's where we need to start. The only problem I see is that the brain we want to use is too big to fit into the medical bot's head."

Pointing to a small bot near them, Kent said, "We can put it in the body of that bot there. After we pull everything out, we can reshape it and make the body into a backpack. Then we can just weld it on the back of the medical bot."

Jeff liked the idea. "We would have to put some additional stabilizers into the medical bot so it could walk properly."

Kent agreed, "That would work. Medical bots never walk far. They just need to be able to move freely around a medical bay."

For the first time since he ran away, Jeff looked directly into his father's face. "Let's get started."

As the two worked, they didn't talk much. But this silence was different. Jeff felt like a thick fog had been flushed from the room. When Kent came into work the following day, he and Jeff even chatted about Jeff's experiences with the crew. It was a welcome change.

Things changed in other ways too. At dinner, Barbie approached Jeff and demanded, "What did you do to Little Miss Linmei?"

"What are you talking about?"

"Linmei. And the others. They're all nice to me. Kind of. Not really nice. But nicer. What did you do?"

"I just told her you were my friend and that she really doesn't have a reason to dislike you."

Jeff wasn't quite sure what the look on Barbie's face meant. After a pause, she asked, "Why would you do that for me?"

Shrugging, Jeff replied offhandedly, "Dunno. Just seemed like the right thing to say."

"You're weird, Arcology Boy. Nobody does things like that."

Jeff smiled. "I'm ok with being weird," he told her. Standing up he continued, "I'm done eating. Let's go riding." Together, they headed toward the AR suite.

26

"Hi Harriet. I got your vmail. That's too bad about your sister breaking her ankle. I hope she doesn't get in trouble for injuring that spectator. I can't believe she jumped on top of him to hit the ball. But she was always kinda wicked at powertennis. I've never seen anyone hit the ball like she does. It's more like shooting it from a gun."

Jeff wasn't sure how to proceed, but he decided the best thing was just to be honest. "In answer to your question, yes I've made some friends. And yes, some of them are girls. One of them thought we were more than friends, but she saw the watch you gave me and started asking questions. Now things are straightened out. She understands that she and I are just friends."

"It's been nearly four weeks since I left. It seems so much longer. I guess because so much has happened. But things are going a lot better with my dad and me. He apologized for wanting to leave me at the Albany Transfer Station. We're working on a medical bot together. So far, we've got a new processor matrix for it. Dad's not so good at programming, so I uploaded the medical bot's programs to the new brain and got it running. Now we've just got to get the body fixed. We already got the welding done. And we found new eyes for it and built a new leg from parts of other bots. But we're having a hard time replacing its missing arm. The arms on this thing have to be really high precision so it can do surgery on people. Dad says we might have to make it from scratch. That would be hard to do."

"Anyway, I finally got a letter from Akio. He's still on the way out to the hypergate they're taking to the New Tokyo system. He says he's bored so he's teaching his brother some martial arts."

"I got a letter from Akio's mom too. She said Akio misses me and wishes I was there. She says he gets into a lot of trouble when I'm not around. He and Akifumi figured out how to make all the toilets in the passenger module flow backwards. They were just lucky the crew never found out who did it or the whole family would have been kicked off the ship. Akio's mom doesn't let him out of her sight any more."

"We'll get to the hypergate tomorrow. The hypergate to the New York system drops us out about a week away from the Albany

Transfer Station, which is right next to the gate we'll be taking to the Ohio system."

"Chief Connors says that's the way it always is. The exit to the wormhole that the hypergate creates is one light day away from the next hypergate. One light day is the distance that light travels in one day. It takes this ship one week to travel that far. He says that as long as the ship moves from gate to gate, it can cross space pretty quickly. But on this trip, the ship is going to the planet New Oxford for some reason. He won't say why. I think we're going to pick something up, but I'm not sure. I don't know why they would move the ship all that way into the Far Oxford system instead of just having whatever it is shipped out to the hypergate so we could pick it up there. It's going to take a month to get clear in there and another month to get back out. Dad says he doesn't mind. The extra time made the tickets cheaper. Everyone else who wanted to go to the Colorado system was booking themselves onto ships that got there in only three months. So they gave us a big discount to get us to ride the Ellsworth. I don't know. It doesn't make sense to me. But whatever."

"It probably seems strange, but I've actually made pretty good friends with Dirk's younger sisters. The little one, Denise, she's six. She calls me Sirsen Jeff. I don't know why. I don't go into the passenger module because I just don't want to deal with Porsche and Dirk. But the passenger module has an AR suite and so does the main crew module. The AR pods in the two suites can talk to each other, so I meet them in AR programs and we do stuff. I'm teaching them to swim and ride horses. I even teach guitar to Denise. Little kids are fun."

Jeff hesitated, and then said, "I miss you Harriet. Bye."

27

The following day, the entire ship had to undergo a safety check before going through the hypergate. Continuing the work on the medical robot, Jeff tried to keep out of the way as much as possible by leaving the bots only briefly at mealtimes. Kent didn't come to work that day because all of the passengers were confined to the passenger module. The entire crew was working at a fever pitch. Jeff felt a bit like an outsider. 'But things will be different if I join the crew permanently, I guess,' he thought.

At exactly 3 p.m. the Captain announced on the ship's comm system that the hypergate was opening and they were cleared to line up to go through. Jeff hurried back to his quarters, scooped up his datapad, and plunked himself on his bunk. Connecting to the ship's external cameras, Jeff gasped at the size of the hypergate. 'That has to be at least a quarter of a mile across,' he thought to himself.

The gate was a huge cone, with the wide part at the front. The inside was covered with gigantic spheres. "Gravity mirrors," he murmured out loud. The huge mirrors bent and concentrated gravity that was generated by bright coils lining the front edge of the gate. The coils were glowing a pale blue color. But as Jeff watched, they shifted to bluish white, and then to bright white. Small bright spheres that looked like pulsating blue stars formed around the front rim of the gate. As they did, they slowly fell toward the point of the gate at the back. There they collided together and formed a large wobbling ball of liquid-looking light.

Jeff watched intently as the shining blobs formed at the front of the gate faster and faster. Soon, they were falling so quickly to the back of the gate that they were nothing but throbbing streaks of light. The ball at the back grew larger and more stable. As it did, it also got brighter. Suddenly, it appeared to fall away from the front of the gate. Startled, Jeff saw that the ball was now tunnel. It looked as if the tunnel should go right out the back of the gate. However, Jeff knew that if he were to take a shuttle and fly around behind the gate, all he would see would be a large cone. The tunnel was actually a wormhole—a tunnel through hyperspace that would get them to the New York system in less than a day. If this ship tried to cross the distance in normal space, it would take about 120 years to reach its destination.

Connecting to the comm system, Jeff listened to the chatter coming from the gate's control center. A large passenger liner was ordered through the gate first. It approached the wormhole slowly until it got right to the entrance. Abruptly, it appeared to accelerate away so quickly that it became a streak. Then it was gone.

One by one, the ships ahead of the Ellsworth moved through the gate. Each one zipped away as soon as it reached the wormhole. At last, it was their turn. The Ellsworth, like the other ships, slid gracefully into the front of the massive gate. It glided gently to the mouth of the wormhole. In a flash, the ship was completely enveloped by the shining blue tunnel through hyperspace. There was no sense of movement at all. The ship was carried forward like a leaf on the surface of a gently-moving stream.

Jeff continued to watch for a while, but there was no more excitement. The Ellsworth seemed suspended in the glowing wormhole that whizzed by with incredible speed. Other than that, there was nothing to see.

Jeff spent the evening in his quarters puzzling over how to build an arm for the medical bot. He was still at it when Kent showed up after lunch the next day. By then, they were already out of the wormhole and back into normal space outside the New York star system.

"I spent the morning taking an inventory of the parts we could use to build the arm," Jeff told Kent. "There's a few good parts here, but not all that much."

"That's ok," Kent assured him. "I sent a mail to the manufacturer on Ganymede last night. The answer just came a couple of hours ago. This robot is out of date. They were surprised that we're trying to fix it. They even offered me a discount on the new model."

"Anyway, they gave me diagrams for manufacturing the arm. I've checked with the Chief and he says that the tools we need to make it from scratch are all on board. He was pretty surprised we wanted to try it, but he was very positive about us making the effort."

Jeff asked, "When do we start?"

"Right now," Kent answered. "We'll go down to Engineering and get the tools."

Jeff followed his father eagerly. As they walked, he thought, 'If I take a job on this ship, I won't get to do things like this with Dad.'

Within two days, they had the arm fabricated. It worked perfectly. "But," Kent told Jeff as they finished testing the arm, "the hand is going to be much, much harder."

"Why?"

Kent explained, "This robot has to be able to perform microsurgery with tools made for human hands. The movements of the wrist, hand, and fingers can't be jerky *at all*. They have to be very smooth and very tightly controlled. Any slip of a laser scalpel could mean someone's death."

Their first attempt at a hand failed badly. The parts they created were not nearly good enough. As soon as they turned the robot on, it went through an automatic self-check. Red lights flashed all over the control panel on its chest. "Don't worry," Kent consoled. "We'll try again tomorrow." Jeff went back to his quarters depressed.

Three more tries over the next three days also failed. Jeff tried to make himself feel better by sending a long letter to Harriet. It helped, but not much. That night, Jeff lay in bed staring into the darkness. With only two days left, he knew they had to try something different.

Finally, at 2 a.m. he got up, dressed in the dark so he wouldn't wake José, and went back to the cargo bay. Sitting on the pile of remaining robot parts, Jeff stared at the medical bot and fumed. "There are just too many parts in that stupid hand," he said out loud. "There are too many chances for us to screw up. It would be nice if we didn't have to do everything from scratch."

After a long time of frustrated pondering, Jeff heaved a sigh and started toward the door. As he walked, he stumbled over the broken foot of a domestic robot. Turning to face the mangled heap that was all that was left of what once had been a maidbot, Jeff gave its foot a good kick.

"Arg!" he screamed, limping. Jeff pulled off his shoe and squeezed his toes. They didn't seem to be broken. As he put his shoe back on, he noticed the maidbot's hand. It was completely intact. Quickly, he grabbed some tools and pulled the hand off the bot. Examining the hand closely, he found that is was very similar to the medical bot's. He set the hand near the medical robot and went back to bed.

When Kent came in for work, he found Jeff intently working on the hand. "Where did you get that?" he asked.

Jeff pointed. "I pulled it off that maidbot. That bot is made to look kinda female, so the hand is smaller with longer fingers, like the medical bot."

"Yes, son," Kent countered, "but a maidbot's hand doesn't have near the fluidity of motion for a medical robot."

"Yup. But that's ok. I made adjustments to the motors in the hand this morning. And I made the palm slightly bigger. They all pass the robot's self-check. But the maidbot's hand doesn't have as many micromotors as the medical bot's hand. We have to make some more."

Shaking his head doubtfully, Kent told him, "The micromotors are the hardest. So far, only about 1 in 10 of the micromotors we've made have been good enough. There must be 30 or 40 more of them that we'd need to get that hand working properly."

"How much do they cost to make?"

Surprised, Kent responded, "The micromotors? Not much at all. They're very cheap. Why?"

"Let's make a batch of 500. That way we'd be sure to get enough good ones."

"500? Just to get 40 working micromotors? What'll we do with the rest?"

Jeff pointed to the pile of robots. "Throw them on the pile."

Kent thought for a moment and then smiled. "Sure. It could work. But we'll be up most of the night making them so that we can have a working batch for tomorrow morning. If this bot is going to work, it has to be finished by the time we reach the Albany Transfer Station tomorrow night."

Jeff responded enthusiastically, "So let's get started."

Kent and Jeff worked through the rest of the day and into the evening. Mark came looking for Jeff about 7 p.m. that evening. "Hey, Jeff," he asked. "Are you gonna play basketball tonight?"

Shaking his head, Jeff answered, "No. Me and my dad are trying to finish this robot before tomorrow. We've been at it non-stop all day. Thanks anyway." Mark waved as he left.

A short time later, Barbie and Linmei entered the cargo bay carrying trays. Linmei explained, "Mark told us you've been working non-stop on your robot. We thought we'd bring you some dinner."

Embarrassed, Jeff glanced from the girls to his father. Kent smiled broadly. "Thanks, girls," he said. "It's nice to know Jeff has such thoughtful friends."

Barbie quickly handed her tray of food to Jeff. Casting a frown in Barbie's direction, Linmei handed hers to Kent. They both thanked the girls and dug hungrily into their meals. Linmei quickly left with a shy, "Well, bye Jeff." Barbie lingered for a moment.

"It was actually her idea, you know," Barbie told Jeff as soon as the door closed behind Linmei. "She's still after you."

Jeff gave her a sly smile and accused, "But you decided to come along and give her a hard time."

"You know it, Arcology Boy," she laughed. Then mimicking Linmei, Barbie said a mockingly shy, "Well, bye Jeff," and left.

Kent chuckled. "Looks like you've got yourself quite a drama going onboard."

Jeff could feel himself blush, but he smiled anyway. "Maybe a little."

More seriously, Kent asked, "What about it Jeff? Do you want to stay here or go to the Colorado System with the rest of the family?"

Uneasily, Jeff answered, "I don't know."

Silently, they continued eating.

When he was nearly finished with his food, Jeff asked, "Do you think you'd let me stay if I wanted to?"

Kent didn't reply at first. He just carried on eating. After a moment he told Jeff, "You know, after what happened the day we boarded the ship, I understand that what's gone on between you and Dirk is a lot more serious than I thought. And I know that Porsche hasn't helped the situation. She has a real blind spot when it comes to Dirk. But I'm still hoping the two of you can put these things behind you and we can be a family."

Kent paused, chewing thoughtfully. Then he said, "You have to learn to let go of things Jeff. If you hang on to anger and bitterness, it eats you up. When ... when your mother died, I was pretty broken up, just like you. I felt a lot of bitterness at having to face life without her. There was even a time I was angry with her for leaving me behind."

Jeff couldn't believe what he was hearing. Kent saw his expression and said, "You'll find, Jeff, that that's a normal feeling survivors have when their spouse dies. Grieving a spouse's death is a complex process. Feelings like that are one part of the grieving process and are very normal. You get over them. But I was angry. Angry at life. At times, angry with your mother. And mostly angry with myself because the whole trip was my stupid idea. If I'd left well enough alone, she would be here with us right now."

"No, Dad. You can't think that ..."

"It's ok, Jeff. I've had years to work all this out. One thing I learned along the way is that you have to let go of anger and forgive. It's hard to forgive others." Looking away, Kent continued, "It's hardest to forgive yourself."

Jeff didn't know what to say. After a few moments of silence, Kent finally told him, "I understand if you want to stay on board. I can see you're making a good life for yourself here. These are good people who'll take good care of you. Both the Chief and the Doctor have had some serious talks with me about you. You'll get a better education here than I can give you. Lots of opportunities. But you know, you're the only thing I really have left of your mother. I'd really be happy if you'd stay on with your old dad for another few years. Maybe I'm being selfish but ..."

There was another silence as neither Jeff nor Kent looked at each other. At last Kent stood and said, "Well, shall we get back to it?" They laid their trays aside and started to work.

Their efforts continued through the night and into the early hours of the morning. At 3 a.m. they finished all 500 micromotors and began testing to see which ones could be used. By 4:30 a.m. they had all that they needed and threw the rest away.

Kent stood up from the workbench and stretched. "Let's call it a night, kid. We'll finish the rest when I get back."

Yawning, Jeff nodded. He stumbled wearily out of the cargo bay and shuffled to his quarters. Slipping in silently, Jeff eased into bed.

It seemed like only a moment later when the ship's computer began playing music and said, "Good morning Jeff. This is your wakeup call. I hope you had a good rest."

Groggily, Jeff dragged himself out of bed. As usual, José was already gone. Jeff showered and staggered to the cafeteria, still exhausted. Blearily, he ate breakfast and then dragged himself to the cargo bay. Through the morning, Jeff fitted as many of the micromotors as he could into the hand. He left the harder ones for Kent, who had more experience.

After lunch, Kent arrived and looked over Jeff's work. "Well done, son. Take a break for a while. I'll get the rest of them in."

Working until nearly dinner time, Kent mounted the rest of the micromotors. Jeff took a nap on the floor until the hand was finished. Together, they put the hand on the robot. With great anxiety, Jeff threw the switch that powered up the robot.

It seemed like it took an eternity, but finally, the last of the self-checks was finished. "Ha!" Kent shouted. "We did it. This thing is absolutely perfect. It's completely checked out!" He grabbed Jeff in a big bear hug and thumped him on the back.

As they walked lightly toward Engineering to tell Chief Connors of their success, Jeff thought, 'This is one of the best moments of my life.'

Upon hearing their report, Chief Connors was astounded. He shot out of his office and almost ran to the cargo bay with Kent and Jeff trotting along behind. In the cargo bay, the Chief quickly grabbed a hand-held scanner from the workbench and began studying the medical robot intently. After nearly an hour, he set the scanner down and said, "Perfect. This thing is in nearly new condition. I am absolutely amazed. Congratulations to the two of you." With enormous pomp and ceremony, Chief Connors shook hands with each of them in turn.

"We must tell the Captain immediately," the Chief said. He seemed to freeze momentarily. "The Captain would like to see you both right now. Let's go."

Confused, Jeff gazed at his dad. Kent pointed toward the datacrown on the Chief's head. Jeff understood instantly. Chief Connors was able to interface with machines through the crown-shaped computer he wore on his head. The Captain had one also. The Chief had sent a message directly from his brain, through the datacrown, across the ship's network, and to the Captain's datacrown in that moment he stood frozen. 'It's almost like telepathy,' Jeff thought as they walked.

When the door to the ship's main bridge slid open, Jeff felt almost as if he were entering someplace holy. Even his breathing was hushed. Chief Connors guided them toward the Captain's office, which was at the rear of the bridge. The office door opened as they approached.

Captain Vorless looked to Jeff to be about sixty. She was a slender woman with short, white hair. When they entered, she rose. "Please sit down," she instructed, indicating the chairs in front of the large wooden desk. Timidly, Jeff sat in the chair nearest the door.

"Congratulations to both of you," the Captain told them warmly. "I never would have believed you could fix *any* of the robots in that pile, much less the medical bot. It's amazing."

'What?' Jeff thought. 'What does she mean? She didn't think we could fix *any* of them?'

The Captain noticed Jeff's surprise. "I'm sure the Chief told you that those robots were considered too damaged to bother to fix," she said. "Didn't he?"

Jeff shook his head.

Startled, the Captain glanced briefly at Chief Connors. Then with a knowing smile, she looked back at Jeff and said gently, "Jeff, I've never met a 14-year-old that could do anything with a pile of junk like that. But I knew you couldn't hurt anything either. And when the Chief said he'd pay your salary to do the work, I had no objection to him hiring you."

Jeff looked at Chief Connors, stunned. The Chief grinned furtively and winked.

Turning to Kent, Captain Vorless asked, "Did you know that the Chief was paying your salary as well?" Kent shook his head. "Well, I know Chief Connors considers you one of his oldest and dearest friends. And I know I'll embarrass him by telling you both this, but he did a lot to ensure that you two had a chance to reconcile. I see that you've not only done that, but you've succeeded together at a nearly impossible task. Congratulations. The sale of that medical robot will bring in enough money on this trip to offset the losses that we'll incur by going into the Far Oxford system. That's a significant savings to us."

The Captain addressed Chief Connors, "Chief, the ship will now pay the salaries of these two. And you'll be credited with everything you've paid them so far." The Captain and the Chief froze for a few seconds as they gazed at each other.

'They're talking through their datacrowns,' Jeff realized.

"Jeff, Chief Connors tells me that it was you who reprogrammed the medical bot. Have you ever thought of becoming a computer specialist rather than an engineer?"

"N ... no Mamsen," Jeff stammered. "I always wanted to be an engineer, like my dad."

Smiling, the Captain reassured him, "I can see why. Your father is a gifted engineer and fine craftsman to have fabricated so many parts for a surgical-quality robot. And I know you helped too. But getting the other robot's neural processor matrix to accept the medical bot's programming was just as amazing as anything your father did. You're a very gifted programmer. Our crew needs talented programmers right now. We're working on a very special project, and I think Chief Connors should assign you to it as soon as possible." The Chief nodded in agreement.

Addressing Kent, Captain Vorless implored, "When he first approached me, I tentatively agreed to the Chief's request of possibly offering your son a position on this ship. That offer is firm now. If you will consider trusting us to take care of and educate your son, we will do the very best we can for him. He's a gifted young man. You must be very proud."

"I am, Captain," Kent beamed. "Indeed I am."

"Before you leave, I think it proper to offer you a bonus for the great job you two have done. I'll have your accounts credited as soon as we dock at the Albany Transfer Station."

An idea flashed through Jeff's mind. "Um. Mamsen, Captain, Mamsen?" he interjected in a quavering voice.

"Yes?"

"C ... can I have something else instead?" Jeff asked, heart pounding. "I ... I fixed a butlerbot, you see, and I was thinking ..." Jeff's voice trailed away.

Captain Vorless finished his sentence for him, " ... that you'd like the robot as your bonus? Of course, Jeff. The butlerbot is yours. You deserve it."

The door behind them slid open. Jeff understood that it was time to go, so he stood. As he did, he said, "Thank you Mamsen. Thank you for everything."

The three of them exited the Captain's office and the bridge. Kent stopped just outside the bridge door. He placed his hand on Chief Connors. "So Darius," Kent said softly, "you were paying us?"

The Chief smiled, but looked away. "I guess you know how things ended between my father and I," Chief Connors said distantly. Kent nodded. "I couldn't let you and your son end up the same way."

"I can't tell you how grateful I am for what you've done for Jeff and I."

The Chief turned back to Kent and looked at him with mock sourness. "Don't get gushy on me now. You know I hate that."

Kent slapped the Chief on the back and laughed. Together, the three of them walked to the cafeteria for dinner.

28

"Hayayayayayayayayaaaaaah!" Jeff screamed as he jumped from the second story balcony of the inn. Landing lightly in front of a group of grungy, armor-clad bandits, Jeff whipped out his sword and slashed it back and forth through the air threateningly.

The largest bandit, who was obviously the leader, waved his giant war hammer in response. "You will not keep us from pillaging this village, Brice Yee!" growled the bandit. "We will pulverize you and burn this village to the ground."

Instantly, Jeff kicked the nearest bandit and sent him sprawling at the bandit leader. The two of them tumbled to the ground.

"KILL HIM!" commanded the bandit leader as he struggled to his feet.

"Frenzied feet of flaming fury," Jeff called out, "ACTIVATE!"

Using the special abilities the game gave him, Jeff sliced his sword and kicked his feet so fast that he was almost a blur.

"Hayayayayayayayayaaaaaah!" he screamed as he sent bandits flying in every direction.

Hours later, Jeff sprawled on his bunk and grabbed his datapad. He tapped an icon to record a message.

"Hi, Akio. I just had to vmail you after what's happened. My dad and I finished the medical bot and they sold it for a *huge* amount of money at the Albany Transfer Station to some guys from the Buffalo Mining Colony. Even though the New York system is pretty crowded, they have trouble finding doctors who want to live that far out in the Ontario Asteroid Belt. So they were willing to pay a lot of money for the bot."

"I got to see the captain of the Ellsworth and she gave me a butlerbot that I fixed as a bonus. He's an RVX series 5—pretty old. I call him Arvix. Here's a picture." Jeff attached a picture he took of Arvix to the message. "I haven't really used him much yet. Chief Connors, my boss, gave me two days off while we were at the Albany Transfer Station. The first day, Dad and I went around the station together. It's *huge*. Not as big as Lunar Central, but still huge. The second day, I took Denise and Danae around the station. It was pretty fun."

"Anyway, we left the station yesterday and got through the hypergate early this morning. José, my roommate, told me that we took on a lot of cargo at Albany. Mostly tools and stuff for building farms and houses on the outer colony worlds. We're in the Ohio system now, moving toward the hypergate to the Far Oxford system."

"José says we're stopping at the Youngstown Deep Space Port to pick up more cargo. All this stuff goes to the newer colonies like the Colorado and Montana systems. He said we're getting loads of farm animals. They keep them frozen, but they're still alive. 'Cryogenic stasis,' José called it. They're in like a frozen sleep that they can stay in for years and years, but they don't get any older."

"Tomorrow I start work in the programming department in the ship's Central Computing section. Barbie's sister, Stacey, works there. Chief Connors introduced me to my new boss, Sirsen Huntington. I'm going to be working on a kind of secret project they've got going. They call it 'the Living Ship' but I don't know what it's about. It has something to do with the thing we're picking up in the Far Oxford system. They told me Sirsen Huntington's father used to teach there. He started the Living Ship project at Oxford and Sirsen Huntington's been working on it since he graduated from the University."

"My birthday is the day after tomorrow. I used some of my money and bought some sheet music on my datapad. I can already play one of the songs on my guitar."

"I got a letter from Harriet. She says you haven't written her yet and she wants a letter. I told her the story you sent me in your last letter. She didn't think it was funny. She said, 'Little brothers should not be used as basketballs.' I told her the ship's doctor fixed Akifumi up really good, but she still didn't think it was funny."

"Anyway, we'll be at the Youngstown Deep Space Port in a few days. I'll mail you again after we get there. Tell your mom and dad I said hi. And tell your mom I miss her too. Bye."

Jeff turned off the recording as José entered their cabin. "Are you still using that thing?" José asked incredulously.

"What? My datapad? What else am I supposed to use?"

"Almost anything," José joked. "That model of datapad was old tech when my grandfather was a kid. People have been using computers like that since the 21st Century. Seriously."

Going to his chest of drawers that was set into the wall, José yanked open a drawer and fished through its overflowing contents. He pulled out a handful of databands. "Here," he instructed as he threw one at Jeff. "Use one of my old databands. They're not as good as the new ones, but they're a whole lot better than that datapad of yours."

"Wow, José. Thanks. Are you sure you can afford to give me this? These are expensive!"

José shook his head. "Not when you live on a freighter. We can buy almost anything at lower prices than you pay in stores. I buy a new one about every other year. That's why I've got so many. It's no big deal."

"Thanks, José. Thanks a lot."

29

Jeff reported to Sirsen Huntington's office in Central Computing the next morning right after breakfast. "I'm glad to have you on the project, Jeff," Sirsen Huntington greeted him as he showed Jeff to an unoccupied workstation.

"This will be your workstation," Sirsen Huntington explained. "It's a dedicated station we bought specially for working on the Living Ship project. Now I want you to know that the Living Ship is our top-secret project; you have to keep it quiet. Don't talk about this with any passengers and don't send anyone mail about it."

'Uh-oh,' Jeff thought, remembering that he had mentioned the project in his vmail to Akio the night before. 'But I didn't really say what it was. I didn't know,' he told himself silently.

"My father and I started this project when he was teaching at the New Oxford University and I was a graduate student there," Sirsen Huntington explained. "After he retired, I got permission to continue working on it here. We work in conjunction with a few other private groups, some universities, and the New Tokyo Shipyard."

Sirsen Huntington paused, and then asked, "Jeff, do you know what nanobots are?"

Shocked, Jeff replied, "Sure. Everyone knows that. They were used as weapons in the Third World War. Nanobombs tore people apart molecule by molecule. Why?"

"Because that's what you'll be working on."

"For real? I thought they were illegal!"

Nodding, Sirsen Huntington agreed, "They are in the Solar System and in most colonies. However, they're legal at some of the major universities."

"Universities?" Jeff asked. "Is that why we're going to planet New Oxford? Because the New Oxford University is there?"

"Exactly, Jeff. We have a special permit to pick up nanobots for a test in deep space late next year. What we're trying to do is create a ship that grows from a kind of egg-like seed that's about the size of a basketball. It uses nanobots to mimic the way that living things grow and heal themselves. If we succeed, we'll be able to embed a shipseed into an asteroid and just wait. In a few months, it will grow into a fully-operational spaceship about three times the size of this one."

Jeff couldn't believe what he was hearing. "You gotta be kidding me. How can a ship grow from a seed?"

"It uses the same techniques that living things use. Do you know what a whale is?" Sirsen Huntington asked. Jeff nodded. "Think how huge a whale is. And every whale grows from just a single cell. The Living Ship will be the same. It will grow from a seed and be able to heal itself from all but the worst types of damage. This will be a revolution in spaceship design and production."

"And you want *me* to work on this? But nanobots are dangerous. If I make a mistake, they could eat this ship and everyone on it—just like in World War Three."

Sirsen Huntington smiled. "Don't worry. You won't actually be working with the real nanobots. This workstation is a simulator. It lets us program simulated nanobots and then test them out. They do everything the real nanobots do, but they only do it to simulated materials, not real things like people or ships. It's just like blowing simulated things up in AR games, nothing real gets hurt."

"Oh," Jeff said, relieved. "I guess that sounds ok. So what do you want me to do on this project?"

Looking past Jeff, Sirsen Huntington called out, "Stacey, can you come here please?"

A girl in her early twenties rose from the workstation she was at and approached. Jeff had met her before. "Hi, Stacey," he greeted. Stacey was Barbie's older sister. Like Barbie, Stacey had purple eyes. However, unlike Barbie, Stacey's hair was pink with purple streaks.

"Hi Jeff. I hear you're going to be working with us from now on," Stacey said warmly. Jeff nodded.

"Stacey," Sirsen Huntington instructed, "I want Jeff to start by running the tests for the programs you write. In a few weeks, he can start programming the plumbing systems for passenger modules. That'll give him an easy task to start on. Can you help him get up and running?"

"Sure," Stacey replied cheerily. "Have a seat at the workstation, Jeff. I'll show you what to do."

Jeff sat down as Sirsen Huntington left. Stacey explained, "All the programs we write for nanobots have to be tested on this simulator. We send the results to the New Oxford University for review. If they like the results, they send it on to the New Tokyo

Shipyard in the New Tokyo system and the Federated Alliance headquarters back on Earth. And if *they* like the results we can get permission to try the programs for real. The whole process takes a long time, so if we get backed up, it can delay the project for years."

In about half an hour, Stacey had Jeff running simple tests on the software she had written a few days before.

"I'm really glad to have your help, Jeff," she told him. "The senior staff wants to finish these tests as soon as possible after we pick up the nanobots so we can do the first live trial later this year. Having you around to run these tests will really help me keep on schedule. Oops, look at that." The workstation's display showed a bright flash, and then went black.

"What happened?" Jeff asked.

"The test we just ran was on the nanobots that build the fusion reactors. The reactors weren't built right, so when they started to operate, they blew up. That happens a lot. It just means that I have to work more on my programs." Heaving a sigh, Stacey returned to her workstation.

Following her example, Jeff turned to his workstation and ran the next test in the list. It didn't turn out any better than the previous one. He recorded the results and moved on.

For the rest of the day, Jeff continued running tests. Most of them were kind of boring, but every so often, his workstation displayed a nice explosion or other disaster. But apparently that was normal for nanobot programming.

At the end of their shift, Stacey and Jeff went to dinner in the cafeteria. Barbie and Mark met them there. Jeff was a little surprised that Carmen wasn't there too. After dinner, Stacey asked, "Jeff, Barbie and Mark are going to the AR suite with me. I just got a great new program when we were at the Albany Transfer Station. José and Wendy will be there too. Do you want to come along?"

"Sure. What kind of a program is it?"

Stacey smiled. "You'll see. It's my favorite."

José and Wendy were just arriving at the AR suite when Jeff and the others got there. They all quickly got into pods and entered the program. Jeff was unimpressed at first. Apparently, the program was nothing but a gently-sloped plateau about a half a mile above a green and verdant valley. Jeff peeked cautiously over the edge of the sheer cliffs that ran around the entire plateau. The lush countryside stretched to the horizon in every direction. In the distance was a golden coastline. Warm winds rustled through the knee-length grass that covered the plateau.

"Um," Jeff began, trying to be polite, "this is nice. It's a nice spot for a picnic or something."

To Jeff's amazement, José, Barbie, and Mark howled with laughter. Wendy and Stacey smiled kindly. "Jeff," Stacey explained, "In this program, you learn to fly."

"I can already fly. I'm licensed to fly four different classes of aircraft and spacecraft."

That only brought more laughter from José, Barbie, and Mark. Jeff was indignant until Stacey told him, "Jeff, I want you to imagine that you have wings and a tail like a bird's."

"Huh?"

Barbie broke in. "Just do it, Arcology Boy," she said, still chuckling.

Dutifully, Jeff imagined he had the wings and tail of a bird. And suddenly, he did. Seeing his shock, Barbie again laughed.

Stacey said, "They work just like your arms and legs, Jeff. You just will them to do what you want them to do. Try stretching your wings."

Pausing momentarily, Jeff glanced at his right shoulder. The program he was in had created an opening in his shirt so that his wing could pass through it. It was the same for his left wing. He imagined there was now an opening in the seat of his pants for his tail, but he didn't want to crank his head around to try and look with everyone watching him. He decided not to think about it right now.

Unsure of himself, Jeff stretched his wings. The gentle breeze filled them and pressed him backwards slightly. He could feel the warmth of the air as the wind rustled through his feathers. The sensation was electrifying.

Jeff watched as José, Wendy, Barbie, and Mark sprouted wings and tails, leapt from the cliff, and sailed into the vast blue sky. They chased each other upward as they danced on the wind.

Stacey led Jeff up the slope of the plateau. After a few minutes of instruction, Jeff was able to get off the ground and glide down the hill to the edge of the cliff. With a few practice runs, Stacey told him he was ready to go over the cliff.

"If you want it to, the help system will give you advice as you fly," she instructed. "Just want the advice, and you'll hear a voice giving it."

Even though he knew he was in an AR program, Jeff was still hesitant to leap from the cliff. Looking nearly three thousand feet down, all of his senses told him he was on the edge of a real precipice. Everything inside him told him that jumping off was bad. But Stacey was standing there gazing at him expectantly. The others were already far across the blue expanse. So Jeff anxiously stepped to the edge of the cliff, spread his wings, and jumped.

Jeff's brain screamed with panic as he plummeted downward with the wind blasting past him. Suddenly, his wings caught the air and he floated forward. He whooped as he sailed upward effortlessly on a current of rising air. Just as suddenly, a downdraft sent him plunging earthward again. Flailing his wings against the unexpectedly hostile air, Jeff pitched toward the sheer cliff wall. Realizing he couldn't keep himself from slamming against the hard stone, he closed his eyes and braced himself for impact—only to open them seconds later and find himself standing again not far from the edge of the cliff. Jeff teetered slightly, and then plunked into a sitting position on the ground, his tail stuck out behind him.

Stacey trotted toward Jeff and called out, "Not bad. On his first flight, Mark hit the cliff wall right away. Try again."

Gazing up at her, Jeff almost asked Stacey if she was out of her mind. But then he remembered the feeling he had in those few seconds when his wings were lifting him gently skyward. Shakily, he stood. Steadying himself and squaring his shoulders, Jeff strode resolutely to the edge of the cliff again, spread his wings, and jumped.

The warm air wrapped its invisible arms around him as Jeff wafted upward. The soft touch of the air currents through his feathers made his wings tingle. Unsure what to do next, Jeff wished for some advice. Immediately, a woman's voice came to him saying, "You might try flapping your wings gently. Don't overdo it. Oh, that's very good."

Deciding to practice his turns, Jeff zigzagged his way toward the ground. After a while, Barbie and Mark rocketed down from above and came abruptly to a near halt in the air beside him. Calling out her brand of slightly mocking encouragement, Barbie spiraled slowly around Jeff as Mark hung in the air nearby. After a few minutes, they pounded the air with their wings and gained altitude again, leaving him behind. Jeff was alone in the expansive blue of the sky.

It took Jeff the better part of an hour to reach the ground. His landing was less than spectacular. At least he managed to curl into a ball and roll across the soft grass. Brushing himself off, Jeff stood near the seashore and peered up at the cliff he had jumped off of. It was now far across the rolling landscape.

"How do I get back up there?" he asked himself out loud. The program responded by putting him instantly back on top of the cliff. 'Of course,' he thought, 'I just have to want to be back here and I am.'

This time Jeff marched confidently to the edge of the cliff and jumped off. As he rode an updraft, Jeff searched for the others. He located them far across the green valley. "Man, I'll never catch up with them," he said. Again, the program responded by moving him to where he wanted to be. Jeff found himself drifting lazily not far above the others as they chased each other back and forth. They seemed to be playing some kind of game. Jeff decided to just continue watching from above. As he did, he tried to copy some of the turns, dives, and other moves they were making. 'Next time we do this,' Jeff thought, 'I'm joining in.'

At the end of the evening, Stacey asked Jeff, "So what did you think? Was that a good program?"

"The best," he responded. "Can I use it again?"

"Sure, any time." Stacey told him. "Anyone can use it. Have fun." She smiled and waved to the group as she and Barbie left the AR suite.

As Jeff and José made their way back to their quarters, José asked, "So I hear tomorrow's your 15th birthday. What are you going to do to celebrate?"

"Fly. I'm definitely going to fly."

30

Jeff began the morning of his 15th birthday by cleaning up cow manure. The ship was making the jump into the Far Oxford system. It would spend two days in the wormhole before emerging in British space.

Because Jeff's workstation was shut down for the transition into hyperspace, he helped out on the ship's farm. The cows would have to spend the entire two days of the wormhole traversal in their stalls instead of the corral. So Dr. Darnelle assigned Jeff, Mark, and Barbie the task of cleaning the stalls and getting them ready.

Although somewhat smelly, cleaning the stalls wasn't as bad as Jeff expected. By lunchtime, the cows were safely in their spotless stalls and munching contently on their feed. After showering, Jeff ate lunch with Mark and Barbie as they watched the jump into hyperspace.

"Can I ask a question?" Jeff queried after the ship slipped into the wormhole. Mark nodded.

"How come I see you two together so much lately? What does Carmen say?"

Barbie flashed one of her wicked grins while Mark looked embarrassed. "Carmen and I aren't going out any more," he explained to Jeff.

Jeff was surprised. "So you two … ?"

Looking triumphant, Barbie told Jeff, "I can't be held responsible for lost or stolen boyfriends." Her wicked grin returned. Mark shrugged and continued eating.

Once Jeff's workstation was back up, he went to Central Computing and worked through the afternoon. To his surprise, Kent appeared in the door to Central Computing just as Jeff's shift was ending.

"Happy birthday kid," his father said as he handed Jeff a large box.

"What's this?"

"It's your present. Open it."

Jeff pulled the top of the box open and removed the flat rectangular slab inside. It had data connectors on one end.

"What's this?" Jeff asked again.

"That," Kent explained, "is a neural processor matrix blade. It contains a million computer processors. I picked it up from a place on the Albany Transfer Station that sells used parts for ships." He smiled.

Jeff gazed at his father blankly. "Uh, thanks," he stammered.

Kent chuckled. "It's for your robot," he informed Jeff. "You put this cable ... ," Kent grabbed a cable from the box. " ... onto the data connectors on the processor blade ... ," he connected the cable to the processor blade. " ... and run it up from Arvix's back, through his neck, and you connect this other end to his processor matrix." Kent pulled another rectangular object from the box. "Then you put the blade in this and weld it to Arvix's back to form a backpack just like we did with the medical robot. There's some additional stabilizers in this box that we'll need to install into Arvix as well."

"You mean this is extra brains for Arvix?"

Kent nodded. "Exactly. And I got Sirsen Huntington to add some artificial intelligence code he got from an old public domain AR program. Now Arvix will be able to learn just like characters in AR programs do. He'll be nearly as smart as those high-priced domestic robots you see following rich people around."

"Wow, Dad. Thanks!"

"You're welcome. Happy birthday son." Kent started to move toward the door.

Jeff asked, "Do you want to come and eat dinner with me?"

Kent hesitated, "Why don't you come eat dinner with us? Today is also Denise's birthday. Did you know that?"

Surprised, Jeff asked, "Denise and I have the same birthday?"

"That's right," Kent replied, "and we're having a bit of a party for her. You could come and join us."

Now it was Jeff's turn to hesitate, "I ... I don't think so. I'll just eat dinner in the cafeteria."

Jeff could see that his father was disappointed. Kent struggled to suppress it as he replied, "Ok, son. Have a happy birthday." He left.

Somewhat sadly, Jeff went to the cafeteria for dinner.

"SURPRISE!"

Jeff took a step back, stunned. Standing in the cafeteria entrance, he saw a huge banner hanging over one of the tables that read, "Happy Birthday Jeff." All of his friends on board were standing underneath it congratulating him. Awkwardly, Jeff edged forward. Linmei approached and hugged him. With her usual wicked smile, Barbie did the same.

The group cheered as Sirsen Darnelle, the head cook on board, and some of his staff brought out a special dinner for Jeff. "Have you ever seen this before Jeff?" he asked pointing to a large flat brown thing on the plate.

"No, what is it?"

"It's Beef Wellington. Eat it all and then come by the kitchen and tell me it's the best thing you've ever had in your entire life."

Smiling, Jeff told him, "It will be, I'm sure."

Sirsen Darnelle was right. It was the best meal Jeff ever had. After dinner there was birthday cake with ice cream. As his friends said their goodbyes and wished him another "Happy Birthday," Jeff had an idea. Slipping into the kitchen, Jeff approached Sirsen Darnelle.

"Thanks for the dinner, Sirsen Darnelle, it was the best," Jeff said.

"You're welcome, of course. It's always a pleasure to cook for people who are as appreciative as you."

"Sirsen Darnelle? Can I ask a favor?"

"Sure, Jeff. Anything for the birthday boy."

"I know someone else who's having a birthday today. Could I take her and her sister some cake and ice cream?"

Sirsen Darnelle gave Jeff an understanding, almost sad look and answered quietly, "Sure Jeff. That's very nice of you. Go ahead and help yourself. I'll give you disposable plates and silverware so they can just throw them away when they're done."

A few minutes later, Jeff wended his way to the ship's long main corridor. At a communication panel he stopped and called Danae. When her image appeared on the screen he said, "I heard it's Denise's birthday."

"Yeah, we just finished a little party for her. She's really excited. But she really wanted to see you too."

"Can you bring her to the forward-most door of the passenger module? I've got something for her."

"Sure Jeff."

Arriving at the passenger module door, Jeff set a plate down on a nearby conduit and placed his hand on the palm reader in the doorframe. The double doors slid open.

"Sirsen Jeff!" Denise squeaked as she bounced toward him and wrapped her arms around his waist.

"Hey Little Mouse," Jeff greeted her. "This is for you. Happy Birthday." He handed her the plate as she released him.

To Danae, Jeff said, "I've got one for you too." Retrieving the other plate, Jeff passed it to Danae.

Denise stared at her plate. "What is it?" she asked.

"Cake and ice cream."

"This is cake?"

"Sure. Haven't you ever had cake for your birthday before?"

To Jeff's surprise, Denise shook her head. He could understand her not recognizing the ice cream. Food like that cost too much money for most people these days. But everyone at least had synthcake on their birthday, didn't they?

"Try it, it's good."

Denise nibbled at her cake. Her entire face lit up as she tasted it.

Smiling, Jeff told her, "That stuff there is strawberry ice cream. It's cold, but it's really, really good. You have to eat it slow, though. You get a headache if you don't."

Danae broke in, "A headache? Why?"

"Beats me, but that's what happens when you eat cold stuff fast."

Both girls sat on the floor. As Denise ate her ice cream tears streamed silently down her face. Surprised, Jeff asked, "Denise? Is something wrong?" She shook her head and continued to eat.

Danae explained, "No, Jeff. Nothing's wrong. She's crying because she's happy. Our family's never had birthday parties since my dad left. We never had money for stuff like that. You and your dad are the first people that have ever given her things for her birthday."

Embarrassed, Jeff stammered, "Well ... glad to do it. I mean, it's no big deal. I just wanted her birthday to be fun."

Finishing her cake and ice cream, Denise drew near Jeff and pulled on his arm until he stooped down to her level. She grabbed his neck in the biggest hug she could manage. "Thank you Sirsen Jeff," she said and she kissed his cheek. She turned and left, still crying.

Danae surprised Jeff by hugging him as well. "You're the best brother we ever had," she told him. Tears filled her eyes as she said, "Happy Birthday Jeff." Scooping up both plates, Danae followed Denise through the door to the passenger module. A stunned Jeff looked after them for a moment. 'This is a really good birthday,' he thought as he placed his hand on the palm reader to close the door again.

Back at his quarters, Jeff checked his mail and found birthday greetings from Harriet, Akio, Akio's parents, and some of his friends back home. After viewing their messages, he sent each of them a thank-you. Just as he finished, there was a beeping from

Jeff's databand. When he answered it, Jeff saw an image of Chief Connors and Porsche floating above his wrist. They were in the Chief's office.

"I normally don't accept office visits from anyone other than my staff and the captain this late in the evening," the Chief told Porsche. "What can I do for you?"

Oozing charm, Porsche explained, "I was wondering if you had a chance to review Dirk's application for employment? I think he would be a valuable addition to the crew, just like my husband and stepson have been."

The Chief didn't reply for a long moment. He sat behind his desk gazing at his hands. At last, he said, "Your son has no skills that my engineering staff can use. I can see from the letter his YPA flight instructor sent that he has an exceptional skill at piloting, but that's not what we do."

Undaunted, Porsche pressed on. "I was hoping you could train him, like you've done for Jeff."

"Jeff needed no training. He came with a skill set that few people twice his age have. He's exactly what we look for in crew members."

Porsche showed no disappointment or discouragement. "The captain offered my husband a job today. I'm sure it would be easier for him to make a decision to stay if both of his sons were employed on the ship. Is it possible for you to talk to the captain and find something for Dirk?"

Chief Connor's face became stony. "Have you discussed this with your husband?"

Hesitantly, Porsche replied, "Well ... not exactly."

"When you submitted the employment application for Dirk, you authorized a background check. Did you know that?"

Wide-eyed, Porsche nodded but didn't say anything.

The Chief said, "I've had letters from Dirk's teachers, school principal, the sector council where you worked, and the sector police. Not one of them has a single good thing to say about your son. Upon further investigation, I've found that Dirk has committed numerous criminal acts, including theft, felony hacking, and felony assault. I must hand it to you. You've been very skilled at keeping him out of jail. But in the Captain's own words, 'Dirk is a person you can trust only as far as you can spit him.' Which is her way of saying he can't be trusted at all. In fact, after seeing the information I've collected on your son, she's seriously considering withdrawing her offer of employment to Kent. I think that's very unfortunate. Your husband is a fantastic engineer and I need engineers now. He's also one of the best friends I've ever had."

Porsche sat in shocked silence. Chief Connors continued, "The sector police have also informed me that you have been sending a continuous stream of letters blaming Jeff for the assault on a boy named Hubert Benson, as well as a number of Dirk's other crimes. They've told me that they've repeatedly sent replies telling you that they have an eyewitness who swears that she saw your son commit the assault. They don't believe your excuses for Dirk and neither does anyone in this crew. The Captain has declared that your son is an especially dangerous person to have in an environment like this. Her expressed desire is to get him off the ship as fast as possible."

As Jeff watched, he realized that Porsche didn't know anyone could see what was happening. The Chief must have opened the comm channel silently with his datacrown.

Chief Connors continued, "Because your son's not yet an adult, we asked you to authorize a background check on yourself as well and you agreed on the application. I see that your original name was Henna Kwak. You changed your name the day you were married to your first husband."

Smiling sarcastically, Chief Connors speculated, "You named yourself after that singer that was so popular back then, didn't you? The information I have is that you grew up in a rather ugly section of the city outside the arcology you and Kent lived in. You married Dennis Highborne, a rather wealthy 25-year old resident of the arcology, on your 18th birthday. You're a very attractive woman. I suspect you of marrying him to get yourself off the streets. I also suspect you of marrying Kent to get yourself off Earth so Dirk wouldn't be prosecuted. Kent is my good friend. But you and your son are not people I want to have anything to do with."

Without a word, Porsche whirled around and stomped angrily from the office. The Chief turned toward the comm panel in his office wall and said, "I hope revenge is a good birthday present. Goodnight, Jeff." His image disappeared.

'She's still blaming me?' Jeff thought. 'She never quits. But I'm glad there's an eyewitness. I wonder who it was and why it took so long to come forward?'

The next few weeks passed uneventfully. Jeff started pre-Academy classes in the AR suite with several others his age. He worked hard on the Living Ship project and put in his shifts on the farm. Occasionally, he got to work shifts back in Engineering with his dad. Jeff looked forward to those days, which always ended too quickly.

On the day they finally arrived at the planet New Oxford to pick up the nanobots, Jeff was assigned to help load engineering supplies. He brought Arvix along and together with a small cluster of loader bots they hauled in enough containers to enable Jeff to finish his shift early. Jeff spent the extra time in the AR suite flying, just as he did whenever he had any spare time.

The trip back out to the hypergate took four weeks. By then, Jeff was beginning to be a proficient nanobot programmer. Very few of his programs had serious problems. He enjoyed seeing large parts of a ship appear on the simulator when his programs were successful.

As the ship forged its way out of the Far Oxford system and back to the hypergate, Jeff frequently thought, 'This place feels like a good home for me. I really should tell the Chief that I'll stay.' But he never did. Every time he tried to make himself do it, he thought of how disappointed his dad would be.

'Oh well,' Jeff thought as he sat watching the ship enter the wormhole to the Nebraska system. 'I still have time to decide. It's another week and a half before we get to the Loveland Shipping Station in the Colorado system.'

Part 3

THE HOLE IN THE SKY

"It's said that history occurs in cycles and that we're condemned to relive history if we don't study it. That much is true. However, history is more like an onion. It contains cycles within cycles. On the surface, this cycle of history appears to begin with an attack on one boy. Admittedly, this boy was at the center of the storm that swept humanity into the Second Age. But the scale of the attack was ridiculously monumental for the goal of killing one boy. To jump to the conclusion that he and he alone was the motivating purpose behind the attack is a mistake of astronomic proportions." *The Human Race in the Second Age*, Hugh Benson, p. 10.

31

As Jeff sat watching the ships enter the wormhole to the Nebraska system, he did not see a stubby, greenish-grey cylindrical object go into the wormhole together with a freighter that was in line several ships ahead of the Ellsworth. Nor did he see another identical object slide silently in with a passenger liner several ships behind the Ellsworth.

No one else saw the strange objects either. They were each surrounded by a cloaking field that made them invisible. The Space Corps, who built and operated the hypergate, never suspected that unknown and unseen objects might be traversing the wormhole. After all, everyone knew that cloaking fields had never been invented.

Jeff was sound asleep when some of the greenish-grey cylinders suddenly activated themselves. Glowing and vibrating sickly, the devices detonated causing immense waves of gravity and radiation to burst outward in every direction. Gravity waves distort space. They also distort hyperspace. When this happens, any wormholes that might exist in that particular section of hyperspace will fragment into thousands of pieces.

32

"Emergency! Emergency!" blared the ship's communication system. "All crewmembers report to their duty stations. Passengers return to their quarters immediately."

The ship pitched violently, tossing Jeff from his bunk. "Lights!" he heard José shout. The cabin's lights turned on. Hurriedly, Jeff pulled on his uniform as José did the same.

"Get to Engineering!" José ordered. Whatever's going on, they may need help." José ran from the room.

"Arvix!" Jeff called. "Come with me." The robot, which was standing in the corner recharging itself, snapped to attention, unplugged itself from the wall, and followed Jeff as he ran after José. He didn't get far before the ship's long main corridor went completely black. The ship lurched again and tossed Jeff completely off his feet. Behind him, he heard Arvix clatter to the floor.

Emergency lights came on, casting a dim red glow over everything. Jeff struggled to his feet as the ship shuddered and pitched again. "What's happening?" he screamed at José.

"We'll find out," he asserted. Slapping a comm panel on the wall, he tersely commanded, "Engineering." Chief Connors' face appeared.

"Martinez," the Chief directed. "The wormhole has broken apart. We just came out into normal space but we have no idea where we are. We've got damage all over the ship and I've deployed the repair robots. But we need all hands now if not sooner. Take Jeff and go fix some ruptured power conduits in the passenger module."

"Yes, Sirsen," José responded. Turning to Jeff he stated, "We'll get tools from repair bay 7. It's on the way."

Nodding, Jeff followed as José scurried toward the aft of the ship. Hurriedly retrieving the needed tools, Jeff and José entered the passenger module. The blown conduits weren't hard to find.

They set to work immediately, but José noticed that some of the passengers were gathering around. "Folks," he called out. "Please return to your cabins. These power conduits are not safe. We'll get the repairs done shortly and the Captain will announce when it's safe to come out."

Still gawking, the passengers reluctantly made their ways back to their cabins. José and Jeff soon got the conduits fixed and had power flowing to all of the cabins. As they left, Jeff noticed a young, attractive, white-blond woman peeking at them from around the corner. Something about the way she looked at him made him uneasy.

Chief Connors had sent José a message containing a list of repairs he wanted them to do. Hurriedly, Jeff and José went to the central computer core to fix a pressure door that was stuck closed, trapping a few crewmembers. Jeff sent Arvix to get some extra parts in case they needed them.

When they arrived, Jeff pulled the panel off the door control and set to work while José used his databand to contact the trapped crewmembers. 'Ah,' thought Jeff as he examined the circuits. 'There must have been a power surge. The negation displacer is fried." He quickly retrieved a replacement from his toolbox and started installing it.

Suddenly, Jeff heard the zinging of a stun gun. José crumpled to the floor next to him. Whirling around, Jeff found two redheaded men and the white-blond woman he'd seen earlier.

Fearfully but angrily, Jeff howled, "Hey! What do you think you're doing?" With as much authority as he could muster, he commanded, "Get back to the passenger module."

The older of the two men told the others. "This is the target. Take him."

The woman countered, "The target is not known to be a member of this crew."

The older man replied, "We have checked every passenger. If the target is on this ship, he must be part of the crew. A status change has probably occurred since the start of the voyage."

"Highly unlikely," the younger of the two men disagreed. "Spacers in the Federated Alliance are not known to hire crewmembers from among their passengers."

Breaking in more loudly, Jeff tried again. "Look you three, get back to the passenger module! You're in a lot of trouble for what you've done here."

Completely ignoring Jeff, the older man commanded, "Take him. We'll go ahead and process him as a precaution. We can get confirmation later."

Shocked, Jeff saw the younger man pointed a stun gun at him. "STOP!" he screamed. As the younger man fired, Jeff dove to the side. He jumped once more as the man shot again.

Finding himself backed into a corner, Jeff could see that there was nowhere to go as the man with the stunner bore down on him. Abruptly, something whizzed through the air and hit the man on the side of the head. The man thudded to the floor unconscious and bleeding from his head.

Whirling around, the man's companions confronted their attacker. Scrambling to his feet, Jeff also looked down the corridor. There stood Arvix with the container of spare parts Jeff had sent him to retrieve. Jeff was amazed.

Before either of the two remaining attackers could move, Arvix reached into the container and extracted a cryptolink blocker unit that was about the size of a baseball. Moving so fast that he was almost a blur, Arvix pitched the unit at the older man and nailed him right in the forehead. He was out before he hit the floor.

Diving at the stun gun that the younger man had dropped, the woman rolled and pointed the weapon where Arvix had just stood. But Arvix was already behind her. With his fist, he thumped her a good one on the head. She splayed on the floor unconscious.

Still too stunned to move, Jeff stammered, "Ar ... Arvix?"

"Jeff Bowman," responded Arvix in a voice that was his, but not quite like his. "You must hide. You must not be captured by these people."

"Wait ... what?"

Solemnly, Arvix intoned, "Come with me if you want to live." He took a few steps toward the aft of the ship.

Robotically, Jeff followed, still struggling to speak. "Arvix. You can't say these things to me. You're not this smart."

"Correct," responded Arvix. "I am not, strictly speaking, the robot you know as Arvix. I am actually another computer hidden on this ship and I have taken control of Arvix to protect you. However, you may continue to address me as Arvix."

Arvix rounded a corner and stopped short, causing Jeff to nearly crash into him. Motioning for Jeff to retreat, Arvix backpedaled and guided Jeff down a side corridor. "There are more Normans after you," explained Arvix. "They have control of the main corridor into this module of the ship. We have to find another way to get you to safety."

Hurrying through a hatch, they climbed into a junction of the maintenance tunnels. Silently, Arvix pointed upward and began to climb. Not sure what else to do, Jeff followed. Together, they entered a maintenance tunnel and crawled for what seemed a long time. Jeff was jumpy. Every sound seemed to be the footsteps of pursuing attackers. His own breathing seemed to thunder through the tunnel. Arvix's plasteel skin made a click-clack sound that banged through the tube each time he put his hands or knees on the floor. Jeff was sure everyone could hear their movements.

The tunnel widened into an open area filled with pipes. Arvix climbed up among them with Jeff close behind. When he reached a particularly large pipe, he stopped.

"Jeff Bowman," queried Arvix. "How long can you hold your breath?"

"What?" responded Jeff incredulously. Nearing panic, he yelled, "ARVIX! WHAT'S GOING ON?"

"We need to get you out of here, Jeff Bowman. Now."

Slightly more calmly, Jeff demanded, "Arvix, why are those people after me? Who are they? What are they going to do to me? And why are you helping me? You're not really even Arvix!"

"The people trying to capture you are from the Normandy star system. I have insufficient data to explain their purpose. Their intent is to install a cyberbrain in you and make you subject to their mind control. You are correct in stating that I am not Arvix. I am a supercomputer stored in a cargo hold in this ship. I am programmed to protect you. As stated previously, I have no designation so I recommend that you continue to refer to me as Arvix. Response ends."

Taken aback, Jeff wasn't sure what to say or do next. Finally he managed to get out, "Who programmed you? Who's trying to protect me? And why do a bunch of Normans want to mind control me?"

Emotionlessly, Arvix replied, "I have no information on any of those subjects."

"No information? You don't know *anything* more? What do I do? How do I get help?"

Realization flashed through Jeff. "Of course! I need to get help."

Glancing at the databand on his wrist, Jeff called Chief Connors over the communication system. The Chief answered immediately.

"What is it Jeff? I'm very busy right now."

"Chief! Someone's trying to kidnap me! They shot José with a stun gun. I ran away and I'm hiding in a maintenance tunnel."

"Jeff, I don't have time for jokes."

"No Chief, it's real! You've got to believe me." Jeff launched into a description of everything that had just happened.

Surprisingly, Chief Connors believed him. "I've just accessed the ship's internal scanners. They show José lying unconscious in a corridor. I've picked up several armed passengers with stun guns moving through the ship's main sections. The ship's records show that they all originated in the Normandy system."

The Chief grew extremely serious. "This is bad, Jeff. This is very bad. I'm showing that there are two groups of Normans closing in on you. There's no way out. I'm sending armed crewmembers to your location. You have to hide until they get there."

"Where do I hide?"

"Hold on, I'm trying to find you something."

Arvix interrupted, "Jeff Bowman, how long can you hold your breath?"

"Arvix! Why do you keep asking me that?"

"This circular plasteel plate we are sitting on is a valve to the pipe underneath. I have gained access to all of this ship's systems. I can open this valve and insert you into the pipe."

"Put me in the pipe? What's inside there?"

"Water. This pipe is the fresh water main into the passenger module. The flow of the water through the pipe will be enough to push you along until you reach the passenger module. There is another valve there that I can open to let you out."

Far down the maintenance tunnel, Jeff heard voices. His blood turned to ice in his veins. Terrified, Jeff nodded to Arvix.

Arvix asserted, "I will now open the valve. Please remain where you are and take a deep breath."

So saying, the robot climbed off of the valve cover and stood on a nearby pipe as Jeff numbly watched. Realizing what was about to happen, Jeff heaved as much air into his lungs as possible.

Abruptly, the valve cover snapped open from the center like the iris of an eye. Instantly Jeff was plunged downward into the cold water. Managing to keep control of himself, Jeff let the current move him head first through the clear pipe. He heard the valve cover snap closed above him.

It was hard not to flail his arms and legs. Jeff was wild with fear, but he forced himself to keep his arms at his sides and his legs straight behind him. That made him move more briskly. He saw through the glass-like pipe that the rapid current pushed him easily through section after section of the ship. He shot unimpeded along inside the large pipe as it passed through walls and bulkheads.

Heart thudding manically, Jeff tried to keep a grip on himself. Increasingly, his lungs seemed to want to explode. 'I'm not going to make it!' he thought desperately.

But then Jeff reached a wide spot in the pipe. The swirling of the water inside caused him to bounce around. Unexpectedly a valve cover below him opened, spilling him out of the pipe. The water pressure popped a panel off of the ceiling below him. He tumbled through and plopped like a soggy sack of potatoes onto the floor below. Several passengers, who had been using the corridor in which he now found himself, screamed and scattered.

Coughing and gasping, Jeff got to his feet. He found himself near the rear of the passenger module. He wiped water from his face. With an increasing number of passengers gathering to stare at him, Jeff got his feet moving.

'Where do I go?' he thought. 'Where do I hide?'

Like a homing pigeon moving toward its roost, Jeff made his way toward his father's cabin. Dripping a trail behind him, Jeff staggered forward. When he reached cabin 25, he didn't even use the door buzzer. He just tumbled through the door.

Inside, Jeff's dad and Porsche were watching a video feed from the ship's bridge. They nearly jumped out of their skins when Jeff fell into a waterlogged heap on their cabin floor.

Leaping to his feet, Kent cried out, "Jeff! What's happened? Are you alright?"

Shakily, Jeff nodded. As clearly as he could, Jeff explained the situation.

Kent was flummoxed. "Normans?" he asked incredulously. "What do they want with you?"

Jeff just shrugged. "I don't know. But I think I need to call the Chief again."

So saying, Jeff hailed Chief Connors on his databand. Immediately, the Chief's face appeared above Jeff's wrist.

"Jeff," the Chief demanded. "You were in the water reprocessing plant. How did you get into the passenger module?"

"Arvix put me into a pipe," Jeff explained. "Sorry, but you're going to have to send someone to clean up the mess here in the passenger module. The water went everywhere."

"That I know," affirmed the Chief. "We got a flood of calls about a burst water pipe. They told me someone fell out of the ceiling, but I didn't believe it."

"Believe it," replied Jeff. "I've got the bruises to prove it. And sorry again about the mess."

Chief Connors dismissed, "No worries. I've rerouted several crewmembers to your location. All crew over the age of 14 have been issued plasma blasters. They're all trained to use them. I'm having one sent over to your father now so he can have one too."

Kent interrupted, "Darius, what about these Normans?"

The Chief shrugged. "We still don't know much. They got on at Far Oxford. I don't know how they got out of the passenger module or why they're after Jeff. I have no idea where this supercomputer that Jeff talked about is. But it seems to have been in all of our systems since we left Lunar Central. It probably came aboard when you did."

"But why?" Jeff wondered.

"To protect you, I think," Chief Connors speculated. "Most of its activity seems to be about monitoring you."

"Who would want to protect me?"

"I don't know, Jeff. But I'm glad they do. I realize now that it was because of that computer that you became a crewmember in the first place. Now that I know it's there, I've run a low-level network diagnostic. I can see what that computer's been doing in our system. On the day you ran away, it disabled several interlocks on the door to the main section of the ship. That's how you were able to get through with just a Swiss ultra knife."

Somehow, Jeff felt insulted.

The Chief continued, "And I don't think it's an accident you ended up on this ship. I wouldn't be surprised if someone put you here so you could have help if you needed it. I always thought it was a huge coincidence that you ended up on the ship where I live. But it seems not."

Jeff asked, "So what do I do now?"

"You and your father need to head to the forward door between the passenger module and the ship's main cylinder. A group of crewmembers will meet you there. I'm talking with the Captain about you. We need to find a place for you that's away from other people—someplace we can secure you until we round up the Normans. Kent, you and Jeff should leave now."

"Will do, Darius," Kent replied.

After somber but hurried goodbyes, Kent and Jeff made their way toward the forward door of the passenger module.

33

"We're sitting ducks here," complained Kent as he peered nervously up and down the long corridor of the ship's main section.

Jeff stood in the doorway between the passenger module and the corridor trying to be as inconspicuous as he could. 'This doesn't make any sense,' he worried. 'Why are people chasing me?' The world seemed to spin around him for a few moments. But with an effort, Jeff got a grip on himself.

From one of the overhead walkways, Jeff heard the sound of a hovercart speeding toward them. 'Good,' Jeff thought. 'The crew is finally here to help.'

Unexpectedly, two men dropped down from the level above. They were descending service ladders with their hands and feet on the outer rails of the ladders, sliding down them like firemen's poles. To his horror, Jeff saw that they were both redheads.

"Normans!" Jeff hollered, retreating into the passenger module.

As the Normans pulled out their stun guns, Kent surged forward. Grabbing a Norman by his wrist, Kent twisted the man's arm behind his back and pulled the stun gun from his hand. Shielding himself with the Norman's body, he aimed the stun gun at the other man and fired.

The first Norman struggled in Kent's grasp and managed to wrap his leg around one of Kent's. After tottering for a brief second, they both fell to the floor. The stun gun bounced away.

Kent and the Norman viciously traded punches. Jeff was terrified. But in spite of his fear, he scrambled forward and snatched up the stun gun. Rounding on the remaining attacker, Jeff fired. He slumped to the floor.

Two more Normans appeared from nowhere. Neither Jeff nor Kent had time to react. As Kent tried to dive out of the way, a tall Norman shot at him with a plasma pistol. His left side hideously seared, Kent screamed in agony and heaved himself between the attackers and Jeff. The tall Norman took aim at Kent.

Realizing that he still held the stun gun, Jeff zapped the Norman before he could kill Kent. The other attacker, who had only a stun gun, shot Kent and knocked him out. Jeff returned fire but missed.

Another hovercart approached on the level above. Jeff could hear footfalls and men talking on the level above. 'More Normans!' he thought desperately. He wanted to run back into the passenger module, but he didn't dare leave his father.

The last Norman rushed Jeff, grabbing at his stun gun. Struggling desperately, Jeff kneed the Norman in the groin, causing him to double over and tumble backwards. With a slight hum, the elevator descended and its door opened. Jeff whirled around and braced himself for another attack. But with an audible sigh of relief, he saw José step off the elevator with several armed crewmembers.

Seeing the Normans unconscious on the floor, the crewmen stopped short. José commented, "I guess you had some trouble while you were waiting."

Panting, Jeff teetered for a moment. Then he agreed, "I guess we did."

"But you looked like you handled it pretty well. Maybe you don't need us around."

"José," Jeff stated somberly, "if you even *try* to leave now I'll zap you a good one with this stun gun."

Grinning, José replied, "Then I guess I'll hang around for a while."

The crewmen with José rolled their eyes. One of them was Sirsen Anderwell. He broke in with, "José, we haven't got time for your jokes. Look! Sirsen Bowman's hurt. Call the medical bay and get Dr. Darnell down here."

"Yes, Sirsen!" José responded crisply. Using his databand, José immediately called for medical help.

Sirsen Anderwell quickly knelt beside Kent. Fearfully, Jeff did the same.

Kent was a mess. The clothing on his left side was mostly ash and the exposed flesh was badly burned. The heat had cauterized Kent's blood vessels, so there wasn't much bleeding.

Jeff could hardly stand to look at his dad's injuries. He wasn't sure he could keep himself from falling apart. He began to tremble. "Is he ok?" he quavered, not sure he wanted to hear the real answer.

"He's not too badly hurt in spite of how it looks," Sirsen Anderwell told him. "See that burn on the wall? That's where most of the plasma went. Your father was burned by the backblast. If he had been hit directly, he'd be dead."

"So ... so he's going to live?"

"I'm guessing the answer is yes. He's got some bad burns. But Dr. Darnell can grow new skin for him and graft it in. We haven't got a bioprinter, so she can't print out new organs if he needs them. But she can make them using cell binders if she needs to. It's not as fast, but it gets the job done."

Jeff really didn't understand what he was saying, but the way Sirsen Anderwell talked made him feel better. At least it seemed like there was hope.

Dr. Darnell arrived moments later in a hovercart with an emergency medical bed floating along behind. Leaping from the cart, she scanned Kent intently. Without looking up, she slowly said, "Don't worry, Jeff. You're father's going to be all right. I'll get him into surgery right away and fix him up." To the crewmen, she directed, "Help me lift him into the bed."

They each slid their hands under Kent's unconscious form and together they lifted him gently onto the medical bed. Hopping back into her hovercart, Dr. Darnell commanded, "You men keep Jeff safe. He'll be able to see his dad in a few hours." So saying, she zipped away with the medical bed following obediently behind.

Without hesitation, Sirsen Anderwell instructed, "Jeff, we need to get you to a cargo bay near Engineering. We'll lock it down so the Normans can't get at you. We've got a hovercart on the level above to get us there quickly."

Still shaky, Jeff followed him to the cart and they started toward the cargo bay. As they rode toward the aft of the ship, Jeff saw members of the Engineering staff closing the ship's huge pressure doors behind them.

José noticed his gaze and commented, "We're locking the whole ship down. Pretty soon those Normans won't be able to go anywhere at all." Jeff felt reassured each time the massive doors slid down behind them.

The hovercart rapidly covered the distance to cargo bay 38. Chief Connors was waiting there. Without preamble he stated, "We've rounded up all of the Normans but one. We don't know where he is, but we're scanning the ship section by section to find him."

José asked, "Where did they get weapons? That's what I want to know."

"The ship's manifest says that there's a load of police weapons that we took on at Far Oxford," the Chief replied. "They must have broken into that."

Sirsen Anderwell commented, "What a coincidence. A shipment of weapons just happens to be available for a group of people who want to use them."

"Exactly," agreed Chief Connors. "There's a lot about this situation that's just too coincidental. But it gets worse."

Warily, Jeff asked, "What do you mean?"

Gravely, Chief Connors put a hand on Jeff's shoulder and told him, "We took on three dozen cryopassengers at Far Oxford. All of them are from the Normandy system."

"What?" interjected José. "Since when do we haul cryopassengers?"

"What are cryopassengers?" questioned Jeff.

The Chief explained, "They're people who are frozen in cryogenic stasis and shipped like cargo. It's cheaper to move people around like that, but most people don't like to go that way unless they have to."

"You mean like the farm animals we picked up? They're frozen so they don't get any older?"

"Exactly," confirmed the Chief. "We were paid a big fee to ship these Normans in cryostasis, so we took them on. Now we know why they were willing to pay so much."

José broke in, "But they're still in cryostasis, aren't they?"

"We don't know," the Chief growled. "The Captain and I think our missing Norman may be on the way to wake them up. We sent an armed team to make sure that doesn't happen."

"But in the meantime," continued Chief Connors before Jeff could get too fearful, "Jeff, come with me. We're sealing you in a bioplasma shipping container."

"A what?"

"It's a shipping container for bioplasma."

"What's bioplasma?"

The Chief dismissed his question with the wave of a hand and replied curtly, "Medical stuff. Don't worry about it. The point is that the container is specially insulated for space. Bioplasma breaks down if radiation gets at it. So the shipping containers are designed so that radiation can't penetrate. That also means that scanners can't see what's inside. The Normans won't be able to find you there."

Making interruption a habit, José asked, "But what happened to the bioplasma?"

Guiding Jeff and José, Chief Connors bit off, "We dumped it already."

Clearly bewildered, José questioned, "Won't our customer be mad that we dumped their cargo?"

Without stopping the Chief shot back, "José, I don't think you realize the situation we're in. When the wormhole fragmented, the section we were in shot through hyperspace in some random direction. We're out in deep space between several star systems. And we may be stuck here. Getting the situation with the Normans under control is only the first problem we have to deal with. We may *never* make it back to the Alliance. No one cares about a little bioplasma since we can't use it anyway."

Both Jeff and José were shocked into silence. They trailed after the Chief without any further conversation.

Arriving at a hulking rectangular shipping container, Chief Connors opened the bulky doors and motioned for Jeff to get inside. Wide-eyed, Jeff complied. To his surprise, Chief Connors handed him a plasma pistol. After quickly giving Jeff instructions on how to handle it safely, the Chief somberly told him, "Jeff, shoot anyone that opens these doors that's not a crewmember."

Anxiously, Jeff nodded.

The Chief pointed to the back of the long container and informed him, "We don't know how long you'll be in here. There's a cot to sleep on, as well as food and water in that pile of stuff back there. Just stay in here and stay calm. The container blocks your databand's wireless signal, so we won't be able to talk with you until it's safe. We don't want to draw attention to this container, so no one will be back here until it's all clear. You'll be on your own. But just stay calm. We'll get this taken care of. And here's a flashlight. Turn it on before I close the door."

Again, Jeff silently nodded, accepted the flashlight, and turned it on.

Chief Connors swung the door closed. Jeff heard it lock from the outside.

"Oh wow," Jeff muttered. "This is just too weird."

Deciding to keep himself busy, Jeff moved to the back of the container and unpacked the crates stacked there. Inside he found the folding cot and some bedding. There was also a portable toilet with a small fusion generator attached. The brochure that came with it said that it was for "roughing it in style."

"Hmph," Jeff mumbled. "I guess people use this for camping."

After reading the instructions, he realized, "Ha! When I do my business," Jeff told himself, "it goes into that fusion generator and the generator uses it as fuel."

Wondering whether the generator's battery was already charged, Jeff pulled a rack of spotlights from a crate and plugged them in. The lights came on. "Well good," commented Jeff. "At least I don't have to wait until I poop to get electricity."

He got the cot and the toilet set up. He also found two 50-gallon barrels of water and a crate of ready-to-eat synthpaste. "Bleh!" he commented when he saw the tubes. "I hope I'm not in here very long."

Plopping down on the cot, Jeff decided to watch a show on his databand. He pulled it off his wrist and set it in front of himself. Calling up the video, Jeff passed the next few hours watching movie after movie and trying not to be worried. But the more time passed, the more fearful he became.

'Why haven't they come for me?' he wondered. 'Why is it taking so long?' Increasingly apprehensive, Jeff fretted over the possibility that the crew and even his family were dead. 'Maybe the Normans killed them all,' he thought. 'And now they're just looking for me. Should I stay here? I'll run out of food eventually. Maybe I should get to a shuttle and run away. But where would I go? We're in deep space.' He knew he would die eventually if he were alone in a shuttle with nowhere to go. 'But if everyone else is dead,' he thought, 'it's just a matter of time before they get me anyway. Is it better to die alone in space than to let them catch me? What do they really want me for anyway? What will they do to me if they find me? Will I really be mind controlled? Is that worse than dying or better?'

Jeff was sweating now. His heart was racing. He clenched and unclenched his fists helplessly. "What do I do?" he demanded of the blank walls around him. "What do I *do*?"

Suddenly, the entire ship shook violently. Like a manic earthquake, the vibrations reverberated through the ship's structure again and again, tossing Jeff around like a rag doll.

When it finally stopped, Jeff picked himself up from the floor. Knowing something incredibly bad had just happened, Jeff resolutely decided that it was at last time for him to venture out and see what was happening. But the container's door was sealed from the outside.

"I'll bet I can get it open with my Swiss ultra knife," he said. Recalling the Chief's words about when he escaped the passenger module, he added, "And this time without anyone helping me."

Extracting his Swiss ultra knife from his pocket, Jeff strode with determination to the container's door. "Hmm," he commented, "I think I'll start with the power decoupler."

Before he could even start, Jeff heard the container's lock click. Scrambling back to the cot, he scooped up the plasma pistol that lay there and pointed it fearfully at the door.

Standing with his feet firmly planted, Jeff tried his best not to let his rising panic overcome him. In spite of feeling like a rat in a trap, he held the gun solidly in front of himself and prepared for whatever might come.

The door swung open. Arvix peeked in. Immediately, the robot requested, "Please do not shoot me Jeff Bowman. I am here to help you."

It was all Jeff could do to keep himself from running up to Arvix and hugging him.

"Arvix! What's happening out there?"

"I have insufficient data to answer that question completely. There have been multiple battles between the Normans and the crewmembers. Most of the Normans are dead. Three of the crewmembers were badly injured and one passenger was killed. There was an explosive gravitational disturbance from outside the ship. The Ellsworth is very damaged as a result. The remaining Normans used a supercomputer just like me to break into the ship's systems. I am currently battling it in an effort to regain control. In the meantime, I have locked the ship down. No one can move inside the ship."

"Then I'm safe for now?"

"No, Jeff Bowman, you are not safe. The Normans are moving along the outside of the ship. That's how they have escaped detection. They're coming here now because their computer was able to break into the communications logs. They found a conversation between Captain Vorless and Chief Connors that told them you are here. You must leave immediately."

"Where's my dad? Where's the Chief?"

"Your father is in his quarters recuperating. His surgery went extremely well and he should make a full recovery. Chief Connors is moving through the maintenance tubes making repairs to the ship's critical systems along with his entire Engineering staff. Most of the rest of the crew are converging on this cargo bay."

"How do I get out of here?"

Arvix motioned for Jeff to follow him. As they walked the mechanoid explained, "You will put on this spacesuit." Arvix opened an emergency closet in one of the cargo bay's walls containing a spacesuit. The closet was at the rear of the cargo bay, right near an airlock to the outside. "You will take this oxygen tank." The robot indicated a large tank that stood next to the airlock's door. "Once you are outside the ship, you will be weightless. You will point the bottom end of the tank toward the front of the ship. You will open this valve on the top of the tank. The escaping gas will propel you at a rapid rate toward the front of the ship. You will travel along the starboard side of the ship. The Normans are moving along the port side. You will get behind them and use your suit's small propulsion thrusters to reenter the ship through the crew module. I will guide you to an electrical junction where we will set a trap for any Normans that may survive."

All of that sounded pretty wild to Jeff. But he did as he was told. It went without a hitch. After he got outside with the tank, he floated in open space. Cranking the valve on the oxygen tank, Jeff held on as tight as he could as the jetting gas rocketed him forward. If his situation hadn't been so dire, he would have enjoyed the ride.

By the time he was approaching the crew module the tank was empty. Jeff let go and the tank drifted away aimlessly. With his suit's low-powered thrusters, he gently aimed himself at the crew module. As he approached, he grabbed onto the latticework of beams that held the module to the rest of the ship.

Pulling himself along hand over hand, Jeff quickly found an airlock and entered the ship. Immediately, he heard Arvix over his suit's radio.

"Jeff Bowman, please proceed to electrical junction AE-35."

Running as fast as he could in his spacesuit, Jeff found the hatch for the maintenance tube that was closest to the junction. Hastily pulling the hatch aside, Jeff climbed in and crawled to junction AE-35. Seating himself on a large conduit, Jeff heaved a sigh.

"Arvix?" he called on his radio. "What's happening?"

"All but five Normans are dead. One crewmember, Allison Kwan, is also dead. Several more are injured and being taken to the medical bay."

"But I'm safe here, right? The Normans won't find me here, right?"

"No, Jeff Bowman. The Normans have already located you and are on the way to your location."

"ARVIX! What did you have me come here for then?"

"You will lead the Normans here. I will overload the power conduits and electrocute them. You will be safe."

Stunned, Jeff stammered, "You're going to kill them? Isn't there another way?"

"No, Jeff Bowman. I am programmed to protect you. As long as any Normans survive, there is a high probability that they will take you. Therefore, I must terminate them all."

"But wait, *wait*! I don't want anyone else to die! This has to stop."

"Jeff Bowman, this ship is lost in interstellar space. There is no help available and the senior crewmembers of the Ellsworth have openly stated that they don't know if anyone on board will survive. I am programmed to protect you. Therefore, I will ensure your survival while I continue to function."

"What do you mean, 'while I continue to function?' What's going to stop you from functioning?"

"I am currently under attack by two computers that are similar to myself but controlled by the Normans. They have been using these two computers to take over the ship's systems and move about without being detected. I have tracked down one of the computers and used one of the ship's repair robots to destroy it. But in the process, I have given away my location. The other computer is also controlling some of the ship's repair robots. We are currently engaged in battle. The likelihood is high that I will lose. All Normans must be dead before then. Jeff Bowman, do you still have your plasma pistol?"

"Y ... Yes, I've got it."

"Then please climb into maintenance tube JRH-161 and wait there. When the Normans arrive, do not move. I will send a pulse down a power conduit that will overload the AE-35 junction. The resulting electrical discharge will kill the Normans. You will be safe in maintenance tube JRH-161."

"Are you sure that this is the only way, Arvix?"

"Yes, Jeff Bowman. It is the only way."

Jeff didn't want to do this, not even a little. He didn't want anyone else to die, even if they were trying to kill him. But he climbed up to the maintenance tube anyway. With Arvix's guidance, he moved to an insulated section of the tube and waited.

Jeff wondered what would happen to him if the computer controlling Arvix died before the Normans. He knew it wasn't alive, but he couldn't help but think of its destruction as dying. And he would be on his own if it was killed.

'I'd better make plans,' he thought hastily. It occurred to him to ask the computer.

"You are right, Jeff Bowman. You will be undefended if I am terminated before the Normans. I will try to program one of the ship's maintenance robots to protect you. But maintenance robots contain specific programming that prevents them from having aggressive behavior. I will have to find a way to override it."

"What about using a different robot? Like the loader bots in the cargo bays?"

"Almost all types of artificial intelligences contain programming against aggressive behavior. The only exception is AIs in games."

'AIs in games?' Jeff echoed in his mind. A thought flared. "Wait," he told the computer. "I have an idea."

34

Jeff strained every nerve to keep himself from running away. He lifted his plasma pistol and waited. His eyes were locked on the entrance to the tube he was in. In fact, it was impossible to look at anything else. From far below his position, Jeff heard voices echoing through the maintenance tubes.

"They're here," Jeff whispered. He didn't get an answer. "Arvix? Arvix are you there?"

"Yes, Jeff Bowman. I am here and ready."

"Are you still being attacked?"

"Yes. But I will be functional for long enough to trigger the power overload. Please be silent and wait."

Reluctantly, Jeff fell silent. 'Here they come,' he realized as their thumping and bumping grew louder. He clutched his plasma pistol in a death grip. Realizing that the safety was on, he forced his thumb to slide along the velvety side of the gun and slip the safety into the off position.

'I'm sweating like a pig,' he thought. The sound of his breath was a ragged thunder in his helmet. Each second was agonizingly long.

Abruptly, another explosion pounded the ship. In the narrowness of the maintenance tube, Jeff wasn't thrown around much. So he was unhurt by the violent vibrations.

Silence fell.

Jeff waited.

When there was no activity at the end of the tube, Jeff still rasping and gritting his teeth, forced himself to crawl to the end of the tunnel. Slowly, carefully, he peeked out of the tube.

Far below him, Jeff could see the prostrate Normans. The power junction had not blown.

'The explosion from outside probably knocked them down,' he realized. With growing dread he thought, 'So they're probably not dead. Which means ... I need to run away RIGHT NOW!'

Near terror, Jeff clamored down to the exit hatch. As he ran down the corridor, he called out, "Arvix! Are you there? Arvix?"

No answer. Jeff was alone. Even though he didn't know where he was going, he kept running.

The emergency lights were on, casting a dim red glow over everything. Jeff struggled forward, his mind racing. Unexpectedly, the ship's artificial gravity field switched off. Feeling like he was falling, Jeff grabbed wildly for anything he could get his hands on. His feet drifted upward from the floor. He continued to flail as he tumbled toward the ceiling.

As Jeff drifted upward, he grabbed onto a 4 inch by 4 inch conduit that ran along the ceiling. He had never noticed it before, but he could see that it contained the power cables for the corridor's lighting. Grabbing the sides of the tube-like conduit, Jeff pulled himself along hand over hand. When he reached the ship's main corridor, he paused and frantically tried to figure out what to do.

Casting his eyes desperately around himself, Jeff could see that there was absolutely *nothing* he could do. All along the corridor, the ship's huge pressure doors were solidly shut. Jeff knew that the doors in the maintenance tubes would be secure as well. The ship's automatic systems had reacted to the violence of the explosion in a way that would best protect the crew and passengers. He was trapped in this section with the Normans. He wondered how long it would be before they woke up.

The artificial gravity came back on. Fortunately, Jeff was floating near the floor. He heard a mechanical groaning noise. As he turned toward the sound, the aft pressure doors slowly opened. Chief Connors came through, his staff and the passengers close behind.

"What's happened Chief?" Jeff demanded.

"Another explosion," the Chief replied. "The ship's very badly damaged; it could fall apart at any second. We've got to get to the cargo shuttles." Chief Connors and his engineers moved quickly to the next pressure door and began opening it.

"But … there's still Normans. There's five of them in electrical junction AE-35."

Chief Connors barked an order to José. "Martinez seal them in." José ran down the corridor toward the junction.

Jeff searched frantically through the thick throng of passengers for his dad. With growing panic, Jeff realized that Kent, Porsche, Dirk, and the girls were not among the crowd. Jeff ran back to Chief Connors. "Chief!" he called. "Where's my dad and his family?"

The pressure doors came open. The Chief turned and waved everyone through. Looking sadly at Jeff, he said, "Jeff, your father and his family didn't make it. They're trapped in a section of the ship that has a hull breach. We've got to save all the passengers that we can. There are four large cargo shuttles that we keep docked near the front of the ship. We're going to have to use them to abandon ship. The Captain is already there with the rest of the crew."

Jeff objected, "We can't just leave them! They'll die!"

"Jeff," Chief Connors repeated with as much patience as he could under the circumstances, "Our duty as crewmembers is to save as many passengers as we can. In space, that sometimes means sacrificing some so that everyone else can live. There's not enough air in those cabins. We can't possibly get to them in time. The whole section's sealed tight because there's a big gash in the hull not far from your family's cabins. I'm sorry, but that's just the way things work in space. We have to do things the way that we do them so that as many as possible can survive. I'm sorry. But you'll have to come with us."

The Chief turned away as the ship shuddered again and strode to the next pressure door. "This is the last one. Get it open and get everyone into the shuttles as fast as possible." The ship shuddered sickeningly. "This ship won't last much longer if this keeps up."

'I'm not leaving my dad,' Jeff thought silently. Before the Chief noticed, Jeff ran toward Engineering again. "There are portable air tanks in Engineering," Jeff told himself. "If I can get down there and get the tanks, I might be able to get them air in time."

Jeff was far down the corridor when he heard Chief Connors yelling, "Jeff! Jeff, what are you doing? You can't save them. Come back." A huge trembling shook the ship again and a pressure door closed behind him. Jeff was cut off.

Running as hard as he could, Jeff sprinted toward Engineering. "I'm not going to make it," he said. "This stupid ship is a mile long. I haven't even gone a third of that."

Suddenly, three Normans exploded from a hatch and dashed straight toward Jeff. Skidding to a stop, Jeff tried to turn around. From behind him, he heard footsteps slamming on the catwalk. Then an explosion of pain seared through him and Jeff fell into blackness.

35

Jeff awoke slowly and painfully. For some reason, he couldn't move his arms. Dragging his eyes open, Jeff blearily saw that his outstretched arms were strapped down. He was lying on a table of some sort. His legs were also in restraints. His spacesuit was off. Five Normans hustled around him setting up medical equipment in a cargo bay.

Terror ripped through Jeff. Exploding into a fit of thrashing, Jeff struggled vainly against the restraints. The Normans ignored him as they continued about their tasks. One of them approached to set up a nasty-looking machine that had several long tubes with needles on the end. The center of the machine contained a clear cylinder full of a sickly-green liquid. Jeff watched with horror as the man set the needle end of each tube by his arms, legs, and neck. He was obviously preparing to insert the needles.

"Please," Jeff begged. "You've got to let me go. My family is trapped in their cabins and they're running out of air."

Continuing as if he didn't hear, the Norman busied himself with turning on the machine and making adjustments to it.

"Please!" Jeff yelled, tugging as hard as he could against the restraints. "They're going to die!" He struggled and strained with all his might.

The man stopped and looked at Jeff. Jeff stopped and pleaded, "Please don't let my family die!"

The man's eyebrows furrowed. Jeff's hopes rose.

"Just let me go, just for a little while," Jeff offered. "I won't run away. I'll let you do anything you want to me. But please save my family."

The man gazed intently at Jeff and then moved toward him. Jeff's heart rose. "Thank you," he gushed. "Thank you!"

The man reached under the table Jeff was strapped to and pulled up another restraint. He clipped it across Jeff's chest so that he couldn't move so much.

"AAAARRRG!" bellowed Jeff in mindless fury. Hopeless and desperate, he thrashed and struggled and twisted and howled and cried. But it was useless. He was trapped.

BAM!

Arvix exploded from an air conduit running along the side of the cargo bay. He tumbled from the high conduit but landed lightly on his feet. "Hayayayayayayayayayaaaaaah!" Arvix screamed as he leapt toward the Normans.

"Frenzied feet of flaming fury," Arvix called out, "ACTIVATE!"

Arvix sliced the air with a length of pipe he was carrying and kicked his feet so fast that he was almost a blur.

"Hayayayayayayayayayaaaaaah!" he screamed as he sent Normans flying in every direction. Arvix kicked. He pummeled his opponents with the pipe. He yelled and jumped and ducked and lashed out against everyone that attacked him. In seconds, the Normans lay on the floor, bloody and prostrate. They were dead.

Delirious with relief, Jeff yelled, "It worked! The Brice Yee programming worked!"

Jeff didn't know whether to be glad of his rescue or sick at the sight of the dead Normans. But he knew he had to keep focused.

"Arvix!" he commanded, "Take off these straps and let me go."

The robot complied immediately and set Jeff free. Leaping off the table, Jeff tore for the exit screaming, "Arvix! Follow me!" Arvix trailed after him.

Jeff didn't get far before the artificial gravity went out again. Launching himself upward, he clasped the handrail of a catwalk that ran along the inside of the ship's long main cylinder.

"Arvix," Jeff instructed, "Reach your hand up to me." Jeff stretched his leg down to the robot, had Arvix grab on, and pulled him up to the catwalk.

"Pull yourself along this guardrail like I'm doing and follow me," ordered Jeff. So saying, he pulled himself hand over hand toward Engineering with Arvix close behind. But his progress was agonizingly slow.

Glancing back at Arvix, Jeff had an idea. "Arvix, come here," he ordered. As Arvix moved close, Jeff wrapped his arms around the robot's neck. "Arvix, pull yourself along that handrail just like you did before." Arvix responded by pulling himself hand over hand toward the rear of the ship.

"Arvix, can you go faster?" Jeff questioned.

"Of course, Master Jeff," Arvix sped up significantly. But Jeff wasn't satisfied. "Go as fast as you can."

Instantly Arvix accelerated with a jerk, almost causing Jeff to lose his grip. The robot's hands were blurs. When they arrived at Engineering, Arvix slowed at Jeff's command.

The Engineering section still had power but no gravity. Jeff rapidly retrieved five air tanks from a storage locker. As he pulled the last one out, the ship wobbled violently again. The pressure doors in the corridor outside of Engineering closed.

"No!" Jeff yelled. "How am I going to get back to the passenger module?" he demanded of no one. Tears filled his eyes as he thought of his dad and the others trapped in their cabins. Except for the hum of the power generators, a deathlike silence fell across the ship.

Wondering what to do next, Jeff searched frantically around Engineering. When he caught sight of a space suit locker, he had an idea. Hurriedly, Jeff opened the locker and jerked on a suit. Activating the suit's electronics, Jeff checked his air levels. He was good to go.

Jeff darted to the air lock and opened the inner door. He turned on the suit's external speaker.

"Arvix, put those air tanks in this airlock and then get in," he commanded. As the robot worked, Jeff obtained some long straps and a toolbox. Entering the airlock, Jeff strapped the tanks together and then hooked them to Arvix. Using a connector on his spacesuit, Jeff clipped the toolbox to himself.

"Arvix, when I open the outer door, you start pulling yourself, these tanks, and me in whatever direction I point. When I raise my hand like this," he put up his hand with the palm forward, "you stop. When I point my thumb up like this, you go faster. When I point it down, you slow down. Understand?"

"Yes Master Jeff."

Jeff slammed his hand on the button that sealed and cycled the air lock. Within moments, the outer door opened.

The ship hung in the unending, unnoticing night as a blazing sea of pinpoint stars shined out their cold, diamond-like glow. Jeff pointed to the latticework of beams that ran along the entire outside of the ship. Arvix moved in the direction he pointed. Jeff jerked his thumb upward several times. In spite of all the mass he was dragging, Arvix shot forward.

They covered the distance rapidly while Jeff's heartbeat and raspy breathing thundered in the absolute silence of his suit. The display on the visor of his helmet told him his family had only about 30 minutes left. "We're not going to make it," he despaired. He emphatically waved his thumb upward again, but Arvix could go no faster.

They arrived near the front of the passenger module with just 8 minutes to spare. Jeff found a huge, gaping, mouth-like hole near his father's cabin and motioned for Arvix to take them in. As they passed inside, he cringed at the thought that his suit might be cut open by the long, ragged fangs of plasteel that lined the edges of the opening. But he made it though without a problem.

Gazing back at the tear in the hull, Jeff said, "There's no way I can seal that. I can't get the tanks to them without depressurizing their cabins. Now I know why the Chief left them behind." Then he spotted a hatch to a maintenance tunnel. Without hesitating, Jeff yanked it open. Pointing, he indicated to Arvix to get inside.

When the robot and the air tanks were safely inside the junction, Jeff sealed the hatch closed. A panel on the wall showed him that the tunnel that ran behind the passenger cabins still had air in it. Quickly, Jeff opened the valves on two air tanks, which emptied their contents into the airtight junction. When the tanks were empty, there was a thin, but breathable atmosphere. Jeff pressed the button to open the tunnel. Six minutes left.

The suit Jeff was wearing had a scanner built into its helmet. When he thought he was positioned behind the right cabin, Jeff used it to scan the other side of the bulkhead. The display showed three living people. In a flash, Jeff opened the toolbox clipped to his suit and extracted a laser cutting torch. Within seconds, he punched a hole the size of a quarter through the wall of the cabin. The microphones on his helmet picked up a girl's screaming. It was Denise.

Turning his external speaker back on, Jeff shouted through the tiny opening, "It's ok! Don't worry. I'm here to get you out. Just stay away from this wall."

Working madly, Jeff cut the hole to the size of a baseball. Then he made another hole about the same size. "That'll give you some air. Just wait. I have to go cut the others out."

"Arvix!" Jeff yelled. "Bring those three tanks here."

As the robot obeyed, Jeff moved to the wall behind the next cabin and cut a hole. He could hear his dad shouting to him, but he didn't respond. Arvix had towed all three remaining tanks to his side. Jeff opened their valves. The tanks bounced down the tunnel, propelled by the escaping air.

"Dad?" Jeff called through the hole in the cabin wall.

"Jeff? Is that you?"

"Yeah, Dad. Stay back from the wall. I'll have you cut out of there in a few minutes. Are you getting any air?"

"Yes son," he heard Kent pant. "Yes we are."

Within minutes, Jeff cut an opening large enough for an adult to pass through. Kent drew himself out into the service tunnel and then reached back into the cabin for Porsche. Jeff returned to the wall behind the other cabin and cut another large opening. Dirk,

Denise, and Danae spilled out into the tunnel. For a few long minutes, none of them did anything but pant for air. They looked as grey as ashes.

After a while, Jeff could see their faces getting pinker. 'I think they're going to be alright,' he thought.

"Jeff," Kent gasped out as he gripped Jeff's shoulder. "You saved us. You came back."

"Of course I came back," Jeff answered. "I couldn't leave the ship without you."

"Leave the ship?" Kent queried, startled. "Did everyone leave the ship?"

"Yeah. There were some explosions. There's a big hole in the hull not far from these cabins. The crew and the rest of the passengers got into some cargo shuttles and left. Chief Connors said there was no way to get to you in time. But I used Arvix. He got me here fast. I still can't believe Chief Connors was going to leave you behind."

Kent nodded. "That's what they're supposed to do. It's protocol."

"It's what?"

"Protocol. Orders. It's what you do in this situation. The crew has to save as many passengers as possible."

Disgusted, Jeff shot back, "I don't care what the proto-whatever says. It's mean to leave you behind–to leave all of us behind. He said he was your friend."

Waving his hand, Kent cut Jeff off. "He did what any good spacer would do. Did you scan any of the other cabins for survivors?" he demanded.

Dumbfounded, Jeff shook his head. "No. I didn't think about it."

"Do it now," Kent ordered.

Jeff moved rapidly along the corridor and scanned each cabin. "No other signs of life," he reported. "There were some people trapped in the next few cabins, but we didn't make it in time. They had four in each cabin so they used up their air faster. We're alone."

A sickly silence fell over the group.

Kent queried, "Jeff, where do these maintenance tunnels go? Can we get into a part of the ship that's pressurized?"

"There was a map on a panel at the junction," Jeff remembered. "I think there was a tunnel that runs forward to the next junction. Now that this section has air, we can use that to get back into the ship's main corridor. But the pressure doors are closed all through the ship. How will we get to Engineering?"

Kent stated, "I can get the pressure doors open long enough to get us through. Just show us the way out of here."

Jeff led his family out of the service tunnels and Kent used the manual overrides on the pressure doors to move them through the ship. There was only one spot where the readouts told them that the space on the other side of the door was depressurized. They crawled through a service tunnel to get around it. Soon they arrived at Engineering.

"Right," Kent began authoritatively as he gazed at the status panels. "The air system in here is functioning and so is the plumbing. This," he said as he pressed a button, "turns the regular lights back on." The burning red of the emergency lights flickered out and the soft glow of the overhead lighting returned. "That's better," Kent commented.

"Now we'll get gravity working—at least in this part of the ship. Jeff, you'll help me. The remaining power generators aren't enough to generate gravity for anything but Engineering and maybe the section in front of it. We have to cut the connections to the gravity net in the forward parts of the ship. After that's done we can feed power to this part of the gravity net and get it working."

They quickly obtained the tools they needed. Jeff and Kent then wended their way in and out of the maintenance tunnels that surrounded Engineering, clipping connections as they did. It took nearly two hours, but when they were done, Kent was able to restore gravity.

"What's next, Dad?" Jeff asked as they sat at the primary control panels. "Can we call someone for help?"

For long moments, Kent stared at the computer's data readouts. Sensing something was wrong, Porsche, Dirk, and the girls gathered around them.

"What is it?" Porsche asked. "What's the matter?"

Heaving a sigh, Kent explained slowly, "We're in a real tough situation here." Jeff could tell by the expression on Kent's face that the situation was more than tough.

Kent continued, "According to the data that the main computer sent to Engineering just before it went down, the wormhole didn't just collapse. It broke apart, sending pieces of itself spinning all through hyperspace. We basically fell into the sky. I have no idea where we are. We could be ten thousand light years from the planet Boulder by now."

A shocked silence fell. Kent continued quickly, "But on the plus side, the ship has reentered normal space just outside a star system." No one seemed to consider that a big plus.

Kent turned his gaze away from them, "Before the ship's main scanners went down, they picked up signs of a couple of planets that might be habitable. If we were on the cargo shuttles, we might be able to get there. But there's no sign of them. They may have already headed there. I don't know. In any case, we can't move the ship and we have no ships that can make the trip."

Porsche queried, "Why can't we move the ship?"

"Whatever caused those explosions sent out massive waves of gravity. The ship's gravity mirrors are fried."

Porsche fell into silence. But Dirk asked quaveringly, "Does that mean we're stuck here? We'll die here, won't we?"

"Yes, Dirk," Kent answered bluntly, "unless we can get the ship moving, we're stuck here. And if we're stuck here, we can only continue to live for a while. Our food, water, air, and power will eventually run out."

No one said anything. Kent fell deep into thought and muttered, "We can't fix the gravity mirrors. How can we move this wreck? There's nothing to use, not even an old-style rocket."

A light went off in Jeff's brain. "Rocket?" he blurted out. "We can make a rocket. We had a lesson on that not long before school let out. Those old spaceships in the 21st Century used water rockets. You heat up water and it builds up pressure in its container. Then you open a valve and let it go streaming out the back of the rocket. They did that on the early missions to Jupiter."

Kent brightened immediately. "You're right!" he agreed. "This ship's high-efficiency fusion generators are powered by purified water mixed with seaboricite. There are three huge tanks of it on the outside of this ship that are nearly half a mile long each. We could use some of the 1000-gallon tanks in the plumbing system as boilers to heat the water in. All we need to do is run some pipes from one of the fuel tanks to the boilers. Each of them would heat their water, let it burst out the back, and then refill. The other two fuel tanks will provide fuel for the fusion generators. The electricity from the generators will power the boilers."

Surging toward a computer panel, Kent exclaimed, "It may not work, though. We may not be able to get enough thrust to move the ship fast enough. If it's too slow, we'll take years and years to get to a habitable planet …" He didn't have to finish his sentence. Everyone knew they wouldn't last years on the badly-battered ship.

Using the Engineering's main computer matrix, Kent ran the calculations. He didn't look happy with the result, so he started again. Jeff knew they were in trouble when his dad tried it a third time. "How long will it take Dad?"

Kent slammed his fist on the console, and then fell into a frustrated silence. After a few moments, Porsche asked, "Kent?"

"Twenty years and a couple of months," Kent shot back. "Twenty years, no matter what we do."

Once more, everyone fell silent.

"Dad?"

"Yes, Jeff?"

"We picked up animals in the Ohio system that are frozen but still alive."

"Yes, that's how animals are shipped these days. It's called cryogenic stasis or suspended animation."

"A lot of those Normans that were trying to get me were in cryogenic stasis too."

"Of course ..." Kent almost exploded with happiness. "YES! Of course it works on people too. We can put ourselves into cryogenic stasis. We won't need any food, air, water, or anything else. We'll sleep for twenty years and not grow any older at all. Yes, Jeff. I think you just saved our lives."

Kent hopped to his feet. "I'll need help with this," he stated as he swung into action. "First we need to see if we can repressurize the parts of the ship between here and the aft cargo bays that don't have air. We need to be able to get to those stasis units without having to go outside. Then we can start tearing out parts of the plumbing. We'll build the steam rockets in cargo bay 31 because it's right in front of Engineering. We can use the big cargo doors on the outside of the bay to get them onto the outside of the ship. All we have to do then is weld them on and run some plumbing and wiring."

With his hands moving rapidly over the computer panel, Kent said, "There's a hull breach a few sections forward of us. It's not too big. I'll go out and seal that. Yes, this will work. There's hope for us yet."

Seizing a large tool kit, Kent grabbed a spacesuit and got in. His external speaker came on. "I'll be back in an hour or so. You guys see if you can find some food and water around here. As I remember, José said once that he keeps some food stored in a locker somewhere. But it might be pretty well hidden. Chief Connors would have had a fit if he ever found out."

With that, Kent moved into the air lock and closed the door. Jeff stood staring after him for a moment and then glanced uncomfortably from Porsche to Dirk. "I'll get a hand scanner and see if it'll help us find food. If the plumbing still works, there's water in the bathroom over there." Jeff pointed. Turning away, he dug through a tool locker and retrieved a scanner. By the time Kent returned, Jeff had located José's secret stash.

"Wow," Kent commented when he returned and saw the pile of goodies. "I didn't know José was such a junk food junkie."

Porsche commented cautiously, "This isn't going to last us very long. How long will it take to build your rockets?"

"A couple of weeks," Kent answered.

"*Weeks?!*" Porsche gasped.

"Honey, this is complicated stuff. Even with everyone helping, it will take that long. Jeff, you're going to have use Arvix to get back to our cabins. Our supplies of synthpaste are still there. That'll solve our food problem."

Jeff recoiled at the thought of eating synthpaste again. He had grown way too used to real food. "Couldn't I get real food from the ship's kitchen instead?" he objected.

Shaking his head, Kent smiled and chuckled. "We're stuck who knows how far away from the nearest habitable planet on a ship that we're going to have to move with water-powered rockets, and this kid worries about having to eat synthpaste." Kent smiled and heaved a sigh. "Sure. Go get us the best food you can find. That will help make everyone feel better anyway. Put the food into airtight containers. That'll keep it in good shape. Dirk, you come help me get some of these pressure doors open."

Jeff strapped two containers onto Arvix and exited Engineering through the airlock. This time, he didn't have Arvix move as fast. He had some time to look at the universe around him. A vast, green, cloud-like nebula filled about a quarter of the sky above his head. Far below his feet, an angry swirling orange mist surrounded a small group of stars. Thick pools of stars filled the sky. 'I wonder if that means we're a lot closer to the center of the galaxy than people have ever been before?' Jeff pondered ominously. He couldn't pick out the star they would be moving toward. All of them seemed infinitely far away.

Arriving at the crew module, Jeff found an airlock and entered. There was still air inside and the emergency power was on. Jeff packed as much food as he could get into the containers he brought and had Arvix pull him back to Engineering. When Jeff brought the food inside, everyone's eyes bulged. Kent found a large empty container he turned over for them to use as a table.

"What *is* this stuff?" Dirk asked as Jeff laid a meal out on their makeshift table.

Jeff answered, "It's stuff for making sandwiches. There's lots of other things too, but I thought it would be better to get everyone something fast instead of trying to make something fancy." Jeff demonstrated how to make a ham and cheese sandwich, and then took a bite of his creation. Kent made himself a sandwich and started eating heartily.

After sandwiches were made for everyone else, they ate in silence. When they finished the meal, Kent directed, "We're going to rig up temporary quarters for ourselves in cargo bay 37. It has a lot of colonization supplies. There are mattresses and blankets there. I checked with the computer. We can rearrange the containers to leave some open spaces. Those will be our rooms. We'll use the bathrooms here in Engineering."

Standing, Kent told them, "It's been a long day. Let's go make our sleeping quarters now. Then everyone can have a chance to rest. We'll start working on our rockets first thing tomorrow."

The entire group followed Kent to cargo bay 37. Upon entering, they saw towering stacks of cargo containers clamped tightly into racks. Kent stepped up to a small computer pad on the side of one rack and began entering instructions. When he was finished, the rack ponderously heaved itself to one side, opening up a space between itself and its neighbor. Kent continued to shuffle the racks around until he created three square, room-like spaces among them. Each one had an opening they could use as a door.

"These will be our rooms," Kent informed them. Stepping up to another rack he continued, "Here's our bedding." He tapped instructions into the pad and three containers slipped out of their racks and opened themselves. Inside, they found mattresses, blankets, sheets, and pillows. "I brought some cables from Engineering. We can use them to hang blankets across the openings for privacy. That'll be the only real doors we have for a while. Girls, you take the room on the right and you boys take the middle. Your mother and I will have the one on the left."

Dirk shot a smoldering look in Jeff's direction, grabbed his bedding, and dragged it down one of the long rows between the racks of cargo containers. "I'm sleeping back here," he announced flatly. Kent was clearly disappointed as he watched Dirk pull his things into a nook between some containers far to the rear of the cargo bay. Jeff pulled his bedding into his room, and then helped Denise and Danae with theirs.

After hanging blankets for doors, everyone retired to their beds and Kent put out the overhead lights. "I'll leave the lights on in the corridor and the cargo bay door open," he told everyone.

Jeff told Arvix to go to Engineering and find a wall socket to recharge himself. When the robot left, Jeff lay in his bed and pulled his blankets tightly around him. Anxiously, he wondered, 'Can we really make it to a planet we can live on? And if we do, what kind of life will we have so far away from all other humans?' Then the thought came to him, 'What will Harriet think? Won't she think I'm dead? And Akio too? I'll never see them again.'

Then faintly, Jeff heard a woman crying. He realized it was Porsche. 'She must be thinking the same things as me,' Jeff thought. And for the first time, Jeff saw Porsche as something other than an enemy. As Jeff listened to Kent's quiet attempts to comfort his wife, exhaustion overcame him and he fell into a deep sleep.

The following day, they ate a quick breakfast and set to work. Jeff sent Arvix, who had learned to make his own way outside the ship, back to the crew module at the bow of the ship to get more food for everyone. Under Kent's direction, the entire family spent the day gathering parts they would need to build the rockets. They carried the parts they found to cargo bay 31. Jeff returned with Arvix to the family's cabins in the passenger module to retrieve everyone's belongings. He made a side trip to his own quarters in the crew module to get his possessions.

Kent started work on the first boiler the next morning. The others now had a familiarity with what Kent needed, so they were sent to scavenge parts on their own. They spent the next few weeks looking for parts and helping Kent however they could. Often, Jeff took time in the evenings to make up games and play them with the girls to keep their spirits up. As the rockets took shape, the entire family grew more hopeful.

After weeks of work, all five rockets were ready. Kent, Porsche, Dirk, and Jeff all put on space suits. Kent turned off the gravity in cargo bay 31 and opened the large cargo doors. Together with Arvix, the four of them moved the rockets to the outside of the ship where Kent welded them on. The next day, Kent and Jeff began work on running plumbing from one of the fuel tanks to the rockets. It took a full week to get it all connected, and then Kent tested everything.

"It looks good," he reported happily after the first test. "I've got to make some adjustments to rocket number 3, but overall it looks fine. We're getting real good thrust, and Jeff's written a program to control it all. It seems to be working great. We're already starting to move toward that nearby star system. I'll watch it for a few days and make adjustments, then we'll go into cryostasis."

The entire family had a huge meal to celebrate. Even Dirk seemed to enjoy himself. Jeff noticed that for the first time ever, Dirk talked and joked a little with Kent. Three days later, Kent declared, "Everything's working perfectly. Today's the day we go into cryostasis."

With some trepidation, they all followed Kent to the cryogenic stasis units he had brought from one of the cargo bays with Arvix's help. "Danae and Denise, you two can share a unit. Climb in and lie down."

Looking a bit fearful, the two girls got into a stasis unit. Kent pulled a hypospray out of his pocket. "Hold out your arms," he said.

"I don't wanna shot!" Denise wailed instantly.

"Denise," Kent told her soothingly, "You have to have this shot. It's what keeps you alive when you're frozen." With the mention of being frozen, Denise only cried louder. Eventually, they got her calmed down enough to give her a tearful injection. The others quickly received their shots as well. Kent sealed them all into their cryostasis units and started the sleep cycle. Lastly, he programmed his own unit and got in.

The shots swiftly took effect. The family drifted immediately to sleep. A profound quiet fell over the entire ship as systems automatically shut down to conserve power. At regular intervals, the boilers of the handmade rockets filled with water. Each boiler superheated the water, building the pressure inside itself to maximum. Then a valve at the rear opened, allowing the steam to escape through a tube out into the infinite night of space. Each time it did, the crippled ship was pushed slightly toward its destination.

As the ship made its slow progress toward a distant, unknown sun, the six humans inside gradually stopped breathing. Their hearts stopped beating and ice crystals formed on the inside of their stasis units. To the casual observer, they would have looked dead. But the displays on the stasis units showed they were still very much alive.

The computer turned off the lights in Engineering and a deep darkness enfolded the entire ship. Outside, the rockets continued to send spurts of superhot steam into the vacuum of space as the hulking freighter slowly accelerated toward the nearby star.

In the tomb-like silence of the cargo bay, Jeff and his family slumbered dreamlessly. The cryostasis pods monitored them attentively and waited with infinite patience for the day when the humans inside would wake again.

Don't miss Book 2 of the **Possessor Wars** series! You can find it at:
http://possessorwars.com/the-series/book-2.html

Official Web Site: http://possessorwars.com/
Facebook: https://www.facebook.com/chad.spencer.165
Twitter: https://twitter.com/PossessorWars
To be notified of new releases, please sign up for the author's newsletter at:
http://possessorwars.com/subscribe.html

.

www.ingramcontent.com/pod-product-compliance
Lightning Source LLC
Chambersburg PA
CBHW070834120626
46556CB00002B/758